PARIS
STILL LIFE

ALSO BY ROSALIND BRACKENBURY

Novels

Nonfiction

Poetry

PARIS
STILL LIFE

for Margaret —
in NY, April 2018.

ROSALIND BRACKENBURY

Rosalind Brackenbury

LAKE UNION
PUBLISHING

Text copyright © 2018 Rosalind Brackenbury

Published by Lake Union Publishing, Seattle

www.apub.com

Amazon, the Amazon logo, and Lake Union Publishing are trademarks of Amazon.com, Inc., or its affiliates.

ISBN-13: 9781477809006
ISBN-10: 1477809007

Cover design by David Drummond

Printed in the United States of America

For Miranda

1.

That morning was gray with the cool washed gleam you often wake up to in Paris. It was a Monday, and I suppose that was why they chose it to film on rue Mouffetard. I went out to buy bread and to top up my phone, but of course everything, even the local boulangerie, was closed. There'd be one open higher up the street, most likely, but the way was barred. A young woman was shooing people along rue Saint-Médard, explaining quite patiently, over and over, that it was a film and that they couldn't take photos using flash while filming was going on. The street had been transformed into a 1950s street, with shop fronts put up over the modern ones, with *"Boucherie"* and so on in antiquated writing. There was a smell of hay and animals. They even had tiny birds in cages, although they turned out to be fake, with little wire claws. It was all old France, men in brown suits and flat caps, women in skirts and thick heels and makeup, carts everywhere, only the cobbles and the shape of the street unchanged, its crooked path that has been there since the Middle Ages. People stood watching, about to disobey the rules and use flash on their cameras. Someone murmured that Juliette Binoche was coming, or was it Julie Delpy, then someone else said it was an American film—they would all be Americans. Watching the film being made, even this very small part of it, was like watching a performance in itself, in which people raised and lowered lights, pulled thick ropes of electric cable after them, pushed objects this way and that. It all seemed very slow. The actors sat about on chairs and had their faces rubbed by makeup people, their hair patted into shape, their clothes tweaked, then they got up and walked about talking on their cell phones, outside the world of the movie. Then they were on set, and their movements changed. The cameras hung and swooped, and the makeup people ran after the actors, dabbing their faces, pulling at their clothes. They were all making an alternative reality, there on the street. It seemed an incredibly laborious way of doing this. When you are a kid, you can just say, *This part of the floor is the sea, this table is a ship, and there you are, at sea.* This moviemaking, this creation of play for adults, was an unwieldy version of make-believe in which nothing, not even the smallest detail, could be left to the imagination.

I stayed there fascinated, watching, in the frail late-morning sunshine—yes, the light was spreading, a pale egg of sun had emerged. It was my first week in Paris, and the light seemed filtered after the brilliance of Florida, the air unusually cool on my skin. I thought of how different people looked who did not have cell phones clamped to their ears. Just people walking, talking. In those days, in the forties, the fifties, you could only talk to the person next to you. Or go somewhere special and use a heavy black Bakelite telephone. The world of instant connection—of cell phones, of Skype and Wi-Fi and taking photographs with your tiny phone, all of which now seems so necessary—none of it had been either invented or expected. We are living in science fiction, and we don't even notice.

I was thinking this, idly. And then I saw him. He was just a little way away from me but on the other side of the barrier that divided the street. He had his back turned to me and was staring back up the street in the direction of the Place de la Contrescarpe. I could only see his black corduroy jacket and a white crest of hair. Then he turned around. He could have been with the film actors, or with the crowd of onlookers; he stood just where the two joined. Like a divided sea, with a parting. Flat caps and working blues on one side, cell phones and cameras on the other. The young woman in a flowered dress and leggings with high-heeled boots shouted out, *"On va tourner! Pas de flash!"* and two of the actors whose clothes had been most recently adjusted began walking up the street, chatting quietly to each other, past the fake boulangerie and the *quincaillerie* with all the old-style pots and carpet beaters hanging outside. He was facing me now, curved nose, white hair standing up on end, slightly bent shoulders in an old corduroy jacket, tanned face, sunglasses. My skin prickled on my scalp, as if each hair shifted. Then, after a long, tense minute in which only the two actors moved, and a flurry of cameras on long stalks, we all began shuffling on up the street. Time fast-forwarded. It was a May morning in 2008, not 1951, and he had vanished. My father. I could swear it, but it would be no use. Before I could reach him or even call out, he had gone out of sight.

I stood to one side in the crowd that had collected and simply stared at what was all around me, a film set, a historical fake-up, actors who had not been born in 1951 any more than I had, and a place and time in which I had just seen my father, who died six months ago in England, looking completely healthy on a Paris street. Then the woman from the film crew waved her hands again to shoo us all down rue de l'Arbalète.

I didn't know what to do with what I had just seen. I wanted to run after him and shout, *Dad, it's me, I'm here, it's Gaby!* But the wooden barriers were still up across rue Mouffetard, and he had vanished. I sat down on the nearest empty chair outside the Café de l'Arbalète and asked for a coffee and a glass of water. I could still see the movie set from here, on the other side of all the parked vans and snaking wires and heaps of extra baskets, wheelbarrows, wine flasks, and other French fifties paraphernalia. The movie land ended at one point in the street, and the land of the twenty-first century took over. I was stuck here between the two.

Had he, the person I had seen, my father, been part of that past? No, ridiculous thought. He looked just the way he had when I'd last seen him, not the way he would have looked in 1951. *Anyway, Gaby, don't start going over the top here. They are making a movie. This is reality, the twenty-first century, where you sit.* I sipped my coffee after I'd stirred sugar into it and wished I still smoked. You can still smoke outside cafés in France, and nobody stares at you as if you were a suicide perched at the edge of a high building, the way they do in America. I remembered that I had seen a film in which Juliette Binoche did sit in this very café after a car crash in which her husband and child died. But, oh, God, where was real life and what was it, and where did that vision I had come from, and what could I do? It must have been someone else. He did have dark glasses on. But that jacket, the one he'd had for decades, worn black corduroy over old jeans—a sixties dresser, my father, a very old brand of chic. That jacket, I remembered. I closed my eyes for a moment. I could even remember its smell. Cigarettes and aftershave, and sharpened pencils, and varnish, and himself.

My phone went off in my bag then, and I had to rummage, the way you do, while the first notes of some great musical masterpiece sound tinnily and everybody else is too busy listening to their own devices to care. I pressed the green arrow and heard my sister's voice. "Gaby? Hello? Gaby, are you all right? Are you in Paris?"

"Marg! Yes, why?"

I thought, *I can't tell her.* She would think me even crazier than she did already. I said, "I'm sitting in a café, outside one, actually."

"I had the weirdest dream about you." She had called me to tell me about a dream? I don't think people should tell you when they dream about you, as it is really all about them, and it puts you in the strange position of starring unwittingly in their drama. But I didn't say this.

I said, "I'm fine. How are you?"

"Fine. I just had to check. I was worried about you. You know how it is."

My sister used to be always tiptoeing into her children's rooms, to see if they were still alive. I said, "Yes, no, really, I'm fine. But thanks for asking." I still couldn't say, *I have just seen our father on the set of a movie*, so I said, "How are the kids?"

"Fine. Gaby, I'm sorry to hear about you and Matt."

I had wondered if she was going to mention him. "Yes, well, I need to take some time on my own right now. Did Phil tell you? I hoped it was okay with you about coming to the apartment."

"Yes, I was beginning to wonder why we kept it, since none of us ever has time to go there."

"You'll come here when the kids are grown up. Meanwhile, it's great to have it."

"Good. Gaby?"

"What?"

"Take care. You sound weird."

"Just surprised to hear from you."

"Well. Keep in touch."

I said, "I will. And don't dream any more scary dreams about me, okay?"

"I'll try not to. Do come and see us. We'd love to see you. It's been ages."

"I don't know yet, I've only just got here, hmm, yes, maybe. I'll call you, okay?"

"You sound so American!"

"Well, I'm not, not really. Or maybe I am. I've just lived there a long time."

I put away my phone after we had said our goodbyes, remembering how my sister always did this to me, how I let her, how something out of our childhood had hung on and distorted any adult relationship we could have had. She had to sound critical; I had to sound abrupt. This time, it was as if she was annoyed with me for appearing in her dream, as well as for sounding American and not confiding in her about Matt. I tried to focus back on the scene around me and thought not for the first time that cell phones allow us to be removed from what is real. But what was the reality around me? A disguised street, actors and film cameras, a man who had disappeared into the crowd who I was sure—almost—was my dead father. Perhaps Marg, in England, with her questions, was more real than all this. I finished my coffee and left the coins to weight the bill in the saucer provided and watched the huge film truck across the square being filled with boxes of props. A crate with real hens in it went onto the flatbed, and some bales of hay were tossed on board. The people doing the lifting and tossing were in black like mimes. A young woman went past in clumpy shoes and a 1940s suit, smoking, her hair in a roll and a hat pinned on top. Above it all the Paris sky cleared of mackerel clouds and their tentative luminosity. Blue began to spread between the chimney pots and the steep chimneys with their vertical ladders like staples punched into them for chimney sweeps and steeplejacks to climb. Even looking at them gave me vertigo.

Then I remembered the time when I was about twelve and came here on a school trip. When everyone else went up the Eiffel Tower, I pleaded that I felt sick, to be allowed to stay on the ground. I went to a café with a kind teacher who told me he felt the same, and he bought me a hot chocolate. That was when I learned the word *vertigo*. It was good to have a name for it. Later, when the Eiffel Tower danger had passed, we went to a gallery on the Right Bank, along from the Louvre, and I saw a picture, a painting of a horse done by a Chinese artist. It was a picture that appeared everywhere, only I didn't know it. I loved horses, and this picture was meant to be mine. I didn't have nearly enough money to buy it, so I sadly left the gallery with the others, and we all went back to our hostel and played Truth, Dare, Force, and some girls were made to take their knickers down, only of course the teachers never knew. When I got home, my father said he had something for me, that it was in my room. There, done up in brown paper, was my picture. The Chinese horse hung for years on my wall in my parents' house, and I only lost it when moving flats in London. How had my father known about that horse? He simply said, "I was in Paris, wandering down the

Rive Droite after lunch one day, and I saw it in the window of some touristy gallery or other. I thought that's what my Gaby would like, and I went in and bought it."

"But, Dad, I was on a school trip that weekend, we went into that gallery, I saw the horse, I didn't have enough money, and then when I came home, there it was!"

"Darling, don't expect me to remember where you go on school trips. It was Bath in my day—all we did was hang around in the rain trying to pick up girls. Not Paris, worse luck. Hadn't a clue you were over there too. Funny thing, life, isn't it? Full of coincidences. Jung called it synchronicity, you know, but I don't suppose you've got on to that yet."

I hadn't got on to it, no. But that morning in Paris, that Monday, I thought that perhaps it was time I did.

2.

When I arrived back at the apartment, I discovered that a thin envelope had been slid under my door, with my name written on it in precise black pen. Who could have written to me? I opened it and saw the signature. André Schaffer. A friend of my parents, I remembered, who had visited us more than once in England. He had written me a note to ask me to meet him at Les Deux Magots the following day. I was pleased, both because I longed to see somebody who had known my parents and because they would have loved to think of me there, in the place of pilgrimage where Sartre and Simone de Beauvoir had spent so much time. I still didn't know what to make of that appearance, that fleeting impression of someone—could it really have been someone?—who looked exactly like my father. Would I tell André Schaffer? He would probably think I was deluded, a poor child; he would not know what to say.

I took the *métro* to Saint-Germain-des-Prés the next afternoon and walked across to the café. We hadn't met since I was a teenager, and I remembered him as a burly man with a lot of dark hair. He seemed to have shrunk, and his hair was white and sparse, and I would not have recognized him if he hadn't waved across at me immediately, seeing me come in, in my jeans and short green leather jacket. *Who do I look like?* I wondered. *Him, her, or neither?* Did he just recognize my American

clothes, my English face? We sat inside, because of all the crowds outside, and he bought me a glass of orange juice.

"How are you, Gaby?" He'd stood up to greet me, then we slid onto
our banquettes opposite each other. He folded his hands on the table as
if we were doing an interview.

"Well, okay. Not great but getting better. Glad to be in Paris. How
are you?"

We spoke English to each other, because with my parents he always
had.

Immediately, he told me a story. As I had guessed he would. People
here told stories before they ever asked a direct question; the courtesy
of the indirect way, a thing you rarely encountered in America. It was
the story of a film script he had written, based on the events of May
1968 in Paris, a love affair that ended when the events ended, when
de Gaulle came back and tried to put everything back the way it had
been. There was a car crash in it, and the sudden death of one of the
lovers. I realized, late in the story, that the lovers were both women,
one a university professor, one a working-class student. He gave me the
story, urgently, because he couldn't make the film. He hadn't been able
to get funding from anyone, and now it was too late; everyone was up
to here with May '68, this year of its fortieth anniversary. All the films
had already been made and produced. So, the story needed to be told.
It was a story about love and death. I sat across the narrow table on the
bench seat in Les Deux Magots and received it, making it in some way
my own, although I wasn't there, had never been in love with a woman,
had never had a lover who died in a car crash, although my mother had
done just that. Once again I was aching with unshed tears. Was it for
a film that couldn't be made, a project that went nowhere, a love affair
that ended, a man who was devastated by being stopped from making
the thing he loved? I fished in my bag for a tissue, and he looked at me
directly, and blushed.

"I'm so sorry," I said. I blew my nose.

He said at last, "I was so sorry to hear about your parents. It must have been terrible, one and then the other, in so short a time. They were too young to go. I can't believe I will not see them again."

I looked at him across the table. As if these words lay in wait for me everywhere. As if the whole of human language led here, to the place of loss. But where else was there to go?

"Gaby, I am so sorry." He said it again, leaning in closer.

"It isn't your fault. Everything still makes me cry. You could tell me any story, more or less, and it would have the same effect."

"It's not surprising."

"André, when did you last see them?"

"When? Well, let's see, I saw your father on his last trip to Paris. Last summer, in fact. He used to come here several times a year, you know. Your mother, oh, I think I hadn't seen her since we all spent Christmas together one year. You had already emigrated, I remember."

I wished then that I had asked for a glass of wine, not juice, as if I were a child, as I stared at him out of the shipwreck of my life. I longed for him to give me something, tell me something I hadn't known. But what could he give me? Whatever he said, he couldn't give me back my parents.

I said, stubborn and trying not to go on crying, "Yes, and I have just separated from my husband."

"He is American, your husband?"

"Yes. I only left a few days ago."

"And you think it can't be mended? You can't go back?"

"I'm not sure. I don't think you can ever really go back, do you? But maybe it's possible to find another way forward." I wanted to ask him, *What do you think? Is there a film that talks about this? Come on, you are French. Is there a theory, a story, a clue, to how life may be lived?*

"So, you are living in your parents' flat in the *cinquième*, right?"

"Yes, except it's mine now. Ours, I should say. My siblings are all busy, married with kids, mortgages, all that, so they don't mind. We were going to rent it out, but we didn't, thank God."

"I see. And what will you do, here in Paris?"

"Get a job, eventually. Write too. I have a book of poetry to finish, though probably nobody will want to publish it." My first one, I now thought, had probably been a fluke, even though the prize I had won for it was three thousand dollars, good money for poetry, and it had been put forward for a National Book Award.

"Ah, like my film."

"Yes. What happens to all the films and books that don't get published? All the ideas? Does it make a difference that we have made them, do you think?" *Does it make a difference that people live, and then die?*

He said, "I think so. Sometimes films are found decades later. In cellars, in ruins. You know, someone found *L'Atalante* in a cellar, decades after it was made? You know it, Jean Vigo? One of the best films ever made."

"I haven't seen it, no."

"Ah, you must, you must. Rent it. I am sure you can find it—1934, it was, before the war. Beautiful. And it could so easily have been lost, buried in rubble, dust, the debris of the war. A lot of things are lost, but not all of them forever. I am sure that what you write will see the light of day, and of course if I didn't believe that about my films, I doubt that I could go on."

There was comfort in knowing that he had known my parents years ago, when everything was safe, when I was young. It was like being close to the wall of a house that the sun has warmed, that after sunset still stands at your back like a radiator. I could put out my hand and touch him, and almost warm myself at him. But I was no longer safe, nor young. I couldn't base my whole life on somebody one day finding a torn manuscript of mine in a cellar. Neither could I tell this man I hardly knew, what—or whom—I had just seen.

I said, "I suppose Jean Vigo never knew that people found his film."

"No. Of course not. He died young. But it lives on, that is the point."

"André, tell me about them. My parents. Anything you can remember? Anything I might not know."

He looked across at me, a whitened man with a sweet mouth and pale-blue eyes behind thick glasses. He saw my hunger. Crumbs of information, even meaningless scraps of memory, would do. Then I could go away and, like the people who painstakingly put that film back together scrap by torn and faded scrap, create what I needed, a coherent story, in order to live.

"Peter was somebody who was never content with things as they were, I always thought. It was as if he always wanted something more, or different. He was a restless soul. But your mother, she couldn't have been more down-to-earth. I think she connected him to reality, in a way. Would you like something else?"

"No, thanks, that was fine."

"I knew your father better than I knew your mother. Though I was very fond of her too. It was partly because he came here on business. I always felt he was someone who had a hidden life, not exactly secretive but as if something was going on behind the scenes. I knew about his other woman." He paused and looked at me. "Forgive me for mentioning her, Gaby, but it was partly why he came here. There was a journalist. I never met her, but she was part of his life for quite some time, I think. Also, I think he would have liked to be a painter himself, not just a dealer. There was some disappointment in his youth, I think. His father wouldn't allow him to go to art college, you know. You look very like him, by the way. But, Gaby, I'm afraid I shall have to go. I have another appointment. I'm so sorry. I had forgotten when I suggested this. Can we meet again?"

His other woman? I was stunned by what he had just said. I wanted to hold on to him, make him tell me more, but I didn't know how to without seeming impossibly needy. I said, "Yes, of course," which is something you often find yourself saying in Paris. (A journalist? She was part of his life for some time . . . But who? What? How?)

I asked him instead, "How did you know I was here?"

"I know one of your neighbors, in your building. She said she'd seen someone, a young woman coming and going, that your apartment was inhabited, so I guessed it would be you, not your sister. I gave her the letter, as I thought you might not think to look in your mailbox. Your sister lives in London still?"

"Cambridge. She's married, with kids, so, yes, it was more likely to have been me."

We wrote e-mail addresses and phone numbers on small squared pages torn from his notebook. Outside, the crowds on the boulevard Saint-Germain slowed and massed, and the tempo of the afternoon had changed. The striding and pushing had slowed to a saunter, and I remembered the French word for strolling, *flâner*. I had not been able to do much flâning since I had arrived a week ago. Living in south Florida had made me take sunshine as a right, like orange juice, like the ocean, like not having to wear a coat.

"André, thanks for the drink. Thanks for asking me."

I noticed that he frowned as I took his hand, in the weak sunshine outside the café, where there seemed to be well-dressed bodies flung onto every possible chair. Once this place must have been empty, quiet, a suitable café for two middle-aged writers to meet and talk. Today, the rush-hour traffic on boulevard Saint-Germain roared past.

"Gaby, are you all right? What you have told me makes me worry about you. I mean, I know you are grown up, but I can't help thinking of Peter and Helen and that they would want to know you are all right. Will you come to me if you need anything, the smallest thing, it doesn't matter. Call me. Or write me an e-mail. I'm here for the next two weeks, then I have to go and see my mother in Normandy. Promise, if there's anything at all."

"Thank you, André. It's good to see you, and good to know that you are here." Another thing I have learned lately is that people like to be thanked, and like to be important, even necessary. I couldn't think what I would ask him for, what the "smallest thing" would be, but I could say wholeheartedly that I would let him know.

"I am sorry, but did I shock you, telling you about your father's other woman?"

"Oh, no, I always knew. It's okay," I lied, because I didn't want to admit how shocked I was, even to myself. "And thanks for the story." The quick thud of my heart, the sweat in my armpits, were the real effects of what he had told me.

"The story?"

"The story of your film. It's safe with me. Even if it never gets made, I have it all in my head now. Better than in a cellar, perhaps."

He smiled, and after a hesitation, we kissed on both cheeks. He went off to the *métro*, and I to wander down rue de Seine, past the statue of Voltaire grinning to himself in a little garden, and along the quai des Grands Augustins toward Place Saint-Michel. I needed to walk it off, to shed tears as I walked, to be invisible in the faint glow before sunset, to digest what I had just heard about my dead parent. Ask, and you get told. Want information, and you get a piece you never wanted. Had I known? I began to remember all the times my father had not been there, and both we and our mother had seemed to find it perfectly normal. But what had I left out? What had remained invisible? I walked along the quai Malaquais, then up the Montagne Sainte-Geneviève and past the Panthéon, the monument to all those *grands hommes* that always feels too big and bulky for its site, and home through the Place de la Contrescarpe and down the crooked familiarity of rue Mouffetard. It seemed that I would have to begin to remember everything differently. But you can't undo memory, you can only reinterpret it.

Paris took me back into its heart as I walked. I remembered walking the banks of the Seine all those years ago when my parents had shipped me off here as a teenager, to spend summers speaking French with friends of theirs, the Beuchets, who lived on rue des Rosiers in the Marais with their daughter, Sophie, who was my age. Sophie and I had walked and walked, partly trying to lose weight, partly to exchange eye contact with young men in cafés and be invited to join them. I thought of her now—where would she be? We had lost touch, or lost interest in each other, yet those first walks across the city, all the way along the Seine, up to Trocadéro, sometimes into Belleville and up to Montmartre, sometimes along the Canal Saint-Martin and all through the Marais, had been a sort of pilgrimage for me, and she my guide in a first heady taste of Paris—and freedom.

Back at the apartment—my apartment, as I was beginning to think of it—I made tea and boiled an egg to calm myself down. I dipped toast fingers into my egg, as my mother had showed me when I was a small child, and as I had eaten my eggs ever since. I thought of her and wondered: Had she known? Had she been miserable, in private, without any of us knowing? My father had lied to her—he must have. Did she discover the lies? Was she unhappy when she drove her car out that day, when a truck had driven into her? I would never know, now. Tears dripped into my egg as I ate. I felt furious, betrayed, myself as well as her, myself where I was her, her child. Yet, I was his child too, and I could also imagine him here, alone but about to go out and meet a woman—who?—somewhere in Paris.

Later, as I was trying to get to sleep, dosed with melatonin and red wine, the light still picking its way in between the shutters, I thought again about May '68 and the two lovers who were women, student and teacher, and the car crash, and the way love flames up and then is brutally extinguished, like revolution. You can tell a story so many different ways, you can leave things out, make things up, change the characters, you can play with it endlessly. But the story I had just been presented with, the real one, was about my life. It involved me; it had involved me for years, without my knowing. It was, had to be, my story now.

3.

My father, Peter, was a secretive man, as André had said, but I knew he loved my mother. Or I thought I knew, until now. You could see it in his face when he looked at her. Sometimes he frowned and scowled, but then there was always the beseeching look, saying, *Helen, love me, I need you, I want to know you are near.* But was needing someone the same as loving her? If my father had not loved my mother but someone else, all my notions of what love was would have to be revised. I would have to forget everything I thought I knew about them. I would have to tell it all otherwise.

I was in America when he died, last November, as I had been at the time of my mother's death, two years earlier. I booked a flight from Miami and arrived at Heathrow on a wintry evening and took the train as fast as I could to Norwich, not very fast because all the trains now are called "Cross-Country" and tend to stop arbitrarily in the middle of nowhere, so that you have to sit and stare at banks of nettles. I arrived just in time for the funeral, which my brother Hugh had organized. My father had died suddenly. A heart attack, I was told. He was sixty-five, and it ran in the family. I knew he'd been taking pills and trying to do meditation for a few years, at a doctor's suggestion, after many years of drinking and eating exactly what he felt like and in between flying all over the world, taking long, fast walks along the cold beach that ran in front of their house on the east coast. He had quit smoking too, saying that there was no point now, it was not a mark of freedom but of simple idiocy. He'd been lonely since my mother died, no doubt, and my sister and brothers could only visit so often. The house was cold, isolated, uncomfortable, but he wouldn't move from it to a smaller place in Cambridge, near my sister, Margot, which had been suggested. I used to call him from Florida and listen to his ranting about George Bush and American politics, his jibes about how he didn't know how anybody in her right mind could live there.

"Dad," I'd say, "what about Margaret Thatcher? You didn't leave the country when she was in power."

"Ah, but we were militant. Labour was militant in those days. What are the Democrats doing? Nothing at all. I don't know how you can put up with it, darling. Florida, of all places. I suppose the weather must help. When are you coming over, anyway?"

And then he was dead. Hugh called me, and then Phil. None of us could believe it. He had been found out in the marshes near Blakeney, as if he'd been a vagrant. Facedown in some reeds, his old coat spread around him. It made me think of Magwitch in *Great Expectations*. At the funeral in the flint church that reared up out of the marshes and summoned everyone with its peal of bells, the way it had announced shipwrecks for centuries, there were not many people. Hugh, Phil, and I; and Phil's twins; and Marg and her husband and children; and some neighbors, the Blacks, who looked after the cottage when he was away; none of his friends from London; no one from the gallery; certainly no one from Paris. At the time, I thought it was strange. I asked Hugh, "Didn't you put it in the papers? Didn't any of his friends know?" I couldn't believe there wasn't anyone who knew him at work. My father had had a gallery on Cork Street for many years and had traveled widely, buying art. He was always having drinks with one person, dinner with another. Amsterdam, Paris, Rome. Friends, colleagues, mysterious people with strange names. Where were they all?

I thought back: there had not been a strange woman at the funeral, in black, standing apart, looking like the French actress Fanny Ardant; I would have noticed.

Hugh said, "I put it in the *Times* and the *Telegraph* and phoned a few people who might not read newspapers, and we got quite a lot of letters, you can read them when you have time. Nice letters. People missed him, they minded. But I suppose nobody wanted to travel to the wilds of Norfolk on a cold November day and catch their deaths themselves. That's all I can think."

I wondered whether André Schaffer had been one of the people called. He had seemed very calm about his friend Peter's death—not the reaction you would expect from a contemporary, a man nearly the same age.

I remembered the cold in the church, and then, just when we were getting used to it, a blast of hot air as the central heating suddenly kicked in. From freezing, we sweated. Young, spotty-faced men from the undertaker's heaved my father's coffin up the aisle as the organ wheezed out its traditional hymn tunes, and I'd thought of how English this was, all of us in our winter coats—mine one I'd left in a cupboard in my parents' house for years, with moth holes in it now—rubbing our hands together, watching the plain pine coffin shouldered up the aisle, dreading going to the crematorium, dreading the tea afterward in the cottage; there would be the whisky bottle passed surreptitiously from hand to hand, the slight sniffs that stood in for tears. Then, the sudden blare of heating, so we were all red in the face and sweaty in the armpits, panting to get out. The church was one of the East Anglian churches built when this part of England was rich in sheep and wool. A wool church. It was where my mother's funeral had taken place, only two years earlier. Yet somehow because Dad had still been there to organize it, none of us had felt quite so bereft. We were not yet orphans, then, nor were we the chief mourners. I remembered the feeling from that time, the sheer astonishment that our mother was no longer there to try

18

to organize our lives, she from whose control I had fled, at seventeen, never really to return.

Our father's coffin had looked strangely small as it was set down. Phil, the younger of my two brothers, nudged me suddenly and said, "I wonder if it's really him in there?" and his son Andy immediately said, "Maybe it isn't him; maybe it's someone else!" and Hugh, tall and frowning over his hymnbook, shushed them both.

"What happened to the dog?" I asked Hugh at the tea.

"The dog?"

"Muffin, whatever she was called. Dad's dog. He wouldn't have gone for a walk without her. Did she come home alone, or sit there nobly with the body, like dogs in movies?"

"You know, I haven't the slightest idea. I never thought of that. I wonder where she is?"

After my father's funeral, I went back to Matt and to Florida and tried to take up my life as it had been, but nothing worked. I began to detest heat, palm trees, the traffic in Miami, people's accents, the sameness of days; I began to detest my husband. I knew that none of this was his fault, that he had not changed during my brief absence, but I was unable to love him, unable even to talk to him. I was more depressed than I knew: cast adrift, as I felt it, on the uncaring tide of American life, stunned by the glitter and speed of the city, horrified by its highways that I had to negotiate in order to go anywhere, in hiding from the brightness, the hard surfaces, even from the unending blue of the ocean. *Matt, I have to go, if only for a while, I have to leave you.* I practiced saying it in whispers, to myself in the bathroom; then I said it to him. He hardly argued. I realized that I had been, for many weeks, an intolerable presence in his life. He looked at me across the breakfast table when I said it aloud, then he simply got up, left his plate of scrambled eggs and toast, took his coffee cup with him, and walked out of the room. I didn't follow him. I looked at congealing scrambled eggs and heard the front door slam. If there had been a conversation, would it have been different? At the time, our whole marriage seemed to be expressed by that refusal of his to talk, even to defend himself.

"I love you." It was the last thing he said to me, on Concourse D at Miami International Airport, where he had insisted on coming to see me off. The first time someone says these words to you, they go through you like an electric shock. The last time—well, it sounds so plaintive. In America, it is supposed to be the magic word, the phrase to end all argument. The open sesame, if you like. Lights go up when you say it, music plays. Where it is used more sparingly, in England, for example, it does not have this instant argument-ending power.

I didn't say, *It doesn't work like that.* Or, *Love isn't enough.* I love you. I know, people say it all the time, at the end of phone calls even, light and meaningless as "have a nice day," leaving the *I* out of it, so that it comes out subjectless, disconnected from themselves. Love you. But we did, once, and perhaps we would again. I did not know.

I chose Paris to run to, because it was home and yet not home. It was where I had first felt free, anonymous, a person in my own right, during those long summer vacations with Sophie on rue des Rosiers, where we two, at fourteen, fifteen, walked all day and were never asked by her busy parents where we had been. These days, although I often woke still weeping in the shrinking dark, I felt that my parents' apartment held and comforted me. I walked out early into the chill gray mornings, and had a cup of coffee and a croissant at the nearest café as soon as it opened. Sometimes the woman was still washing the floor, and would go out to the bakery opposite for my croissant, leaving the floor to dry in islands around me. I sat in a corner with my notebook, one of those black Moleskine ones with an elastic band that Picasso, Hemingway, and Bruce Chatwin are supposed to have used and everyone else has now. Boys' notebooks, evidently, but useful and chic. Outside, the vans were still unloading. Inside, the chairs were still stacked on top of each other. The lights were all on, long yellow lanterns hanging from the ceiling, and it was warm inside; on these chilly days leading up to summer, they still had the heating on. Radiators ticked and sang. Men came in carrying stacked boxes with lettuces packed in them, leaves showing green in the cracks. The waiter came out from the kitchen, a round tray balanced on one hand, wiping tables with a rag held in his other hand as he went. He uncoupled the chairs and pushed them into place. People came in gradually, wearing raincoats and scarves, in the drab colors of Paris. There was a man who perched up at the end of the bar on a stool each morning reading *Libération* or *Le Parisien*, drinking a glass of white wine that the waiter set before him without being asked. The café smelled of coffee and new bread, and people unfolded their thin crackling newspapers and set out their laptops, and the market stalls outside were covered still—like tents in a nomads' camp.

I sat at the same table every morning and sipped my good coffee and looked around me and, because I was alone, was able to feel part of it all, a little more each day. It was like being invisible, yet allowed to belong. I began to notice things again. One day at a time, isn't this how it goes? Perhaps this was the start of feeling alive.

There were moments during that first week in Paris—when I had turned the key to let myself into the apartment—when I could hardly get through the door before I began to sob. I paced, sobbing, talking to myself. I felt slightly crazy, doing this, but somehow justified. It was what I had tried to hold in during my months back in Florida, as if by sheer willpower I could stop the full pain of loss, and guilt. Lights went on in the buildings across the courtyard, I could hear footsteps overhead and people letting themselves into their apartments, and I wondered if they could hear me. I turned up the jazz program on the radio, just in case. I howled, sobbed, blew my nose, poured myself a glass of wine, sat down to try to read. It was a process, I knew that. Everyone had told me so. I knew about the phases of grief, in theory: you suffered every day, several times a day, then every other day, then once a week, then once a fortnight, and so on. I just had not allowed myself to cry like this, as if the life I led in Florida forbade it. Now I opened the floodgates. I was alone at last and could cry any time I wanted for the loss of these two people who had loved me more than anyone else ever had, or would. The loss of Matt was small by comparison, but similar, like an echo of loss, a way in. I thought of him, his voice, his body, his hands, things we did together, the immense innocent hopes of marriage, and the wrenching sounds began. I thought of him going to bed alone, waking alone. Standing in the bathroom naked, looking beautiful. I saw him bend to feed the cat, who hadn't understood that I had gone. I thought of the cat not understanding, receiving her plate of kibble from Matt's hands, and the sobs began again. I paced, muttered, sobbed, threw myself down on the off-white sofa that my mother would never have bought, and cried—for the cat, myself, my young husband, my dead parents, life as it used to be, for being forty, for not having children, for the tragedies of the world—and then I blew my nose, poured myself another glass of wine, took a handful of cashew nuts, and began to think, should I have an omelette or pasta for supper? Outside, the evening turned very slowly dark, not like the sudden curtains of dark that come down after a quick sunset in Florida. I knew that grief had an end, and I thought I knew how to get there. It seemed to be a valuable thing to have learned, even if so far it was only in theory. All the therapeutic theory I had heard since my mother's death had been about closure, moving on, moving through, but how this actually worked, I'd had no idea. Her death was still raw in me when I had to face my father's. But I simply believed— deep down, rightly, as it turned out—that one does not cry forever.

4.

Peter and Helen Greenwood, my parents, met in London in 1960 and were married in 1963, when I think she must have been already pregnant with Hugh. He was a student at the Slade and she was training as a teacher in a postgraduate program at London University. He lived in Fulham, she in Chelsea. They met at a party. It seems that their lives were full of parties at that time; I imagined them: men with beards from the Slade or Chelsea art school, well-brought-up young women from the home counties and East Anglia, the cheap wine, the cheese, the crumbs, the music, Buddy Holly and then the Beatles and then the Stones. If they didn't tell me the details, they were there in the myth of the sixties—in the films of the time, the fashions, all the stuff, the posters and the records, the casual references, the habits that lived on in their later lives. We who came next were never quite going to get what the sixties were all about. We were never there, or if we had been there, it was only at table height, as toddlers, dressed as baby hippies in strange offbeat colors, standing there while all the debates and discussions and arguments went on above our heads, in the fumes of cigarette smoke and then pot and the smells of spilt wine and patchouli. My parents didn't stay this way all their lives, but there was something about them that didn't change, that echoed that way of life; it was on them like a faint odor, it was there like Dylan heard from another room. You could say, and some of my contemporaries have, that they never really grew up. But they were my parents, so of course for me they were the adults. Until I became an adult myself, and could see them from higher than table height, and began to wonder what lay behind all the in-jokes and the references, the way they were together, kissing in public, fighting in private, and what was particular to them, the people who had come together to make us, to make me, to make the society in which I grew up.

They had bought the Paris apartment in about 1980, to use for weekends and then longer periods of time, when he was buying paintings over here and she collecting things to fill up their house in England. I had been here several times before, first with them, when they made Phil and me follow them all around the Louvre, the Jeu de Paume, and then the Pompidou, at an age when we had no interest in looking at rooms full of paintings; then with a boyfriend from London for a rather unsatisfactory first-sex weekend; and once again with my sister when we had tickets to a Pink Floyd concert in the eighties. It felt, now, like a different place, but I could not remember enough of the former rather shabby décor except that it had been full of things bought by my mother from antique and junk markets all over France.

When I saw the *"Brocante"* signs about the antique market that was going to be set up in the street that weekend, I thought of her and her collector's passion: how she would have loved all that chipped old china, those smooth-handled knives, the debris from emptied houses and barns all over France, these old heavy lace-embroidered cotton nightgowns of which there always seems to be an endless supply. She used to wear them, when I was small, and she always used Opinel knives in the kitchen, and big Le Creuset pots that nearly broke your arm when you tried to heave them off the stove. My mother was an addict of *brocante*. She bought French linens and odd spoons, jugs with cracked cheeks made in Quimper, bowls for drinking coffee, pots with *"Sel"* and *"Farine"* and *"Café"* and so on written on them so that when I was small I knew these words and what they were: the soft shift of flour, the grain of sea salt, the strong, dark smell of coffee. Again, heavy to lift off the shelf, and the shelf itself made of heavy stripped pine—everything, dresser, table, chairs, made of stripped pine, and the floors, cold to my bare feet and presumably hers, quarry tiles always, never anything soft. My mother, ruthless in her passion for getting things right. Like the brown quarry tiles, she was hard-wearing, serviceable, with no concessions made to comfort. But she loved me, I did know that; she swept me up off those hard floors to embrace me when I was small, she slapped and then kissed, she shouted and then handed out bread straight from the oven. I associated her with warm crusts, as well as cold floors. The words of love songs, as well as feet clattering in clogs and legs marked with dark hair that for years she refused to shave.

In this apartment on rue des Lyonnais, there's nothing old, chipped, or uncomfortable now. Perhaps Dad insisted. Or perhaps there was only any point in old French rustic if you carted it back to England. Perhaps he redecorated after her death. I don't know. But now there are white plates, white cups, white bowls, plain rush matting on the floor, and absolutely no Quimper pottery or old chipped saucers with curled edges and flowers on them. It could be that he was so distraught by her death that he simply went out and bought everything new, so that no signs of her were left to sadden him. Perhaps he had had more than enough of French rustic. Perhaps it was to clear the decks for the other woman in his life. I'd wondered what he did when he came here alone, apart from wandering around galleries looking at paintings, and meeting other dealers. Now I thought I knew.

My two Parisian friends René and Marie-Christine had been e-mailing and texting me since I'd arrived. I'd met René when he worked for my father in London as a student. He had spent one summer trying to learn the business, running around after my father, answering phones and paying bills. It was the year that I worked for my father in the gallery too, having left school abruptly and gone to London, the year he rescued me from my chaotic teenage self. I remembered René as a gangling young man with spots on his neck and a prominent Adam's apple, but nice gray eyes; now he was as I was, all grown up. Marie-Christine was the latest in a long line of his girlfriends; they had been together for several years. They invited me round, and we sat at the kitchen table in René's apartment on rue de l'Arbalète and ate pork chops and green beans and drank our wine. I noticed that French people were careful about asking Americans about politics these days, or were until Barack Obama began gleaming at them on posters, on the front of the *Nouvel Obs*, and on TV. They realized, I think, that we had been feeling battered by the world's hatred of our government, the one we hated so hopelessly ourselves. They also didn't ask questions about why I wasn't with my husband, only nodded when I said that he was not joining me. We just ate, and drank our wine, and talked about films. People seemed to talk a lot about films in Paris and were always telling each other their plots and going on about their directors. It was a way, perhaps, to talk about life indirectly; like all the theories French people have, it was a structure within which people could live.

"Gaby?" Marie-Christine called out to me across antique furniture, old postcards, shawls spread across chairs, baroque-looking clocks, and boxes full of keys. We were wandering through the market that sprawled across the Place Saint-Médard and up the avenue des Gobelins, that last weekend in May, and I was thinking again about my mother and how she would have adored it, and that I myself would never buy any of these old, worn things. "Where are you? Don't get lost!"

They were looking after me, the orphan who wandered with them through the debris of French bourgeois society, fingering things, turning things over to look at prices, not wanting anything. The light of early summer made faces pale and sharply lined, and it fell in shafts on the shabbiness of the antiques, the worn rubbed surfaces of all these objects. Velvet-backed chairs, lace tablecloths, darkened pitted silver. Enamel and pewter, brass and copper, the real and the fake; old carpets with rose-pink, sky-blue patterns; garish new ones in tan and orange. As if nothing mattered. As if everything were the same, and for sale, with price tags on little white cards and men who lied systematically about the prices, pretended to haggle, pocketed wallets full of notes, and locked up their cashboxes.

"I'm not buying anything today," Marie-Christine announced. "I haven't seen the right table, so I'll wait." She wanted a certain size and height, to fit exactly into a corner of her tiny apartment. She had been looking, she said, for years.

I thought, but did not say, *How can you care, how can you want to buy furniture, or anything?* Perhaps American consumerism had cured me of ever wanting to buy anything again. Or perhaps it was that my parents' house, emptied of all its furniture, had been sold without me, and everything of theirs dispersed.

I saw Marie-Christine's glance at René, her pursed mouth and raised eyebrows, signaling, *How can we make her want something?* She showed me a jade pendant that lay in the palm of her hand, a black ribbon threading it.

"Only ten euros, look, isn't that pretty?"

I bought it, not because I wanted it but because I did not want to disappoint her. I paid, and let her tie it around my neck.

"There, it really suits you. It makes your eyes look green, like the jade."

For them, I smiled. I looked in the cracked little mirror the salesman held out, saw my fading tan, my eyes, not red as they felt, but green, and the contrast of the black ribbon against the skin of my throat.

"Très jolie," said Marie-Christine firmly. *"Très, très jolie."*

5.

Over the next few days, a cold late spring turned toward summer, and blue sky blazed above Paris almost the way it does above Florida. Everyone was in floating dresses or shorts, with sandals, baring flesh that rarely saw the sun. I felt my body relax; when you have lived in the tropics for years, cold never can feel normal, and gray skies make you feel as if something is wrong with the world. The film set on which I had glimpsed my father, or his double, had disappeared instantly to make room for the *brocante*, and that had disappeared to leave the usual rue Mouffetard food market. René, who'd also been there at the day of the filming, remarked that it had all looked much too rural for Paris in 1951, and too retro, with stuff from the forties on view that would have been gone, or outmoded. Hay, birds in cages, ancient carts, it was all a bit overdone; but then, it was an American film. You used to be able to rely on solid objects to tell you about reality, but not anymore; anything could be faked, copied, reproduced, put there to fool you. I didn't tell anybody about my vision, or whatever it was, but still I walked about with a kind of sixth sense operating, eyes in the back of my head, an abnormal sensitivity of skin. I would feel it if he appeared again. I found myself staring at elderly men in the *métro*, on buses, in lines in the market, outside cinemas, in crowds pushing home on rue Claude Bernard in the evening. *It couldn't have been my father. It must have been my father. My father is dead. How do you know? You never saw him dead. People don't make that kind of mistake, don't be absurd.*

When I was young, my father did conjuring tricks at our birthday parties, making things—a knotted handkerchief, a string of beads, an egg—disappear and reappear. He swung us upside down and twirled us around until the world dizzied us into orbit and we saw stars and fireworks and our mother told him to put us down. He made up stories about things that had happened to him, like being cast afloat on an ice floe and lost in the Sahara desert, and I knew by the time I was ten or eleven these things could not have really happened, that he wasn't exactly lying to us, just making life more exciting. Once, he sold a forged painting by mistake and nearly got into serious trouble. Other times, he showed us how to forge signatures, make copies of documents, use invisible ink made with lemon juice for writing that you had to warm with an iron to read. But it was for fun; I don't believe he would ever have deliberately faked anything that mattered. He invented codes and wrote to us using them; he laid trails for us to follow, using gnomic rhymes and passwords to lead us to where the treasure was. My father the trickster. I began to see this all in a changed light now. But surely he wouldn't have gone so far as to fake his own death? Why? What would be the point? And if he had, what was he doing in Paris, on a film set in our neighborhood, not even noticing me?

I was his youngest, and he'd always had time for me, when he was at home. I remember his winking at me, his smile across the dinner table, as if he wanted to let me in on secrets. There was always that slightly baffling complicity, that question: What did he want of me? I laughed when he wanted me to, flattered by his attention. But there was always a secret I was never to know: a further ruse, an inner joke. He teased me, pulling handkerchiefs that were made into rabbits with ears from the pockets of his trousers, hiding things in full view, so that I stumbled upon them with delight and surprise, giggling at the incongruity of a cauliflower on a mantelpiece, my school uniform rakish on my mother's tailor's dummy, a single shoe on a place setting at the table, an empty coat hanging on a peg in the hall with shoes below it and a hat above, making a hollow man to scare and thrill me. Was it because I was a child still, and my siblings had already grown away from him, mocked his own childish humor, scorned his tricks and jokes? He'd had me, I thought now, in the palm of his hand. And when I became an angry teenager, when I ran away from home to find a possibly dangerous life in London, he came after me, pinned me down, gave me a job, spent his lunchtimes sitting on a desk in his messy office where I was supposed to type and make lists of clients, and gave me his full attention. "You're like me, Gab," he used to say, "You're a wild one, and we have to calm you down a bit, don't we?" I was pleased, to be like him, to be thought wild. I wanted it, to be his true daughter. I modeled myself on him in those days, charismatic Peter Greenwood, whom everybody loved.

Days passed, my jet lag passed; I no longer looked quite so red-eyed and exhausted. I walked back and forth from the apartment to shops and markets, to meet my friends and go to movies with them, to eat in restaurants and sit in bars, and all the time I was looking out for him. It was like being a spy. The three of us, René and Marie-Christine and I, went to see a film about May 1968, the one that had been made instead of André's, and I told them that I had been born in May 1968, it was my month and year. When I was a child, my mother was always introducing me to people as a child of the revolution—her own piece of street cred, you might say. I couldn't help thinking that André's film would have been more interesting, because he had seen behind the obvious details, the barricades and rock throwing, the obligatory political stances. He had gone for something personal, something fragile: an unlikely love between two women. That was why his film had not been made. As we were coming out, Marie-Christine said, "Gaby, are you all right? You seem rather nervous."

"I'm fine."

"You're not worried about something?"

"She's still sad," René said. "It's our job to cheer her up."

"We aren't doing a good enough job," Marie-Christine said. "Shall we go for dinner somewhere? A drink?"

I said, "I don't sleep very well, that's all."

"It's normal," Marie-Christine said, in a tone that was probably that of her mother.

They exchanged a glance across me. They knew about Matt and me, and what they did not know, they guessed. *It's normal,* she meant, *if you have nobody to sleep with, when you are used to sleeping with your husband.* They smiled at each other, possibly thinking up a further plan to cheer me up. I shook my head, *no, no, really,* but they only laughed. "Come for dinner tomorrow. We will give you a surprise."

Yves was probably in his late thirties and was very dark, with curly hair and black eyes and a wide-lipped mouth that I liked the look of. He sat in René's apartment on the one big easy chair and didn't get up when I came in but grinned and held out a hand. Marie-Christine was pushing furniture around so that four chairs were free, and René was bringing in bottles and little bowls of olives and nuts. Yves presumably knew as well as I did why he was there. It was all right. People invited other people they knew to hook up with their friends; it was part of the coupling plot that ran the world. It was about helping people to cheer up. In France, it was evidently unconnected with plans for marriage. I sat down next to Yves and suddenly smelled him, sharp and peppery. You don't usually pick up someone's smell like this, unless they are very dirty or wearing perfume, but the smell of Yves came to me strong and immediate and very compelling. I breathed him in, before we had even said a word.

31

After talking about the film, and the one that had been shot on rue Mouffetard, and films in general, and American politics—what did I think of Obama? Hillary? Would America ever elect a black, or a woman, president?—we all moved into the kitchen and sat around the square table there, close to each other because the room was small, our elbows on the table, bread in a basket, wineglasses and a bottle of René's family's wine, and Marie-Christine serving soup. René, like me, could live in the desirable fifth arrondissement because he had inherited an apartment here from his father, who lived here for years before he more or less retired from publishing. We were the children of the bourgeoisie, he and I, however much we might protest; Marie-Christine, who had a tiny flat in the twentieth, on the outskirts of the city, sometimes made us feel it. I never discovered that night where Yves came from, just noticed the way he tore at the bread as if he were famished, and the way his eyes narrowed when he spoke, so that he looked sarcastic—possibly without meaning to be. And the way he smelled. Pheromones, I know. You can't explain them or deny them—they simply are the body's own anarchic signature. I don't know whether the others noticed or not, but we hardly spoke, just eyed each other and ate. He did say that he'd been at Sciences Po and was now doing a teaching job and hoping to get certified, because there wasn't much going for philosophers these days, thanks to Sarkozy and his plan to make everyone in France work harder. The exam he would take in a few months' time would allow him to teach in secondary education all over France, so there was no telling where he might wind up. As he said this, he grinned at me over his lifted spoon and then slurped his onion soup. René and Marie-Christine's matchmaking dinner was already a success. They were soon exchanging raised eyebrows and pursed mouths across the cheese and strawberries, and Yves and I were playing "let's gratify the hosts." A lot of good red wine had gone down, and it was close to eleven, though outside the open windows, the night was hardly even dark, just a greenish cool dusk with swallows and house martins diving and darting between roofs. I was tired and slightly drunk and ready to forget my sorrows at least temporarily, and Yves picked up my hand at last and said, *"On y va?"* Oh, the lovely simplicity of French. Phrases like this flow off the tongue, both exact and ambiguous, and one thing leads easily to another because there are the words for it. It has all been lived and practiced for so long that exactly the right thing happens at times like this, and everybody knows.

They had meant us to leave together, that much was clear, and we were being good guests, doing what was expected. They stood in the doorway against a square of yellow light, like parents, and saw us off down the narrow stairs. I went first, conscious of him behind me. He slipped and slid, loose footed, boyish, but I could feel his eyes on me. We clicked the door open and stepped into the street. His arm immediately through mine, guiding me home—the long way around, I noticed. Down the cobbled hill of rue Mouffetard and across Place Saint-Médard, with the dark trees huddled in clumps around the church, and past the boulangerie, across Claude Bernard on the crosswalk, traffic sparse by now, nobody walking but ourselves, and only the all-night cops outside the Israeli building on rue Broca in their sentry boxes to see us go past.

I said, "Where do you live?"

"Far from here. Near Porte de Montreuil. I'll get the *métro*. But we can see each other again?"

I said, "Yes, okay." We exchanged cell phone numbers. No point, we seemed to be agreeing, in arguing with fate, or pheromones, or other people's plans for us. But in our glance at each other before parting, there was the tacit agreement: *not now, but very soon.*

A day later, after meeting him for a beer at the little café on the corner of my street, I thumbed in the code, and our big gate opened, and we stepped inside. Then, keys in locks, more doors opening, the stairs, my front door. Inside the door, kisses, tongues, clothes sliding, hands grasping, the rapid search of another's body, who are you, where do we fit? No thought of anything but the immediate puzzles of belt buckles, buttons, bras, and tight underpants. He was, as I'd guessed he would be, smooth skinned and slippery almost to the touch, his skin not soft exactly but close-grained, tight. Some people have rough, porous skin, while others are smooth from head to toe. He, with his bush of black hair, a surprisingly hairless body, just a sprinkle around the nipples and a flare of black at his groin. I was hungry, ecstatic, finding him just as fast as I could, and surprised at my own hunger. We fell on the couch and slid off onto the floor, but the rough matting scratched my back, and without saying anything coherent, we made it to the bedroom and fell upon the bed. There, he explored my mouth and then my breasts, and his hand found his way to my crotch, and I grasped his penis, and he gasped, and then he was pulling on a condom with one-handed expertise, and finding his way inside. I couldn't remember when I'd last made love with Matt, but it was not like this. Maybe it had been once. But no, Matt was a slow lover, a deliberate one, and, after all, we had been married for years. There's nothing quite like the dizzy, grasping, messy slipping intensity of the first time. Even if it hurts, and he misses, and you bump noses and get your underclothes tied around your feet, you find your way like a blind person rushing down an alley, in through that door, into the discovery, and he's in you, and you're holding him fast for dear life, and then the movement begins, and you can hardly bear it.

There was a street light outside the window that struck in yellow stripes through the shutters to where we grappled on the bed, and it fell across my eyes and then his, and he threw up a hand across his own eyes and then covered mine, and in the darkness of my closed lids, I felt him come, with a few rapid little movements that didn't do it for me—too fast, too soon, not the slow sweeps I was used to, but it didn't matter, we would get there.

He held me, stroked me, and then lowered his head to begin kissing me with long, sweet kisses, licking and stroking, and then, of course, I felt myself rising and gathering in the way there really aren't any words for, only sensations, and I fell shouting beneath him, my knees shaking, my whole body breaking open. I might faint, it was so sweet and harsh and insistent. Suddenly I remembered Matt talking about it, the American expression, "giving head," and I began to laugh.

What's funny? Nothing. I'll tell you. Oh, God—and from shaking and nearly fainting, I was off into helpless laughter that came close to tears. He held me as if I was breaking apart, and indeed I was. Then we flung ourselves on our backs on the soaked sheets, our heads pillowed together and feet sticking out like two halves of a wishbone. The street lights striped us yellow, and an ambulance went past with its hee-haw note, somewhere a street away.

6.

In the morning, I woke with a familiar sensation of alarm from much earlier in my life, when I had been a teenaged waif in eighties London: What on earth did I do last night, what did I drink, what did I say, who did I go home with? Then I remembered it all. He'd left at three or so, after throwing on his clothes, pushing into his shoes without fastening them, kissing me fast and hard on the mouth, and then nuzzling a little into my neck. We had slept together for an hour or so. He'd said, *"On se téléphone."* I remembered that. Then I woke again close to ten, and there was this panic, this leap into awareness. What had I done? It had all been too fast. Nobody in her right mind had sex on a barely second date. Nobody married, anyway. Guilt threatened—or at least, the unease of having done something precipitous that could not be undone. One other person now knew me this way, the way of the body, and I felt hot as I remembered it. I made tea and dragged the duvet back over me as I got back into bed with my mug. I had made love with someone who wasn't Matt for the first time in eight years or more, and—come on, admit it—I had loved it. But the thought of Matt himself, in America, fast asleep in another time zone without any idea of what I had been up to, gave me a pang. He would get up in a few hours, having slept, having dreamed, having woken without me; he would shower and make coffee and look at the day and maybe think of me, but he would have no idea. In his book, I would have betrayed him.

To me, what I had done seemed to have put me in solidarity with the whole male sex; I simply liked all of them better this morning, including him. It's a strange thing that so-called infidelity can bring you full circle, to think tenderly of your spouse because he is of the same species as the one who brought you so much pleasure, because the blueprint works. Their bodies, their skins, their smells; the fact that they were once all little boys, and will become old men; their anxieties and their performances, not so very different; their desires to please; their fear of failure; their faked insouciance; their swift departures. But I knew that Matt would certainly never see things this way.

I got up slowly after drinking my tea, an English habit that he had once nurtured by bringing me tea in bed on good days—dear Matt, he had learned to boil a kettle and abandon the microwave—and I showered and brushed my teeth and stared into the mirror the way you have to after sex to see if you have changed. I thought of my father, because I looked like him in this raw state, and I wondered if he had used this flat for his rendezvous with that woman, whoever she was. Of course he had. Today, I had to believe it.

I went to my usual café for breakfast because I needed some air and had run out of bread. It was a cool gray morning again, and the gutters ran with water and the pavements were damp. The café was half populated by people reading newspapers, but they were mostly outside. I went inside, because I sat at the same table always so that people would remember me. In a shifting world, these things count. She is the one who sits at the table in the corner and orders a *grand crème* and a croissant and a glass of water, who writes in a little black notebook, who watches the men come in with their stacks of boxes of lettuce and herbs and stares at the other patrons of the café as if trying to commit them to memory. At the same time, my thoughts and feelings remain invisible. I never talk to anyone for long. I just observe them and want them to remember me: two vices of a writer. I didn't know what I would do with the scattered words in the black notebook, what they would become, but they marked my trail, would show that I had existed, even when I did not. Since I won that surprising amount of money for my poetry, it all looked more real to me even when it was flung down illegibly on a small page—and they say that money has nothing to do with art.

My phone rang in my bag, and I fished it out, and when I switched on, heard René's voice. *"Eh alors, ma belle?"* To be called, this casually, beautiful.

"That was a lovely evening, thank you, René."

"So, I gather you met again?"

"Yes. Yes, we did."

"Okay, I understand. You're in public. So I don't get to hear the whole story. I was calling to see if you wanted to come with me to visit my grandmother. She lives on the next street to you; she would love to meet you. I always go on Thursdays, in the afternoon. Are you free?"

"Sure, I'd like to. Come by on your way, then, and we'll go together?" I wondered if there was any particular reason that René was inviting me to meet his grandmother today, apart from our being neighbors. It would give me a chance, anyway, to find out some more from him about Yves.

This small gap in my day was perhaps a good time to review my theories on happiness and its lack. In America, you were supposed to be happy; it was in the Constitution. In England, the best we could do, usually, was, "Mustn't grumble." In France, it seemed that happiness was a philosophical position that you could choose, as long as you were ready to surrender to pessimism when challenged.

My mother had simply said to me when I told her I was going to marry Matt, "I just want you to be happy," in a tone of voice that suggested that it would be most unlikely. My father said dreamily, "I hope you'll be as happy as we have been."

Matt's mother said, "I'm sure he'll make you very happy, dear."

I'd thought I was happy already, no problem, and that sleeping every night with Matt would make me even happier. I couldn't think why everyone was commenting on my happiness; it was just there, like health, like youth, like having enough money for now.

Then—what happened? It began to drain away. There was no solid, lasting happiness, I discovered, only the ephemeral joy of finding the right word, a line in a poem, a final image. When my parents died, too young, one after the other, wasn't I right to be unhappy? When I discovered I lived in a country that took no notice of the Geneva conventions, wasn't unhappiness a correct response? When you were faced with the deaths of thousands, a brutal war carried on in your name, and people cold-bloodedly discussing torture, wasn't happiness an insult, to memory, to humanity, to what made us so fragilely people, not beasts?

Good sex does make you happy, no doubt about it, in a very basic animal way; you bounce up and smile at the world like a dog who has been taken for a walk. To be entwined with another human being, to exchange what are rather disgustingly known as bodily fluids, to slip and slide along each other, skin close, bone socketed, to lick and kiss and giggle and doze, all this has its impacts upon unhappiness and makes it seem irrelevant, at least for the time being. You become part of the human race again, the part that pleases rather than torments each other, that makes love, not war, not pain. You look out on the day with the benign slight boredom of satedness, slowed and settled in all your fibers. Yes, I felt happier from having been to bed with Yves. But the circumstances of my life had not changed. I wondered, as I went to meet René to visit his grandmother, if perhaps the superficial things of life might have power, after all, to change the deep ones, not the other way around. If lightness of heart was the point, rather than the heaviness of taking life seriously. If my father had perhaps felt this too. If it all had to do with sex.

Light things and heavy things fall to earth at the same speed, don't they? Are we humans essentially light, or heavy? And in our headlong fall through life, does it matter which? Can we choose, or are we chosen? A bag of lead or a bag of feathers? A groan or a giggle? A blow suffered or an easy caress?

We walked together up the street, René and I, crossed the boulevard under the bridge that hides the narrow, low-down old streets that once bordered the hidden river Bièvre, beneath the straight broad lines of Haussmann's Paris. There are brass plaques on the pavement to show where the buried river flowed, and where it divided in two. I thought of an underground river, imprisoned there for centuries; surely you can't stop water flowing, it must go somewhere? I minded for it, that its waters could not ever feel the warmth of the sun.

"I didn't know your grandmother lived here."

"She's here part of the time. When we go to the country, she comes too, of course."

When I was with René, I felt the existence of dozens of other people, siblings, cousins, aunts, grandparents dead and alive, and realized what it meant in this country to have family. He really felt he was part of something, a clan, a tribe, French history. When they went on vacation, they went en masse, leaving nobody behind, and it would have been unthinkable to go anywhere but to their house in the country.

"René, will you inherit it all? What will you do?"

"I will inherit with my brothers and my cousins. There will be *le partage*. I'll probably get a house and a bit of land, and the others will keep the rest. Or sell it."

"Would you ever live there?" I couldn't imagine him living the life of a country gentleman, which these days seemed to amount to a lot of hard physical work, because no one wanted to prune trees and chop logs for a living anymore.

"I'll probably go back and forth, from here. I'll keep the apartment too." René had become an architect, not an art dealer, after all, so he presumably had the money to go with this plan.

I wondered how Marie-Christine would fit in with this way of life, she of the tiny skirts and black leggings, the job in a kindergarten, the flat in the *vingtième*. He must have read my thought. "I suppose one day we'll get married, have kids. Marie-Christine would like that." *But not yet*, his tone suggested. At some distant time in the future. He didn't seem to count being in his midforties as time to settle down.

"And you, Gaby, what about you?"

"I really don't know. But I'm here to find out, I guess."

"And with Yves? That's you finding out?"

"Yes, I suppose so. Tell me about him, René."

"You didn't have much time for any conversation, I imagine. Here, this is where we cross. She's on the ground floor, in that building there."

"I don't usually do that, you know, jump at people that way. In fact, I've been entirely virtuous ever since I married."

"Hey, I'm not criticizing you," he said. "We thought it might happen, Marie-Christine and I, so we were not surprised, just happy for you. We thought it might cheer you up. It looks as though it did."

We crossed the street where the impatient little red man switched to the striding green one. "Yves is a funny person. He's not as young as he looks. He's been married. He wanted to be a political philosopher in the grand old French tradition, but once his wife kicked him out, he couldn't survive on political thought. So he's started again, sort of at the bottom, learning how to be a schoolteacher. He's very idealistic, and he thinks that everything that's wrong with the French system begins at school. He wants to make a difference, stop children from being turned into little consumer units, give them some ideas. He's an old-style socialist, sort of son of Jospin, you could say. He's a good man, Gaby, but not an easy one. You'll see, if you stick around him long enough."

I said, "Are any men easy?"

He laughed. "Touché. You'll have to ask my grandmother. Because here we are." He punched in the gate code. It swung open, and we went inside. The door opened on a room like an aquarium, light filtered through plants. The woman who opened this inner door to us stood maybe five feet tall and smiled at us, one to the other. René bent to embrace her, and she reached up to him to receive his kisses on both cheeks, and then one again, all the while smiling at me.

"This is Gaby," René said. "She is your neighbor, *Mamie*. She lives at the other end of your street."

"Beyond the bridge?" She held my hand in hers, and it was cool and soft.

"Just beyond the bridge, yes."

"So, you are in the *cinquième*. While I am in the *treizième*, a bit down market, you could say. Good to meet you, Gaby. Are you English? American?"

"I'm English, but I've lived in America for years now. My parents had a flat here, and I'm living in it for the moment."

"Anglo-Saxons generally come here to mend broken hearts. Or to have them broken again. But I probably read too many novels. That's all I do these days, read and watch films on DVD. My grandchildren gave me a DVD player, so it's like living at the cinema; it's marvelous. René keeps me up with the latest in DVDs. Do you like Almodóvar? I watched his film *All About My Mother* last night. I don't go out anymore, you see. Books, music, films, they are my life now. And the occasional visitor. So I don't get completely lost in the realms of fantasy. You see? René's a good boy, he keeps me in touch with reality—as much as he is in touch with it himself, which maybe isn't a lot. Eh, René?"

"Speak for yourself, *Mamie*."

"I'm ninety-four, so I will. You know, Gaby—I may call you Gaby? Since he didn't even tell me your whole name, you must be Gabrielle. Yes? I never expected to last this long. It's quite peculiar. Nobody ever knows when they are going to die. I say to myself in the mornings, it could be today. And when I go to bed, it could be tonight. But so far, it never is. Now, are you a tea drinker? I have some Chinese tea, rather scented, would you like some?"

When she went to get the tea, shuffling a little into the kitchen, René got up out of his chair and paced around the room. I looked around me. Drawings on all the walls, paintings, sketches. "Whose are they?"

"Hers. She was a good artist."

"She won't mind if I look?" I got up and looked too: line drawings of women, chalk sketches of circus clowns, pen-and-ink portraits, gouaches, landscapes with a tree, a child, a lane, rather in the style of Corot. "They are fabulous."

On the little piano that stood in one corner with its lid closed and family photographs stacked on it, I noticed a big old book, *Masques et Plumes*. Masks and feathers, or masks and pens?

She came back in with a silver teapot and three cups on a tray and set it down on the round marble tabletop. We sat down again, in our low chairs that had perhaps been modern in the thirties but were now old and comfortable, though with clean lines and metal legs.

"I was looking at your drawings. I hope you don't mind. They are wonderful."

"Oh, I was quite good. Yes, people liked them. But I can't do it anymore, my hands shake too much. You have to do what you can while you can do it, and not waste time. Because if you live a long life, which I unfortunately am doing, you are going to have years when you can't do what you want to anymore. I still want to draw and paint in my head, but my body isn't up to it. It's just the way things are. And you, what do you do?"

"I write poetry." Even in French, it sounded a flimsy occupation.

"That's wonderful. Poetry is the purest of all the arts."

Her bright smile, wide lipped, still intense: I imagined how she must have been in her youth, with that dazzling attention. Her hair silver, cut close to her head in a twenties-style straight bob. Perhaps people never change their essential look; it just grows softer, takes on the patina of age. Her hands, small, veined with blue in the white, shook slightly as she grasped the teapot and poured the stream of tea into each thin gray-striped cup.

"The cups are from the twenties. It's a miracle that they never got broken. The teapot is family." *De la famille,* she said, as if it, too, were an old relation. Sitting opposite her, René smiled, his long legs in jeans tucked under him. I understood why he had brought me here: it was about learning how to survive, and have a life whatever happened, wherever you were, and however much you had to give up as you went along.

The tea was transparent and smelled of hay. We sipped, with the gestures these shallow cups with their tiny handles suggested; it was ceremonious, satisfying. René and I, clumsy outsiders, making our attempts to be graceful. His grandmother's grace looked effortless, although she said later, "Everything I do is an effort these days. That's what it's like being this old. I don't really feel like doing anything, but I make myself do things anyway."

I knew what that felt like at forty.

"If I knew how to finish myself off, I would do it," she said calmly. "René doesn't like me talking like this, do you, René? Nobody in the family does. But nobody wants to live beyond a certain point, I really think, and we do have to come up with ways to end the whole thing, if it doesn't come soon enough. I have an old friend who says he's going to hang himself, but I think that would be too disagreeable—also horrible for one's family. So I think about three boxes of Doliprane should do. I don't upset you, do I, talking like this?"

I said, "No, it's good to hear someone being this honest." I meant it. She had cut through layers of pretense to get us where she wanted us: listening to her real preoccupations of the moment, not floundering in small talk. She had this time to make her thoughts and wishes known, and she wasn't going to waste it.

"More tea?"

"I'd love some." The curved spout of the teapot, her hand shaking as she poured, the greenish light coming through all the plants arranged on the windowsill—everything made it essential that I should be here. I was getting messages sent to me from out of the future, out of my own old age.

"Forgive me asking, but are your parents still alive?"

"No. They are both dead. My father died only six months ago."

"Ah, that explains it. You see, I noticed a sadness about you, my dear. You must be still in mourning." I thought for a minute that she expected me to be wearing it. I do wear black, but not consciously for that reason.

I said, "It's strange to be an orphan. Freeing, but also confusing. Now there is nobody between me and the future, if you see what I mean."

"Yes, I do see what you mean. I had a son who died young, unfortunately. One is somehow upset by the order of things being overturned, parents dying young, a child dying before you do. Your parents can't have been very old."

"In their sixties, both of them. Both times, it was a great shock."

"Of course. You must take care of her, René, make sure she is looked after. Grief is very exhausting, and sometimes when we are grieving, we don't make good decisions, because life has confused us, and we feel lost. We need protection."

I sat back, having drunk my tea, and she moved to get photograph albums and show us pictures of her children, her grandchildren, René and his brothers as children, their hair cut in straight fringes, sitting on a hay cart; seventies photographs, their colors fading to orange, of a younger generation who must now be about my age. The house in the country, yellow stone, tall trees; people standing in groups on gravel, the women with their feet crossed at the ankle. Having spoken so openly, she retreated into an old person's occupations, showing photographs, talking about grandchildren. Perhaps she had tired herself. I couldn't tell. But she had seen me at once with an accurate eye; I knew myself recognized.

At last she said, as if to nobody in particular, "I'm not looking forward to the holidays this year. It's so easy here, I have everything I need. My books, films, music, someone to come in the mornings and take care of me. In the country, it's so tiring, you know. All those great-grandchildren, all those people."

I was on the point of saying, *Couldn't you stay here?* but then I realized the weight of family obligation. Grandmothers had to go on holiday with their families, I saw it in René's face. I saw her give in to this, sadly, even if it was not what she wanted. I saw René's eyebrows go up. "*Mamie*, we just want you to be there." I felt the heaviness then of being part of a family. I saw an old woman who was being made, after a long life, to do what was always done. Once again—and was I thinking of my mother?—the sacrifice of a woman's wishes to the generally perceived good. She raised her hands and let them fall back into her lap, on her good dark-blue skirt. "Maybe, for one last time," she said. René nodded, reassured. I wondered what I could say to her, to connect at a different level from the one imposed by the gap of years between us.

René got up to go, saying we mustn't exhaust her; I'd seen him eyeing his watch, so I stood up too. Leaving, we kissed on both cheeks. It was like putting my face close to an old white rose. "Come back and see me," she said. "I can't promise to be here. But here's my telephone number, so do call."

"Thank you. I will."

"You see?" René said when we were out in the street again.

"Why does she have to go to the country with you all when she doesn't really want to?"

"There would be nobody to look after her here."

"There would be the housekeeper, surely."

"Nobody, I mean, from the family."

"There would be me."

"Ah, no, Gaby, I can't have you volunteering to look after my ancient grandmother."

"I have a feeling she would be looking after me." I meant it. I wanted to hear about her years as an artist, about what had happened to all the drawings, the paintings, the sketches she had made; and the husband, who had he been, and the son, what was it like when he died? Could you really look forward to death? Was it in the end what you wanted most?

"I know she's dreading going in there," René said, waving his left hand at the geriatric hospital on the rue Broca on the other side of the street.

"Well, I hope she won't have to go. You can stop that happening, can't you?"

He lifted his hands in a gesture of hopelessness, or accepting fate. "Maybe. But in the end, if she can't live alone?"

"Well, that would be the time to haul her off to the country, wouldn't it, and surround her with great-grandchildren. So she could die *en famille*, like she has to take her holidays. And at least, as she said, she has her store of painkillers." I knew I sounded angry—on her behalf, or mine?

We crossed the street and came down under the bridge that carried the traffic of boulevard de Port-Royal over our heads.

"What's the matter, Gaby?" As usual, he picked up my mood. I had seen him do this with Marie-Christine: a rare perspicacity in a man.

"I don't know, it's just the way women's lives are so seldom our own. We have to toe the line so much, and it made me sad to think she has to go on vacation with you all and be a traditional granny when really she'd rather stay home watching DVDs." I think of what I ran from: my mother's and my sister's lives. In leaving Matt in America, was I running from it again?

"Are you pleasing yourself, Gaby?"

There it was again. That leap, intuitive, sure. I caught up with him on his long stride. "Do you mean Yves?"

"Well, Yves among other things. Is your life going the way you want it?"

"I think it might be getting back on track. I will need to get a job, if I stay here, and I don't know where else I can go. Not England, certainly, and not the States."

"What about your husband, Gaby? Why did you two separate?"

"I don't know if we are separated. I just couldn't stay, after my father's death, and I don't exactly know why, but everything started to grate on me, him included. I felt suddenly homesick, but not really for England. For the past, perhaps, or for their house when we were young, the safety of it, although now—" I stopped. I'd nearly told him about my father's infidelity, how this image of mine—the safe house, the united parents—had been taken away. A childish illusion, perhaps, but it had been mine until the other day, and I missed it.

"Now, what?"

"Nothing, really. I left, and came here. I do have a return ticket, but I still don't know if I'll go back or not."

"Running out of safe houses, eh?" He seemed once again to have picked up on my thought.

"Not exactly. Here feels safe for now. I have what I need here at the moment, a small place, spending time alone, working things out."

"Let me know what I can do to help you," he said as we waited at the crossing for the little green man to light up and the traffic to stop on Claude Bernard. "And tell Marie-Christine, if you can't tell me."

"René, thanks. A granny and a lover, though, and all that good food, it's been a great start. Please don't think I haven't noticed."

"All right, big girl, be on your way, and don't forget to call, whenever. Bye now. *Au revoir.*" He went striding on his way, I to fit my key into the lock of my chosen solitude, and let myself in.

7.

The next time I saw my father was from a bus as it sailed down beside the Seine toward the Pont Neuf. It was only a couple of days later. I was on my way back from a bank René had recommended, where I had been turning my American savings into euros and watching them shrink before my eyes. He was walking and stopped as the bus slowed in traffic; he was looking out toward the thick gray-green flow of the river, and he turned just in time, a slight movement but enough for me to be certain that it was the same man I had seen on rue Mouffetard. But there was nothing I could do about it. I stood up, clutching the bus rail in one hand, swaying among other passengers, trying to see, to grasp the fleeting image as I passed it; I remembered the film of Doctor Zhivago, the part where he sees Lara in the street, years later, and stumbles out of the bus clutching his heart, to fall down on the pavement. Poor Zhivago. Even in Russia, the coincidence wasn't enough, because it wasn't her, and she was gone anyway in the faceless crowds caught up in great historical movements; she was lost to him. I knew how obsession and longing could turn the backs of strangers into the person one most wants to see. I knew that what my eyes saw and what my brain interpreted could be separate, the latter manipulated by expectation and desire. You see what you want to see, and you don't see what you don't want to see. As we passed him, I saw the face, the nose, the glasses, the white hair blown on end, all in the dazzle of light that came up from the river, the face turned up toward me this time, and—was it possible, a hand raised as if in greeting? The black jacket, something white at his neck? He stood backed by the closed black shutters of the booksellers' booths, under trees. I swayed, was about to press the red button to request a stop, but we were already way past, rushing toward the bridge. My legs were shaking, so I sat down again. No point in getting off the bus and running back, I knew; he would not be there. I stayed on while the bus crossed the river and headed along the quai des Orfèvres and toward Saint-Michel, and all the way up to the Jardin du Luxembourg, past the big iron gates, and on until I got off at my stop. Let him pursue me, let what had to happen, happen. I would not run after this man, this probable stranger, and accuse him of looking like my dead father. I would not risk sounding absurd, even crazy; I would not doubt my own sanity; I would not become one of those mad-eyed people pursuing dreams all over the world, grasping at wisps of evidence, memory, hope.

I had not seen my father since my mother's funeral. We did communicate, by phone and e-mail, but he refused the pseudo-intimacy of Skype—"I don't want you looking at me from three thousand miles away, thank you. If you can't be here, be there, and be done with it."

Once he had come to New York when I was there visiting a friend who was in a play off Broadway, and we went together to her first night. But that was in 2003, surely. Five years ago, well before Mum's death. People were out on the streets, demonstrating against the war in Iraq. Since she died, he had not returned to the only city in the States that he could admit to loving, and I, to my shame, had not been to see him in England, believing that we still had time. I remembered a phone conversation, in which he seemed more than usually annoyed by the fact of my living in Florida, "the eternal sunshine of the thoughtless mind," as he called it. I remembered retorting that I was married, if he hadn't forgotten this fact, and this was where I now lived and even had a job, so he might as well accept it and stop being such an old elitist. He laughed with a kind of snort and told me that working for a glossy tourist magazine, I was evidently turning into exactly the kind of moron that Florida produced. Now I thought of how we taunted each other, hiding our love for each other under just such a mocking surface. I realized, too late—oh, is it always too late that one realizes?—how lonely he must have been.

Walking home up my street, I revisited the scene of his funeral and tried to remember it in more detail. Who had seen him before his death? Who had identified the body found in the marshes? Who had signed forms, attesting that it was indeed him? I remembered the house, how cold it was, and the way it felt without him. After my mother's death, he had gone on living there as if he were camping, not turning on the central heating, making smelly fires in the hearth, not doing laundry, coming and going like a cat through a cat door. My sister used to call me and worry out loud about him. "Gab, he's living in such a mess, and I don't think he even lets the cleaning lady in when she comes."

I'd said to her, "He's just reverting to type after all those years of Mum looking after him. It's probably what he was like as a young man. Kind of feral, you know?"

She thought he should be stopped from living like this, that it was a form of depression. I said it was his way of grieving, perhaps, or of reconnecting with himself in some way. He was quite a fit man, and it was none of our business. Once, she hung up on me after I had said that it was not her business. I regretted saying it, and the distance it caused between us. As she had so truly said, it was easy for me on the other side of the Atlantic to do nothing about him at all except quarrel on the phone about what I had chosen to do with my life. Now I wanted more than anything to go back, to know how his last days had been, to see him just one more time, to cut through all the barbed remarks that our family went in for and simply reclaim the love we'd always had. Too late.

Families are all about narrative, the stories we are told when we are young, the ones we begin to tell ourselves, and others, and the ones we argue about, preferring our own versions, unable to believe that a sibling doesn't remember things in the way we do. Our mother, Helen, was the guardian of the stories, the ones she had received from her mother. Our father had few stories of his origins or his immediate family; it was as if he were an orphan himself, or had not been paying attention. So when she died, the narrative died with her, it seemed; there was no one to ask, because he didn't remember, hadn't considered it important, just as he couldn't remember and hadn't made a note of the telephone numbers of their mutual friends. She had been in charge of all that. He had his lists of clients and business associates, people scattered all over Europe and the United States, but friends in England were left to her. I thought about this division of labor, of spheres of influence. I thought about Matt, and the way he never knew our friends' phone numbers, the way he had left me to make social arrangements. If women absent themselves, how do men ever connect up with each other? Is it always our job to provide the links, so that life goes on?

I let myself into the apartment and sat down on the white sofa, kicking off my shoes. My phone rang, I scrabbled for it, and it was Yves. Ah. I had been experiencing that small irritation that soon I would have to stop feeling awed by his existence in my life and begin to be angry with him for not getting in touch sooner. He had reached me just in time.

"Hello, Gaby, bonjour."

"Bonjour, Yves."

"How are you?"

"Fine. And you?"

"Good. I'm sorry I didn't call you before."

"You know where I live. You could have come rushing round the next morning with a bunch of flowers." I hoped my sarcasm worked in French; I had not realized that the anger had been coming to the surface, like the symptoms of a cold, scratchy and sore, for quite a few hours.

"I know. Forgive me."

What could I say to such a request, delivered in an intimate telephone whisper that made me feel as if he were an inch away?

"I was doing my exam. But that isn't what you want to know. I still have the oral, but the written part went well. Gaby, can we see each other?"

"Of course. I forgot about the exam. Sorry. Of course I want to know. When will you know if you passed? When shall we meet?"

"Now? Are you free?"

"Well, I suppose, yes. I've just got in and sat down." It was just what my mother would have said—I've just got in, taken the weight off my feet, made myself a nice cup of tea. "Where are you?"

"At the corner of your street, nearly. I am walking toward you."

"Well, in that case, come. Of course. The code is 5B678."

"See you very soon, then."

I heard him click open the door downstairs and come in and then his feet on the wooden stairs, sounding two steps at a time. His black head appeared, his shoulders. A cone of orange paper with some roses inside. He couldn't have had time to stop and buy flowers because I had asked for them, and now I wished I had not asked. I wanted to be nice to him. I wanted him to think me a nice person. He arrived at the top of the stairs, and I stood aside to let him pass, and as he came in, the incredible smell of him wafted immediately toward me. Pepper and ash. The smell of himself, as he would be, I thought, for the rest of his life, wherever he was. It made me want to nuzzle in to him and sniff it up like a pig after truffles, the way I have heard they snuffle under leaves in the woods. His animal smell made me feel like an animal myself, that happy dog again, hurling itself at its person, barking with joy as soon as he comes home. But I stood back, not doing any of these things, and accepted the cone of flowers. They were yellow and pink roses, tightly furled still, smelling of nothing yet but cool flower shops and green leaves. I cut the string and undid the paper, and found a jug to put them in, the whole business of receiving flowers a ritual, a way of paying attention to something that is not the person, while they have to stand and wait. He took off his jacket and hung it on the back of a chair.

"I am not disturbing you?" I used to think that the French word *déranger* actually meant derange. I am not deranging you? I'm not so sure about that; I think you have begun to derange me quite a bit.

He followed me into the bedroom, and we began the game of taking off our clothes, now you, now me, as if playing strip poker with a lot of kisses in between, and fell onto the bed. It was not as fast and confusing as the first time, but the smell of him and the feel of his smooth skin drove me on. I couldn't get enough of feeling and sniffing him, and he began to laugh at me—why do you sniff all the time? You are like a hound. What are you looking for? And I said, I love the way you smell, I can't help it. He said, you smell good too, like, what are those flowers, azaleas? We tried putting it into words, this sudden imperious nasal attraction, and then we fell wordless, our hands and mouths doing it for us, the certainty of what we both wanted pulling us along.

Later he said, "It wasn't too sudden for you, all this? I mean, we never discussed it, I don't know what you think, whether I have been too direct; but really, Gaby, ever since I saw you come in to the room at René's place, I wanted to make love with you."

"No, it wasn't too sudden, because the same thing happened to me. René said he thought we were both ready for each other. I guess he was right. I don't usually behave like this at all. You must have known they were setting us up, didn't you?"

"Yes, of course. They thought I was sad after my separation. But, you know, it doesn't always work this well."

"You mean, if it's a sort of therapy?"

"I mean, physically."

We were lying across my bed with the windows and shutters still open, so that anybody could have seen us from across the street if they had looked;

but I didn't care. Paris streets are like this, rooms looking into other rooms, people eating, undressing, making love. Silhouettes behind curtains, shadows moving together. We were simply joining in with the other bodies all over this city. The air dried our bodies, and we pulled a sheet over us and turned to look at each other, heads close upon the pillow. Then I told him.

"Yves, I have seen my father in Paris, twice, lately. I saw him this morning, on my way home."

"I thought your father was dead. Didn't you tell me he was dead, and your mother too?"

"Yes, that's just it. I went to his funeral, in England, last November."

"And you say you saw him, here, in Paris? It must have been someone who looked like him, surely."

"Yes, that's the only reasonable thing. Both times, I couldn't move to get closer to him to be sure. The first time the street was blocked off when they were shooting that film on rue Mouffetard, and then today I was on a bus. Both times he was wearing a black corduroy jacket, the same jacket my father used to wear."

Yves propped himself on one elbow and looked down at me. His hand moved across my stomach as if reminiscing. "How can that possibly be?"

"Well, that's what I have been thinking about all week. Either he's someone who looks exactly like him, or he had a twin, or he's a hallucination, or I'm crazy, or—well, I've run out of alternatives."

"What do you think, yourself?"

"Well, it's hardly a thought, really. I just had a gut feeling. It's him, not someone else. So he's either still alive somehow, or he's a ghost."

"Do you believe in ghosts?"

"I don't know. I've never had to think about it before. I know people have all sorts of—experiences. Like hearing the voice of someone they loved, or seeing them sitting on their bed in the morning. But this was so ordinary. He was just a man in a crowd. Not transparent, or weird or anything."

"Maybe he's not really dead. Did you ever see the body?"

"No. By the time I got there, he was shut in his coffin. The others chose not to see him, I think. We certainly didn't go in for that open-coffin stuff. But people have to certify deaths, don't they? You have to get a doctor to sign a certificate, say what the cause of death was."

"What was it?"

"Heart failure, complicated by drowning."

"Drowning?"

"He was facedown in some water. He'd taken the dog for a walk. The dog disappeared. Somebody—a local—called the police, and I suppose they took him to a hospital. You have to, when somebody is found dead, and then he must have gone in the hospital morgue and then to the undertakers. What are you thinking?"

"Have you heard of people faking their own death? Is it possible that your father faked his death? Maybe so he could come and live in Paris?"

"But he could have come and lived in Paris anyway. In this apartment. Why would he go to all that trouble? Nobody would have stopped him. He could have done exactly what he wanted."

"Yes, but he wouldn't have been free of his life."

"Free of his life? What do you mean?"

"If nobody knows you are alive, you are free. You begin again. You are absolved of your past. As if reborn. You see what I mean?"

"He had no reason to do that. He'd never done anything he had to regret." As I said it, I doubted it, strongly. Who among us has no regrets?

"You don't know that. We can't know the inside of another person, no matter how close they are. There were years before you were born. Years when you were a child, too young to know. Then, years when you were already in America. You can't have known him, not really."

It sounded as if Yves was more of an expert on my father than I was. I began stroking the slight dark hairs around his nipple, and felt his penis nudge me and begin to move.

"Okay, enough about your father for now?"

"Yes, enough, for sure."

"It's very interesting. But so are you." He stretched my arms above my head and began licking my armpits, and then my breasts, his hands kneading and then his lips on my own nipples, and I stopped talking and opened my legs to him as if I had known him for years and he was the one I was married to, the one man I had promised never to leave. I love the gifts that one body can give to another: the astonishing gratitude of the flesh as it comes back to stinging life.

There were no more sightings of my father for a while, and I began to relax. Throughout early June, Yves took to visiting me at some point every day, and as my life with him began to take up the foreground, I had less attention for looking for white-haired men in black corduroy jackets. I had friends, a lover, a surrogate grandmother, but no job yet. My poems, strange, short, wriggling down the page, followed one after another in my black notebook; if poems they were. I decided not to interrogate them yet. They were what they were, statements of this time in my life, this place, myself in it. They did not mention my father or my mother or Matt or Yves, but rather insects, plants, animals. A bug on a leaf in the Jardin des Plantes. A bird that dropped its white mess into the courtyard. Perhaps they were a way back into the basic stuff of the world, the crawling, excreting activities we can't avoid, the stink and sting and mess of it all, and if so, I would let them be; they marked a certain trail, and if they led somewhere, I did not need to know where. A poem is a strange by-product of life, appearing as it does both suddenly and for no apparent reason, as if it has come in from somewhere else.

"How do you think you can get a job, while so many French people are out of work?" Both René and Yves lectured me on this. "First, you need papers. A *carte de séjour*, a work permit; you can't just arrive and get a job. You will have to get money from outside. From America. How much do you have?"

"Okay, so no job. What about working under the table?" That was what people with no papers did. My two advisers looked amazed, disbelieving.

"Gaby, you simply can't do that. It is dangerous, if they catch you they will throw you out. Anyway, what can you do? You aren't a plumber or a carpenter, you have no real métier, do you?"

"No. Poet, former gallery assistant. Writer for an American tourist magazine. Not very convincing. I see what you mean."

"I will lend you some, until you can get it from your husband." That was René.

"My husband doesn't have any money."

"But he is American!" That was Yves.

"Most ordinary Americans don't have much money these days. But I do have savings, and I don't need a lot, with no rent to pay."

My father had left me a small inheritance, but it was in England still, tied up and organized by someone called Charlie Baxter, who used to come regularly to tea at my parents' house and reassure them about their shrinking investments, waiting for my father to break out the whisky. My experience of life so far was that there was always more or less enough to live on, if you were careful. In London, in my fugue days, I had lived off chips, eggs, and tea, while hoping to be invited out to dinner by my father, who had favorite little restaurants on Greek Street and in Pimlico, where I tried not to show him how hungry I really was. Here, in Paris, I was doing it again, living off eggs and pasta, coffee and cheap red wine, while counting out twenty-euro notes from my stash that lay in an envelope on a shelf in my closet. It was enough for now, and now was all I could plan for. It would do, until I knew more surely where my real life lay.

The letter had waited in my mailbox for nearly a week, because I had forgotten I had a mailbox. But then I ran into the mail lady again on her way out of our building, and she asked me if I had found my letter all right. I opened the box with the key that had hung unobserved on my key chain, and found a letter in a long white envelope with slanting large handwriting across it: my name and address. *Mlle. Gaby Greenwood.* It had a French stamp and a Paris postmark. It was substantial, good crisp paper, compared with the limp envelope covered in spidery writing that André Schaffer had sent me. Who writes real letters these days? These people, these Parisians, evidently. I took it upstairs with me and slit it open with a knife, the way my mother taught me. She also taught me to bite the stalks off roses and the ends off thread and to eat asparagus with my fingers and never to cut the string on parcels. However much I'd rebelled, these were things I would never forget.

Dear Gaby—if I may call you Gaby. We have never met, but I am an old friend of your father's. When he died, nobody told me, I suppose because nobody knew of my existence; but please let me say now how sorry I was, and am, to hear of his far-too-early death. I have heard that you are currently in Paris. I would very much like to meet you, if that is something you would like. Here is my phone number, and the number of my cell phone, if you would like to give me a call. I live in Montmartre, as you can see. I'm not very mobile these days, but perhaps you would like to visit me here, and have lunch, while you are in Paris. Do, please, get in touch. I was very fond of your father.

With my best wishes, Françoise Lussac

"Well!" I say it out loud, because there is nobody to say it to, only the four pale-gray walls of my apartment. An old friend of my father's. Very fond of my father. An old girlfriend, then, an old flame. *The woman*, in fact. But how had this Françoise heard that I was in Paris? I walked up and down and thought, and decided that, of course, I would call her.

I thumbed in her number and heard the ring. Then a message. I said in French, "It's Gaby Greenwood here, answering your letter." And left my number. Almost immediately, my phone rang again—she must be screening her calls—and a voice said, "Gaby?"

"Oui?"

"It's Françoise Lussac. Thank you for calling me. Does this mean that you would like to meet?"

"Well, yes. Since you were a friend of my father's."

"What about Thursday, for lunch? I live at 5, rue Hermel. It's just behind Sacré-Coeur, a steep street that goes down to the *métro* Jean-Jaurès. Do you know it?"

"No, but I can find it. Thursday, noon?"

"Fine. I'd offer to take you out, but I broke my leg recently, and I've had a lot of trouble with it, especially since we don't have a lift in our building yet, so it's easier to meet at home. I'm not much of a cook, but we'll eat something simple."

"Can I bring anything? Bread, a bottle of wine?" I didn't know this woman from Eve, and here we were discussing groceries.

"No, no, I have somebody who does my shopping for me. Just you will be fine. I do so much look forward to meeting you. I have heard so much about you, over the years."

I wrote her name on my calendar, *Françoise L.* Lunch with my father's mistress. I could hardly believe, let alone imagine it.

Yves said, trimming his nails with my scissors, "What if he faked his death in order to live with her?"

"Well, then, why is he not with her?"

"You don't know that he isn't. What did she sound like?"

"Oh, I don't know. Friendly, welcoming. She broke her leg recently, can't go out."

"Broke her leg? How?"

"I don't know! You sound like a detective on a case, Yves. I'll tell you all about it, don't worry."

With him, I was at that unusual place of backtracking from passion into some semblance of ordinary life. When you have been to bed with someone immediately after you have met him, how do you go back to mealtimes, movies, shopping, talk about work, the everyday? It's like turning back the clock; but it's not really possible, because you already know what there is to know.

That evening he'd said to me, "There is a film I would like to see, *tu veux*?" I felt a certain relief; it was possible to do something ordinary, then. Endless sex, however enthralling, does make you feel somewhat cut off from the world. We went to the old Escurial cinema on Port-Royal, which has photos of dead French movie stars along its walls and a flourish of red curtains. We saw a Palestinian film about a lemon tree that had me in tears again, and came home to make love afterward. At least we had done it, we'd sat beside each other in silence, without touching more than hands, I sniffing, he handing me Kleenex, for the two hours a film takes to run. I bought food, and we ate together. He offered to fix the plug in the bathroom. He cut his nails. We were moving into some sort of ordinariness, from the extraordinary high place at which, like acrobats flying through a darkened space above a circus ring, we had met and embraced. It was both relaxing and slightly disappointing; I wanted to be up on the high wire, soaring, forgetting the complexities of daily life on the ground, and I wanted to know him as a person, not just a seductive body. Sex can be very absorbing—but yes, there had to be life in between: nail cutting, plug fixing, cooking and eating, sleep, and the questions: Who are you? Who are we together? Is this reality, or a pleasant and distracting dream?

⚜

The night before I went to meet Françoise Lussac, he lay sprawled on my couch beside me, and we ate sushi out of little containers and drank beer from bottles.

"You don't have a TV?"

"No, I don't want one much. I don't really like TV."

"In France, it's not like in America. There are some interesting things."

"Well, do you have one?" I decided to let the predictable dig at America go.

"I did, when I lived with my wife. It's good for the news, discussions, things like that."

So, did he want to talk about TV or his wife? I decided it was the latter.

"Who was your wife? How long have you been apart?"

"A year now. She was from a very bourgeois family, she was—is—very beautiful, very intelligent, but in the end, not very nice."

Ah, so being nice—*gentille*—did count for something. Beauty and intelligence, all very well, but niceness was what he wanted; wasn't that true of us all? But I have never liked listening to men running down the women they have loved, so I said, "I have only been separated a few weeks, if that. In fact, I don't really know if it's a separation, or just a pause."

"What about you? It's hard, isn't it? Do you miss him?"

"Well, you get so used to someone. Not always in a good way."

"So, Gaby, what are you doing with me? It's very soon after your leaving him."

"Exploring, I suppose. I didn't expect to get involved with anyone, I didn't ask to meet you, but look—here you are. What was I supposed to do?"

"Yes, here I am. *Me voici!* I didn't expect this either."

He rolled closer and kissed me with sushi-tasting lips, the hot breath of wasabi in my mouth. "Are you glad?"

"Very glad."

"Even if it complicates life?"

"It always complicates life, doesn't it? But who wants life to be too simple?" I said it lightly enough but felt a pang of regret for the apparent simplicity of my life with Matt, in the old days. Where, in our innocence and selfishness, had we gone wrong?

I took the *métro* the next day, Thursday, carrying a small rolled bouquet of gerbera daisies bought on impulse from the flower shop near the station at Censier-Daubenton. Taking flowers to older women you had not yet met, as well as to lovers and friends, seemed to be the thing to do. At least she would have to do all the snipping and separating and finding a vase that would give me time to observe her. I had watched the florist tie raffia around the stalks of the daisies and tighten the knot, after she'd asked me if it was *"pour offrir."* That would take a minute or two to undo. The cellophane was stiff in my hand, my *métro* ticket clasped next to it. I was sweating, not just from the air down there. I came out in the square, breathed deeply, found rue Hermel on the map and began walking uphill. The clock in the square had said ten to twelve. I walked more slowly, Sacré-Coeur's white bulges ahead of me at the top of the street. The houses had art nouveau doors and windows, and the pavements were dirtier than in my quartier, with green-and-yellow garbage bins overflowing. I thought of my father. How often had he walked up this street to this door, flowers in hand, even, and rung the bell or greeted the concierge or, in this age of security, punched a code? I checked the number she had given me, thumbed it in, and the beautiful door with its brass curlicues swung open. The stairs went up to the right, and I began my climb. Every time you visited someone in Paris, you arrived slightly out of breath, at a loss, because they always lived up flights of stairs. I slowed down again, and breathed, and tried to still my heart, which was beating overtime—and not just with the effort of arrival. I was scared, and even possibly angry, but I couldn't let this show. She was on the second floor up, so it wasn't far. The door was ajar; she had heard me coming.

"Come in!" a voice called to me from inside, and a second later, there she was, drying her hands.

"Just washing the salad. Come in. Oh, lovely, these are for me? How kind."

I had expected someone large and blonde, from the voice I had heard on the telephone: a former smoker, a late-night woman, a cross between Catherine Deneuve and Simone Signoret, two of my mother's heroines. But she was slim and dark, an apron tied at her waist over jeans and a shirt, one foot still in plaster with a sock over it, one in a sheepskin UGG boot.

"Sit down, Gaby. Or, if you like, come and help me with these—I love these daisies, they are my favorites—I'm so clumsy these days, it takes me ages to do anything. Oh, and let's have a glass of wine." Her English was good, with hardly an accent.

There was an open bottle of Bordeaux on the kitchen table, and she poured us two glasses and hobbled over to find scissors and a vase. She handed me the scissors—so much for having given her something to do. I felt I had met my match, in some way; there wouldn't be any pretense with Françoise Lussac. She gave me a direct glance, her eyes a strangely violet shade of blue between dark lashes thickened with mascara. Her hair was dark, streaked with gray, and put up in a messy chignon. She could have been sixty, or older, I couldn't tell. Her forehead had lines that met in the middle as if she frowned often, but with concentration rather than annoyance. She was my height, around five nine. Both of us tall women. Both of us dark. But my eyes are greenish-brown, like my father's. I took the daisies that I had chosen and began pushing their thick, furry stalks into a vase she handed me. She sat down at the kitchen table and watched me.

"I see flower arrangement isn't exactly your thing, any more than it's mine. But thanks for them, they are lovely. Now, I haven't got a lot for us to eat, just some pâté and salad and cheese, I hope that is all right, and of course cherries. They have begun to come in from the country, Elise brought me some today. *Salut*, here's to us."

I sat catty-corner from her at the table and sipped my wine. A good Bordeaux, 2005, a good year, as she said.

"Were you surprised to hear from me? I imagine you were."

"Well, yes, since I didn't know of your existence." I thought I wouldn't mention André Schaffer's revelations.

"Ah, but I knew of yours. I have known of yours for many years." This did not sound threatening, as it might have, said in a different tone, but surprisingly reassuring. "It can't be easy, losing both your parents so young. And in such quick succession."

"It isn't. I can't get used to it. You know, I didn't see them often, but they were there. I needed them to be there, without realizing it. When they both died, I felt, I don't know, crippled in a way, as if I couldn't function." I had plunged in here, as I think she meant me to. "But how did you hear about me? How did you know?"

"My dear, I don't want to give you a shock. But your father and I were lovers for very many years."

I had expected it, I already knew, but still the shock I felt as I heard her say it was profound. Her words went in as sudden diagnoses of unexpected diseases do, I imagine, as all announcements must that change your idea of how life really is, of how it has been and will be. I had to hold my breath for a minute, and look away.

"Forgive me, I should have waited."

"No, really, the quicker the better. I want to know everything. I do want the truth. But sometimes it is just rather a shock."

"I know. I do know, believe me. It was like that when I heard he had died. I had to know, of course, but the shock—well, it was hard."

"So, who let you know?"

"I read it in the paper. A colleague here showed it to me. The London *Times*, I believe it was. He thought I should know, and that was how I discovered. None of your family knew me, of course. But I have known you, all of you, from afar."

She refilled my glass, and pushed a basket of bread toward me. "Eat something with your wine. I'll get the pâté and the salad, it's all nearly ready; perhaps you could make a dressing? We have a lot to talk about, and it shouldn't happen on an empty stomach."

I poured the oil and vinegar into the bowl she gave me, and mixed in mustard, salt, and pepper. She placed a thick square of country pâté on a plate, and cut more bread. It was a picnic, by French lunch standards, and I wished she had offered me meat, potatoes, even soup. I was weak with something, perhaps hunger. I drank more wine and began to feel warmer, less shaky. The lettuce leaves went in, and she lifted them gently, turning them over. "People are so often far too rough with salad. It needs gentle turning, only. There."

I thought, *People are too rough with other people too*. I felt as if I had been rushed along on a moving walkway at an airport, with all my luggage left far behind.

"Tell me," I said to her. "I need to know."

"Well. There are things I need to know from you too. But I'll start. We met—let me see—in the late seventies."

I would have been ten or eleven.

"We met here, in Paris. He was buying paintings and taking them back to London, under the noses of French dealers. I was working as a journalist at *Le Monde*, on the arts pages. It's what I do. We met, I think, at an opening of some sort."

I said, "Were you his lover for all those years, then?" My heart sped and I felt a little sick. My history, the family narrative—the loving parents, the family holidays, my parents hugging in the kitchen, their bedroom, his goodbyes, her welcomes—everything was shifting in my mind and turning into something else. There had been something going on during my entire childhood that I had been completely unaware of. "Did my mother know?" I was about to explode into angry tears; my throat hurt, and my hands trembled.

She said gently, "I'm sorry, Gaby."

"No, no, I have to know." Just as I have to hear the dentist's announcement, *This needs a root canal*, or the doctor someday who would tell me, *It's cancer, it's inoperable, I'm sorry.*

"He didn't tell her. Or, I don't think he did. I'll never really know."

"Did you want him to leave her?" Leave her, leave us, leave home? Leave me? Damn her, with her calmness, her so-French assumptions.

"I knew he wouldn't. It was all right. I had part of him, for part of the time, and that part was very good. I didn't have the right to ask for more."

"But you must have wanted more?" Of course you did. You're only human, admit it, go on.

"Eat something, Gaby. We don't have to rush this. We do have time." She paused. "To answer your question, he didn't want more."

I would not tell her that I had seen him in the streets of Paris. I would never let her know. It would be my secret. Let her eat her heart out; I had seen him, and she had not.

"I know, I knew you would inevitably feel angry with me; that's why I told you straightaway. I suppose, there wasn't a gentle way of doing it, really, you know. I could have said we were old friends, colleagues, but I think you would have known anyway."

"Yes, actually, I did know, as soon as you wrote me that stuff about having been fond of him. It could only have meant one thing."

"It isn't a crime to love somebody," Françoise said. The tone of her voice made me look at her, and again there was that clear glance, cool mauve-blue, not giving an inch. She pushed back a black lock of her hair. My match, in more ways than one. A woman who existed simply as herself, who gave herself the right. I thought of that trip to Paris when he bought me the painting of the Chinese horse. Was that what he was doing—seeing her? Everything began shifting and sliding again. There was no memory that could be left intact—not those trips away from us, not those homecomings with presents and bottles of wine, not those seaside holidays on cold Norfolk beaches, not those wedding anniversaries, those parties, those lifted glasses of champagne.

"Did you see him after my mother died?"

"Yes. He was inconsolable. It was such a horrible shock for him."

"But you consoled him, all the same."

"Don't, Gaby, don't hurt us both that way."

"I'm sorry, but she was my mother!" I pushed my chair back from the table like an angry child refusing to eat what has been put in front of her. "She was my mother, and she was killed, in a car crash. Somebody killed her, drove into the back of her, and then he came here to you, and you tried to cheer him up? It's horrible."

I did begin to cry then, the way I had cried in the flat during those first days—noisy, messy, with snot and hiccups. She handed me a paper towel. I took a swig of my wine. Any pretense there had been of us having a politely civilized lunch together had ended.

"I know that she was your mother. And that he was your father. And I was an outsider. But, Gaby, forgive me, you are not a child. Reality is better than pretense, really, believe me. Here, have a real handkerchief. You are simply blowing holes in that paper. You are so like him."

I looked at her. I knew then that she really had known him, his rages, his sulks, all the parts of him that my mother tried to smooth away and ignore. She had seen him trumpet into paper tissues and sob.

She pushed the salad toward me, and I helped myself, and took more bread. Something settled between us. I looked at her, and she looked at me sideways, and then we both began to laugh, I sniffling and blowing and wet-cheeked still.

Perhaps the picnic lunch was to show me she was not the maternal type, was in fact the opposite of my mother, who had made huge soups and stews and fed everyone in sight, whose Bible in the sixties had been a stained cookbook by Elizabeth David, who believed sincerely in the redemptive virtues of French country cooking. Perhaps Françoise was telling me, there was no competition, never had been. She was not a cook but a career woman, she had had no wish for marriage, children, all that—was that the message? We spat cherry stones into our palms and looked at each other.

I thought of my father, and his refuge here in this sparely furnished, rather classical flat with its long windows looking down onto rue Hermel, its few pieces of probably antique furniture—inherited?—and the woman who didn't cook and probably went to Picard, the frozen food shop, for most of her food. There were paintings on the walls that he would have liked, drawings signed to Françoise from various artists I did not know, and a portrait of her glancing sideways, her hair pulled back, her face clear and bony, aged about thirty. What had it meant to him to come here from our various chaotic houses, in Cambridge, in Norfolk? Parallel lives. Was that all we could hope for, to run alongside someone else's life, never knowing its full intensity, its inner solitude? My parents had a marriage that was famous for having survived. We had not, my siblings and I, known the confusion of trekking from one house to another, having to accept other women, other men, in place of one of our parents, being told, *We both love you, we just can't live together anymore.* We had had the warmth and chaos and acceptance of a large, messy house with food always on the table, a parent always at home, a mother in a kitchen poring over sauce-stained Elizabeth David or Julia Child. What, I wondered now, had she decided to ignore in order to give us all this? The dark-haired woman in the apartment in Montmartre. The woman sitting in front of me cutting herself a slice of cheese to eat with a heel of baguette, finishing up her wine. Françoise. Was it a name that ever came between them, was it mentioned in confession, shouted in anger? I would never know. Nobody was here to tell me. The disguise, if it had been a disguise, had been complete. Perhaps he had truly loved both of them. Perhaps for him there had been no conflict, only alternate realities. Men are accused of keeping things in compartments, but perhaps it is the better way—kinder in the end, more discreet.

"Would you like some coffee?"

"Yes, please."

She made it in a tiny Italian metal pot, on the stove, and poured me a sizzling espresso. I dunked in a long rectangle of sugar. Bread, cheese, wine, coffee, sugar: all these things had become listed as poisons in America recently. It was really quite funny how everything shifted once you crossed that ocean. I stirred sugar into my coffee, and so did she, and there was a silence between us for a minute that neither tried to fill.

"I was such a smoker," she said at last. "But at last I managed to stop. One of the hardest things I ever did."

I remembered an early childhood spent in the blue fumes of my father's Gauloises habit. It was okay to smoke if they were French. Something about the way the tobacco was grown, you could see it, he used to say, if you went to the southwest of France, it was all hanging healthily to dry in barns. His clothes smelled of that bitter smoke, and it became part of him as it did so many of that generation: to his children, to anyone who went near him. Then he, too, had stopped. I wondered now if it had been at the same time as Françoise, if it had been a pact. Each one suffering nicotine withdrawal pangs on opposite sides of the Channel.

I said, "Me too. It's almost impossible now to smoke in America. It would almost be easier to shoot up heroin."

"Tell me, why did you go to America?" There it was again, the not-so-hidden question, how could anyone with a brain actually go and live in America?

"I think, to get away from home. I worked in a gallery in New York for a while when I first got there. Then I met my husband, moved to Florida, went to graduate school in Miami and did an MFA. I started getting serious about writing poetry, but, of course, even if you publish, it doesn't make any money. So I got a job recently on a magazine called *Miami Days and Nights* writing about hotels, for tourists. Last year I applied for a job working for Art Basel, but I didn't get it, though I did get an interview. Slightly better than a glossy mag, after all."

"Aha. And what about this American you married?"

"Matt. He didn't tell you?"

"He told me you had married. He told me he hardly ever saw you. Just once, I believe, in New York. It hurt him considerably. He didn't tell me more."

"He was the one who sent me there in the first place. But yes, I feel sorry not to have seen more of him recently. Of course I do."

"I know, you worked for Camilla Verens, didn't you, in her gallery in SoHo?"

"How did you know? Yes, he arranged it for me, after I'd finished at the Courtauld."

"She is a friend of mine too. He had a complicated relationship, you know, with the United States. He needed it for his work, and he always enjoyed New York, but when you decided to live there—in Florida—he was upset about it."

I thought—so, they talked about me. About my choices, my life, all the things that I thought were entirely mine. "He can't have expected me to stay in his orbit forever."

"No, just perhaps to stay in Europe. I think he thought your time in New York was just temporary. Not that you would stay. Once, you know, we went there together. There was something on at the Met, a de Kooning retrospective, and we managed just that one time to go together. We stayed at the Algonquin, imagine that. I had particularly wanted to go there. It was because we knew there would only be one time."

I listened, fascinated, and wanted more. The fact that my mother was probably at home in the kitchen in Norfolk while they were rolling around in the Algonquin pretending to be Fitzgerald and Zelda was no longer uppermost in my mind. I wanted it for them; I wanted them to have had that time. I imagined them in New York, stepping dazzled down Broadway, going to the Guggenheim, the Met, walking hand in hand through Central Park. Like people in an old movie, black and white, with wisecracking dialogue. My father's life, the one I did not know he had. The romance of it, the secret from his pocket, the conjuring trick of his hidden love affair.

We finished our coffee, sipped out of tiny blue cups, and she motioned to me to sit on the cracked leather couch in the sitting part of the room.

"Gaby, is there anything you particularly want to know?"

"Well, you've given me a lot. Paris, New York, the Algonquin. I feel a bit overwhelmed, to be honest. But yes, I want to know how much he told you about us."

"He was happy with you all. He showed me photos, I knew what you all looked like, and your houses and everything, your dog even."

"My mother?"

"Yes, I knew what she looked like, she was in the photos with you all, but he never told me much about her. It was kinder. And he loved her. He loved your family life, the way it was. He didn't want to lose that."

"So you really didn't mind that you didn't have any of that?" I was trying to get my mind around it, the fact of her life here, ours over there, the two sides of his brain making no connection.

"Well, I probably couldn't have children. I already knew that. I didn't want to be married, as I had a good career, and it had to be here in Paris. So in a way I got exactly what I wanted. His company. Never quite enough, of course, and never at Christmas or any of the holidays, but it was all right. I really didn't want that kind of life, Gaby. Do you find that strange?"

"No, actually, I don't."

"Well. So you may understand my point of view."

I did, with what felt like relief. My sister and brothers in England, with their babies, their children, their family cars with car seats, their bags full of stuff, and then their talk of schools, holidays, sleepless nights, in-laws for Christmas—they had absorbed my mother's lesson, uncritically, and lived it out in their lives. I hadn't wanted to. I had not been able to explain to Matt, only told him, I'm so busy, I want to finish this course, then this book, and anyway having children in America is far too expensive, how would we pay for all that? I had never stopped using contraceptives. I had breathed out with relief every time my period began. While he, poor Matt, had early in our marriage talked of our children, and even of having grandchildren, and how wonderful they would be. I had never been able to tell him exactly why, only that we should put it off. It was one of the things that we had gradually stopped talking about, long before I had decided to leave. Now, listening to Françoise Lussac, I knew why.

I said to Françoise, "You know, I don't want the life my mother had either." I wanted to be the woman with the freedom to live alone and do as she liked, who was still alive, not dead in the mud of an English road on her way back from grocery shopping, to be the mistress, with her independence, not the wife. It had never seemed so clear to me.

"Well." She smiled. "Forgive me, but it looks very much as if you don't have it. You are here in Paris. You already left England to go to America. You seem to be looking for something that's far from home. Am I right?"

I was feeling the kind of exhaustion you feel after talking to a kind therapist. I hoped I had not used her as one, but she said only, "I am glad we talked so much, but perhaps that's enough for now? I just wanted to know you, and now I feel I do, a little. Thank you for being so open with me, Gaby. Let's meet again, shall we? If you would like that."

"Yes, fine. Let's call each other. Thanks for the lunch."

She saw me to the door and, when I was about to shake hands, leaned forward to kiss me on both cheeks. I knew it was a formality in France, but it made me feel I belonged, whenever it happened. I could see why my father liked her. I could almost imagine him here, behind the closed double door to the bedroom where I had not been, laughing to himself, biding his time.

"So, what was she like?" Yves wanted to know. I was home, where I had cried briefly and then fallen asleep for half an hour. I had sluiced my face with cold water and lifted the intercom inside my door to let him in. I felt that I wanted to keep Françoise Lussac and my reaction to her to myself for a while, to work out how I did feel about her, but Yves persisted. Sometimes I feel that everything moves too fast for me; it was a sensation I often had in my childhood, particularly at school, and now here it was again.

I made tea, pouring boiling water into a teapot with real tea leaves, Earl Grey, from an expensive shop on rue Mouffetard where they behaved as if tea were gold dust. I needed this ritual from my past, my English upbringing, to soothe and settle me. "She's about sixty, rather beautiful, thin, doesn't cook, had a broken leg, wears jeans, knows her wine, and was in love with my father for thirty years."

He made a French face of astonishment, mouth pursed as if blowing out air. He'd kissed me quickly on coming into the flat; otherwise we were behaving like old friends.

"So, he had a lover here for thirty years, and your mother knew nothing?"

"I've no idea what my mother knew. I'll probably never know. But, you know, coming home on the *métro* just now, I thought, it's the past, and it's their business, not mine. Mine is deciding what to do with my own life. She's nice, she's friendly, she wanted to meet me, but I don't know that we have any more to say to each other, really."

"Aren't you going to tell her that you saw your father here?"

"No! First, I'm not even sure that it wasn't a hallucination. Second, it might upset her enormously. I think she would think I was crazy, anyway." I didn't say that I wanted to keep him to myself—ghost or revenant, person or illusion, whatever he was.

"So, what are you going to do?"

I looked at him across the teapot and our two bowls. "Yves, please don't ask me, I really don't know, and I can't bear being asked all the time, what are you going to do about this, about that?" I felt tears crowding behind my eyes again, and immediately he put out a hand and held mine, and massaged it in his, rubbing gently back and forth across my palm.

"I am sorry. Forgive me. I always ask too many questions. But it's such a fascinating story."

"Yes, I know it is. But it's mine! It's up to me what I do with it. And I have quite enough to deal with as it is just now."

"Yes, of course. Drink your tea, and then let's go and lie down and rest."

I took a big scalding mouthful of tea and breathed in the aroma that would remind me always of my mother sitting down at four o'clock with a sigh of pleasure as she poured her tea and sipped. "Ah, tea, wonderful. What would we do without it?" No American and probably no French person could ever understand the feeling that went into that sigh, that exclamation, the way she sat with her eyes closed for a moment, savoring it. I only had to imagine her for a minute, and tears would come. My mum. My mum at the kitchen table, sipping her tea. She was in me still and always would be, I knew it, whatever I chose to do with my life.

I said to Yves, "My mother used to drink this tea. It reminds me of her. I'm not upset at you, don't worry."

"I know, I know." He could be very soothing. He led me into the bedroom, and we lay down fully dressed on the bed, just touching hands, then arms, then waists, then beginning to feel each other under our clothes.

"You were sad for your mother?"

"Sad that I can't see her anymore. Sad, yes, about how she died, of course. Not really sad because of Françoise. It's almost like my father had two separate lives, and maybe both she and Françoise had what they wanted. One with a house and children, the other with an apartment and a career. It seems possible, at least."

"If you leave jealousy out of the picture."

"Well, yes. I think they tried not to believe in it, in the seventies. Perhaps it worked, who knows?"

Yves stroked my stomach through the gap between my T-shirt and my jeans. His hand went in, stroking, moving lower. I had my hand inside his jeans too, feeling its way. Outside the window, the street moved, traffic and people coming home, and then suddenly we heard a trumpet fanfare, somebody playing jazz trumpet down there just below us. We lay still and listened for a moment. Light moving across the ceiling as cars passed, the jaunty blare of the trumpet, then the subversive little fart of a tenor sax. I thought, I will remember this: this moment, Yves and me lying like this, gently feeling our way to each other, and Paris out there going about its business, and the smell of the tea still in the air, and the music played by gypsy musicians out there on the street. Inside and out. Outside and in. In the thin, barely perceptible places where the inner life meets the outer, there is movement between the two—the outside world gives you the sound and the taste of what you need, while inside you move close to something essential, and are not alone. The thin film between things begins to disappear and is almost gone. There is almost clarity. There is almost peace.

8.

Men, unlike most women, seem to want to know about the other man, the one they may be replacing. Yves had asked me, more than once— "Who is he, your husband?" He was more than curious; he needed to know, perhaps to establish our connection in his mind. Who is this man whose place I am usurping, whom I am pushing aside? Who is my opposite, my rival, the man who is not me?

"He was working on a catamaran when we met, taking tourists out to look at the reef off the coast of south Florida. Then we moved to Miami because we needed to get better paying jobs, and I wanted to do a further degree."

"And, what happened? You didn't love each other, after all? You don't mind me asking?"

I sighed, wondering how to put it. "I think I married him in a hurry, to have a sort of anchor, you know?"

"Just like that?"

"Well, no. It took several years. But you can fall in love, and then discover it's not working, and you don't quite know why. But something has happened. You have grown apart."

"But you loved him at first?"

I thought of that first day, out on the water, nearly a decade ago. I saw Matt dive straight down with the grace of a cormorant while the tourists with their snorkels bobbed around him and the boat rocked at anchor and we were miles, thousands of miles, from anything I knew. I was in the bow of the boat, drinking cold beer from cans, with my friends from New York. He picked me from among all the other pretty tourists, the ones with golden tans and American accents and tiny swimsuits and perfect teeth. I picked him, so unlike the pale men of the north, so unfamiliar that I took his silences for depth of thought, his blond good looks for a sign. We began seeing each other every evening, after he'd docked the boat, that spring when I was down in Florida on vacation. It all seemed a very long time ago. And it could have ended there—perhaps, in retrospect, it should have—but did not.

Sometimes, rarely, you get a glimpse—as if a window slides open—of what seems to be the essence of another person. Isn't that what allows us to fall in love? He let me see him; I saw his love of horizons, and sky, and the knowledge of water. He was competent and practical with the boat and its occupants; I went out often with him on the calm Florida water between the islands and the reef that year, and I saw how he handled both objects and people. We went out fishing, just the two of us, and I noticed the way he pulled in a gasping fish and threw it in the bucket to thrash and turn, how later he knocked it out and quietly gutted it. The way he killed it, almost apologetically, but with skill. Like a surgeon, careful and exact.

He had, I must say, a beautiful body—I did not tell Yves this—but he seemed to be unaware of it; he apparently lacked all vanity, a rare thing in a handsome man. I liked watching him throw out a line, even cut bait. I watched as he hauled up sails, set anchors, opened beer cans one-handed. I wanted him to touch me. I liked that he sometimes blushed.

"He wanted us to get engaged. We were very different, yes, and I wanted that difference. In the end, I said yes." Yes, because I had been saying no to him for so long; yes, because it led somewhere; yes, because he offered me a steady future and a home in that country where I still felt like a stranger.

78

It did seem, from Paris, like another world. It was another world. As was the world I had removed him from, where he was a boat captain, spending his days out on the water. I should not have removed him from that world; I should, I thought now, have left him where he was, and he me. We said we loved each other and then proceeded to cut each other off from the very things each wanted most.

But I did not want to go on talking to Yves about Matt, because to try to put words to my feelings, even in French, seemed to push me toward a decision I was not yet ready to make. You said this, you said that; you said you loved him, you said you didn't—how could either statement stand, for any longer than it took to say it?

"He's a good man. We're just not right for each other, and it's taken me a long time to accept that."

"We don't like to admit mistakes, do we?"

"No. It's like giving up on a dream. We want to go on believing. Until we can't."

Matt believed in my poetry rather as nonbelievers believe in church. It was something that did me good—it was my private religion—it was probably entirely useless, but it could still be admired. When it began to be published, he was pleased and surprised, the way one is if someone wins the lottery, or gets a sudden inheritance. When the book won its prize, he bought California champagne for us to drink at home, but I don't think he told anybody at work; having a wife who was a poet might have seemed just a little too crazy for his world. I don't know that he knew about Sylvia Plath, but husbands can get nervous around women poets and even worry that some of the inevitable angst involved may be their fault. I didn't write at length about his body, or our sex life, as Sharon Olds did about her husband, but I think he was always a little nervous that I might. The idea that poetry might earn actual money had never occurred to him, as indeed it had not to me. After the prize, he saw the point of those solitary hours I spent shut in my study, and when I came out, he looked expectant, as if I might have laid an egg. But the topics of my poems, which even I could not have articulated to anyone except by writing them, these were the footsteps in the forest that led to the witch's house, the dragon's cave. They went to a dark and hidden place that I had to approach alone.

I told Yves some of this. He agreed that marriage was far too hard these days for anyone to undertake, and children out of the question, especially if you wanted to be something as marginal as a poet, or a philosopher.

"So, he believed in your poetry, but he could not let you live the life of a poet. What did you believe about him?"

"That he was some sort of romantic seagoing adventurer, I think. I know, it sounds absurd. Then I made him live on dry land, in the city, and watched him get depressed."

Yves said, "Ah, we all do it. We want to love somebody, and we can't, because we want things for ourselves too much."

"What did your wife do?" I asked him, not wanting to hear her criticized, just out of curiosity, and to stop talking about Matt.

"She wanted more than anything to stay home in the country near her parents, and have children. In fact, she worked in a flower shop on the Right Bank, near the Place de la Concorde, where rich men went to buy bouquets to apologize to their wives after they had been unfaithful. She got very good at advising them what to buy. She would ask about the situation and very tactfully suggest the right flowers, not too apologetic, not too obvious. She was good at it. Still is."

"But you didn't have children?"

"No, I told you, I can't have children."

"Can't or don't want to?"

"Can't afford to. That's why I want to teach other people's children. You see, my mother lives out in the suburbs here, and I have to help pay for her."

I knew that "suburbs" in Paris—*la banlieue*—meant something very different from the burbs in America. It meant poverty, bad public housing, and isolation.

"She is Portuguese, my mother. She came here from Portugal when she was young. My father was French. Is French. I think he's still alive. But we don't see him. I've never met him, in fact."

I thought, that's why he was so interested in my sightings of my father; was he also always half looking out for his own? Parents, the mysteries of where we come from, the people who made us, intentionally or by mistake, and then let us out into the world.

I got up, wound a sarong around me, and went to the bathroom. Behind me, Yves sat up and pulled on his pants. "In fact, I have to go. She is expecting me. My mother. It's a long *métro* ride."

"Is Yves your real name?"

"Yes. No. It's one of my names. I am called Evo. Yves is my French name, the one I use now. Is Gaby yours?"

"Gabrielle. I was called after Sidonie-Gabrielle Colette, my mother's favorite writer. They used to try to call me Jane at school, which is my second name, as it was easier than Gabrielle, but I was Gaby at home from the time I could talk."

"So, we both chose our names. And our lives, perhaps, with them. If you have a different name, you have a chance for a different life, don't you?"

"So, you are going to see your mother now?"

"Yes, I have to get some stuff for her at the supermarket and fix her washing machine. I said I'd go tonight."

"Can I meet her sometime?"

"Sure. I have told her about you. I said I met a funny English girl who likes me and cries a lot."

"You didn't! She'll think I'm insane."

"No, she will like you. Goodbye, Gaby. Until tomorrow. I'll call you, okay?"

When he had gone, I stood looking out of the window at the sky above the rooftops and thought about what he had said. We want to love somebody and we can't, because we want things for ourselves too much. Was it impossible, then, ever to live with and love another human being? All our songs and poems, our literature, our stories, told us that this was the point of life; everything around us pushed us toward this happy outcome. Perhaps it could never be an outcome, only a stage along the way. Perhaps my father and Françoise had lived it as well as anyone could, with his infrequent visits, their brief times together. Perhaps the story we had all been given was in itself a myth. Everyone failed it; everyone had to let it go.

That night, I dreamed that I was old. I was sitting in an armchair in a room like the one René's grandmother lived in, and I was suddenly aware that my life was nearly over. I woke and sat up and turned on the bedside light, and for a moment it still seemed real. I was in my bed, unable to move, and old. Everything had already happened that could happen. It was all nearly over. And I could not remember what my life had been, only that it had rushed past, and I was at its end. I looked at my watch. Four twenty. I got up to go to the bathroom. I sat in the dark, and the thought came: *You must make the right choices, what you decide matters, nothing is a rehearsal, it will not come again. You have to be sure to live your life, consciously, not leaving things out.* Four in the morning here, and only ten o'clock at night in America. I picked up my phone and dialed our number, mine and Matt's. I heard it ring, one tone, far, far away in another world. The buzzes and flickers all over the world as humans try their best to connect with one another: phones, pagers, tablets, all the electronic marvels at our fingertips buzzing and ringing across this planet, as desperate humans try for another chance.

"Matt? It's me, Gaby."

"Gaby? I thought I wasn't ever going to hear from you. I wrote you some e-mails. Did you get them? I didn't have your number. How are you, are you okay?" His voice, the warm American twang, so young sounding, so close, even cautiously friendly.

"I'm fine. I have to talk to you. I had a bad dream. Is this a good time?"

"You called me to tell me about a dream?"

"But it matters, it was about me, about us, about life, about not screwing up, you know?"

"Tell me about it. Are you coming home? People are asking. Hell, I don't know what to say. My wife has left me, or she's just on vacation? Gaby, it isn't okay, I have to know the score. Talk about bad dreams—what do you think I've been going through?"

"I'm sorry." I heard the hurt in his silence, and felt a pang at causing it. "I have to see how it turns out."

"How what turns out?"

"Matt, my father is in Paris, I've seen him."

"Your father? Jesus, Gab, are you going nuts over there?"

"I know, I know, it sounds crazy, but I've seen him twice now, and I have to find out, one way or the other."

"Gaby? What time is it over there?"

"Four thirty. Not a good time to be awake."

"I'm worried about you. You sound weird. This stuff about your father, it can't be him, must be someone who looks like him. It's funny how often that happens, you know, someone who's a dead ringer for someone else."

"A dead what?"

"Dead ringer. It's an expression. Someone who looks just like another person. It happens all the time."

"Well, I have to find out, if it's one of those, or really him. Or a ghost."

"How are you going to do that?"

"Wait and see if it happens again. If it happens a third time, I'll know. I'll make sure, I'll find out. If it doesn't happen again, I'll let go of the whole thing. I will, really. I'll give myself a deadline. Excuse the pun."

"How long a deadline?"

"I don't know. Until September?"

"Then will you come home?"

"I don't think so. I'm not sure where home is anymore. We have to get our lives right, Matt. We have to make sure we don't miss what we are supposed to have. That's what my dream was about."

"Well, I miss you. You're making everything too complicated. It's really very simple. I love you, you know that."

Silence. He had said it, it had come across all those watery miles between us—a statement of himself such as I had never heard before, a rawness, an openness, a willingness to be hurt.

I couldn't say it back. I said, instead, "I miss you too."

His turn for silence. Then he said, "But apparently not enough."

I said, "Now you have my house number. Let's go on talking, okay?"

"What's the point? I thought you want to be left in peace to do whatever it is you're doing over there."

"No, I'll call you again. This matters. There are things we have to talk about. We do have to get it right."

Or, I thought, wander homeless like my father or his solid ghost, through the streets and along the rivers of our past, wondering where we had gone wrong, needing to do it all over again.

Matt said, "You sound as if you're on another planet. I don't know who you are, Gaby, not anymore. It feels awful. I guess I don't really want to talk to you when you're in this mood. Call me when you get over it, okay?"

When we hung up, the sky was just beginning to get light outside the shutters, and I heard the water running down the gutters, the little streams that wash Paris clean overnight. I lay back down again, but was dry-eyed, calm. Somebody said to me once: "You have to prefer reality." The hurt was real, but we were being real with each other at last. There was no other way.

9.

I did not have to wait a month to see my father again. It was only about a week later, as June turned up its heat and everyone was out in the streets wearing sandals and halter tops; and the couples in the Jardin du Luxembourg and along the Seine had installed themselves where they always were, year after year, same places, new people; as the outside café tables filled with people sipping drinks and coffee and turning up their pale faces to the sun. I was on a bus again, and it was turning in front of the Closerie des Lilas before it reached the great sparkling gush of the fountain, just past the statue of Marshal Ney, and about to head down the rue d'Assas toward the rue de Rennes. I was going to meet René and Marie-Christine, to see another film. He was there, on the edge of the pavement outside the Closerie, and this time I rushed to the door like Zhivago, to get out at the next stop and run back; there were people in front of me. I felt bad about pushing an old lady, as I said, "Excuse me, please, I have to get out here." But you cannot get off a Paris bus where there isn't a stop. The next stop was way down rue d'Assas, but I jumped off there and ran back, back toward the Closerie and its pale lilac lights, its hedges, its empty dining rooms and deserted bar. Where was he? I stood and stared around me. There was no one on the pavement, only the green buses turning. I was alone and he was gone again, the man with the white crest of hair and the dark jacket, the man I believed was my father. No sign. He had vanished as suddenly as he had appeared, leaving me desperate, alone, my heart pounding. Nothing for it but to get on the next bus and join my friends. We were going to see a film set in the fifties, about Françoise Sagan. I didn't care now if I missed it, but it was the only fixed point left in my afternoon: a rendezvous to see a film about a dead writer, one in the endless line of dead writers, stretching on like the future kings of Scotland in *Macbeth*, until the crack of doom. I didn't care today about dead writers; I was the one haunted by the ghost of my father. I was in the other play: I was Hamlet, and the ghost was tormenting me, just as Hamlet's father's ghost did, and I could stand it no longer. I stood there outside the famous restaurant where Hemingway used to dine, and now nobody can afford to, and I shouted out, "Come back! Explain! I need to see you!" One of the waiters, young and dark-haired in a white jacket, looked at me around the hedge. Perhaps I looked and sounded crazy. Perhaps I was crazy. Perhaps life had finally driven me over the edge, the one where Hamlet snapped and all the disasters were inevitably set in motion. We humans cannot stand very much reality, Eliot wrote, but unreality we can stand even less. I had to find out who this man was, and confront him; I had to know once and for all that he was not in fact my father, not a ghost, but what Matt had said, a dead ringer, a counterfeit, a fake. Then, perhaps, I would know what I had to do next.

"Can I help you, mademoiselle?" It was not the young waiter but a man who came out of the Closerie, his jacket swung over his shoulder, over a white shirt.

"Excuse me, did you see a man just now? A man in a dark jacket, with white hair? I was supposed to meet him, and we must have just missed each other."

The man—fiftyish, handsome—hesitated. "There was a man in the bar in the Closerie a few minutes ago, when I went in, who would fit your description, I think."

"Where did he go? Please, if you saw him, can you remember?"

"Well, he was at the bar, as I was, presumably having a drink after work. I exchanged a glance with him, you know, as one does with a stranger at a bar, not friendly exactly, just acknowledging each other. Then I think he went out. I didn't notice, sorry."

"But he can't have just vanished! I'm sorry, thank you for your help."

"Would you like me to see if he is still there?"

"Well—if you don't mind." It seemed a lot to ask of a complete stranger.

The man went back into the Closerie—a place I would hesitate to go into as it seems so grand—and eventually came out shaking his head. "Nobody there. Sorry."

"I can't thank you enough for looking. Perhaps he came out and got on a bus, or went down into the *métro*."

"Perhaps. Good luck, mademoiselle, and I hope you find him. Is he your father, by any chance?"

"Yes!"

"I thought so. A certain resemblance. Well, have a good evening."

One man in this city of millions had actually seen my father, or his ghost, or his dead ringer, as well as myself. He had even seen a resemblance. I was not alone. I had not imagined him. I had not made him up. The man with the jacket swinging over his shoulder crossed the wide street and made his way to the *métro* at Port-Royal; I had to hold myself back from running after him.

What to do now? I waited at the bus stop. I got on the next bus, and met my friends, and went to see the film about the dead writer, Françoise Sagan, who, like other dead writers, began young and happy and ended up miserable, ill, and alone. She didn't get a second chance at life. Her first chance, with money and adulation and friends who took advantage of her, was supposed to be enough. Was that what my father had engineered for himself, a chance to begin again, the second chance that nobody gets, because "Life is not a dress rehearsal, Gaby,"

as he, himself, had once said. It is real, minute by minute, made up of
choices you may live to regret. Was that what he was doing in Paris,
having a second chance, drinking in the bar at the Closerie des Lilas
instead of going home to his empty house in East Anglia, taking part
in movies made on the rue Mouffetard, sauntering by the Seine and
pausing outside a favorite restaurant during the long summer evenings?

But why? And how? There were altogether too many questions.
Why was he showing up in all the places I passed in buses, just when I
was trapped behind glass in a moving vehicle, or pushed behind a street
barrier while a film was being shot? Did he see me? Had he planned to
see me? Had he a message to give me? Just what was this about, if there
was any objective reality to it, if it were not simply produced by my
disordered brain? What did Hamlet do, I suddenly wondered. Maybe
I should read the play again and find out. I remembered that he had
been eaten up by jealousy on behalf of his father because his mother
had married again. Funeral baked meats coldly furnishing the wedding feast, something sarcastic like that, he had said. A young man in
a state about his mother. I didn't have to be outraged on behalf of my
mother, because she was already dead. Hamlet discarded Ophelia, and
she went mad and floated down the river. He interrogated gravediggers,
was an insomniac, ended up dead himself. No help there. But what
had Shakespeare meant, I wondered, writing about ghosts, insisting on
their importance in the lives of the living? The voice on the battlements.
The voice in the small hours. *Well said, old mole.* The man in the street
who disappears. They are surely all the same thing. They are the dead,
who know more than we do, telling us what they know, or trying to.
Banquo's ghost, Caesar's ghost on the eve of the Battle of Philippi. We
ignore them at our peril; we listen to them at the risk of our sanity. A
French poet said, by the end of life, we all contain libraries and grave-
yards. It seemed to have happened to me already, my familiarity with
both. I knew I had to get help with this now, and it must be from someone who might understand, because they had a foot in both worlds,

those of life and death. Matt and Yves, René and Marie-Christine, they were all too close to my age. It would have to be someone older, with perspective. Even someone very old, as old as I had been in my dream, when all the choices had been made.

It was midafternoon a couple of days later when I walked down the street to the building where René's grandmother, Amélie, lived. I'd called her beforehand and heard her voice both clear and frail, saying she would be delighted to see me. I punched the code, swung the gate open, walked past pots of geraniums to her front door, and there she was, opening it to me, her silver bob of hair coming up to my chest height. I bent to kiss her and felt her take my hand, hers cool and smooth and small in mine as she led me in. "It's so much easier to move about if I have a hand to hold. You don't mind, do you?"

We went into the living room with its aquarium light, and she gestured to me to sit down on a chair tipped toward hers. "Then I don't have to make an effort to hear."

"How are you?" I asked. "Did you manage to get out of going to the country?"

"Oh, no, unfortunately. But, you know, they would have minded if I'd refused. One of my grandchildren is traveling down with me on the train. My daughter is meeting us at the station. It's all arranged. Maybe next year. Maybe I'll prepare them for it gradually, and make a change. It's a bit of an upheaval at my age, you know, and I do enjoy my time alone. I'm the only friend I've got left! All my contemporaries are gone. I miss them, and I miss my husband, of course, but it does get less as time goes on, and then I surprise myself by discovering I'm really quite happy on my own. But how about you, dear? How are you? I thought you looked sad, on your last visit, and a bit tired. It can be tiring, moving to a new place. How are you settling in?"

"Fine, really. People have been very kind. I really don't feel alone anymore."

"That's good, at your age. I think one needs to get fairly old to enjoy being alone. But you will, one day. Meanwhile, enjoy the company!"

"I wanted to ask you something, if I may?" I wouldn't dare to ask her, if I left it any longer; the words were in my mouth before I knew it.

"What was it you wanted to ask?"

"Do you believe in ghosts? I mean, do you know if they exist? I thought you might know."

Her hands smoothed her skirt over her knees. I saw her decide how much to tell me, how much to withhold. There was a silence, in which I noticed a clock ticking on the shelf and traffic going past on the street.

Then she said, "I think you must be asking me that for a reason. Have you seen one?"

"I think I have. The ghost of my father, in Paris. Either he's a ghost, or he never died, and I had to ask someone. You were the one I thought of, because I can't work it out on my own, and, well, it's very upsetting, not knowing. So I thought I might ask you. I hope you don't mind."

"I do have conversations with people who are dead. And I'm not crazy. But you do have to be very careful about letting people know that, or they will lock you up, especially at my age. Senility, you know. It's terribly easy for people to think you are senile. But this wasn't a conversation, am I right?"

"No, more of a sighting. Three sightings, to be exact. All of them here in Paris, and all of them when I wasn't able to move to approach him. Two from a moving bus, and one when a street was blocked off because they were making a film."

"And did he always look the same, these three times, or had he changed his clothes, for example?"

"No, he was wearing the same clothes. Clothes I recognized."

"Ah, then I think he must have been a ghost. Real people—live people—change their clothes. And they don't wear the clothes they wore decades ago. I think we are talking about a ghost here. You know, it's a word people use, but it doesn't really describe the reality. I mean, the echo of someone who was alive in one universe at a certain time but may well be alive in another. Just, the membrane between the two becomes thin. I think maybe where you saw your father must be significant. You say, from a moving bus. That means, from behind glass. So he was protected and so, to the same extent, were you. And the other time?"

"When a film was being made, on rue Mouffetard. He was on one side of the barrier; I was on the other. I thought he was one of the film people, to begin with."

She spread her thin, pale fingers on her knees and stared at them. The clock ticked, whirred, and then chimed.

"Four o'clock. I will make you some tea. But first, I just want to suggest that the occasions for these sightings were important, because in none of them could either of you contact the other. You saw him. He appeared to you. The glass cut you off from him, like a protection, a statement that you were not really in the same world. Then, the film. It was a film about the fifties, wasn't it? You were not yet born, yes? He was perhaps protecting you by appearing then. Across a barrier, in time, in space, he could give you a sign. But not more."

"But what does it all mean?" My question, as a childish wail. I followed what she said, but it was too strange, too difficult to comprehend; she was speaking in a language that was alien to me, not even looking at me, as if she were reading something written on the air.

"It's hard to say. But I think, Gaby, you should not be upset by it. Think of it as a gift. Your father wants to show himself to you. Now, what is it that you most need to hear from him?"

I thought. "That he's there for me. That he approves of me and loves me. That he thinks I'm making the right choices in life. All that. All that you want from a father. But most of all, I think I want to know that he still exists."

"Well, it seems to me obvious that he is there for you. Your desire to hear from him has made that certain. That he loves you, you must have a good sense of that already, no? But that you are making the right choices in life, only you can say."

It was all harder than I had imagined: the French language, her subtlety, the pressure even of the light through green leaves, the dimness it made between us, making it hard even to see. Amélie continued, "The fact of his existence, well. I believe that nothing, no one, that has existed, can stop existing. It seems only logical to me. But on another plane, perhaps, one we rarely reach in this life. Did you want to know what his life was like? Does that matter? You see, sometimes I think people appear to us because they feel they were misunderstood. Maybe he is trying to give you something important to both of you. Understanding, for him, love and support for you. Or simply information. Does that make sense?"

"Hmm. Maybe."

"I say this because, after my husband died, he came back to me. I saw him at the end of the garden. I met him in the corridor between the kitchen and the dining room. I saw him walking down the road outside our house. I spoke to him. I said, come closer, let me know what you have for me. And he did. He came into the bedroom one night and sat on the end of the bed and said, Amélie, you have to stop mourning me and do your art. There is work for you in the theatre. In the theatre, I said, what have I got to do with the theatre? And then I came to Paris and began making masks. And I did that for twenty years."

"Masks?"

"Yes. I will show you. Theatrical masks. It was entirely his idea. He showed me what to do next."

She got up and walked, holding on to the furniture as she went, into the next room. "Come in!" I followed. The room was papered in red, so that it seemed smaller than it probably was, and the walls were covered in masks. Traditional masks of comedy and tragedy, clown masks, devil masks, white masks with red lips like Japanese ones, wrinkled dark-skinned masks with hair, like African totems. She pointed to the walls. "I made all these. They have all been used at one time or another. Now they just live here, like people I once created. Maybe like the characters in a novel. I know them all, I remember making them."

I stared around me. What would it be like living with a room full of these faces? They stared, they smiled, they grimaced. Amélie took one down from the wall and put it on. She became a grinning satyr. She took it off and smiled at me. "We can become anything, you see. The varieties are endless. I became fascinated with them, and also it paid well. People came to me for masks for parties and balls, in the old days, and sometimes, they still do. I tell them, I'm old now. I can't make them anymore."

"But you still want them here?"

"Of course. They remind me of the old days. And, of course, that whatever face we turn to the world is temporary only."

"They are a little frightening." I didn't know how to say *spooky* in French.

"Only if you let yourself be frightened. It's the same thing with ghosts, and revenants. They are not there to frighten you. But we have such a limited idea of what is possible, we stop ourselves even imagining the existence of other worlds, ways of being."

I took one down from the wall, daring myself, and placed it over my face. A milkmaid, with red lips and arched eyebrows. I looked into the gilt-framed mirror.

"There, you see. You can transform yourself. We have all these selves inside us already. Masks and theatre are only ways to let them out. We are all of us more like each other than we think, and also more different. You see, for instance, an old woman—but look, if I put on the devil mask, what do you think?"

A child-size person with a fiendish face. Hieronymus Bosch, the painters who depicted hell. People with the faces of pigs disappearing into Satan's maw. Disembowelings and rapes. The detailed medieval depiction of what we were all capable of. The photographs of young Americans that had circulated on the internet recently, showing them torturing faceless others, grinning as they did so. The mess and spill of humanity. As she meant me to see, I think.

"Now, let's have some tea, shall we?"

In the midst of these thoughts, I raised my face to her and saw her take pity on me. We left the mask room—"It was supposed to be a guest room, but I never have any guests, only them."

She slipped into the kitchen to make tea, and I sat down on my chair again, after offering rather feebly to help.

"No, no, I can manage." And manage she did, with the graceful silver teapot and the art nouveau cups, just as before. The soothing ritual of tea.

She breathed out, set down her cup. "Gaby, I did not mean to alarm you. Really, those are only theatrical props. I sense that you are troubled, and I only mean to help. If I can, that is."

"You already have. You have given me a perspective that I couldn't have found without you. I mean—it seems that, although you have lived through frightening things, you are all right. And what you said about ghosts, that helped. But what should I do?"

"Do? Do nothing. Observe. Feel. Discover. There is nothing else to do."

"Really? You think I should do—nothing?"

"For the moment, yes. Meditate on what it means to you, your father appearing to you like that. Draw some essential thing from it, yes. But there is nothing you can do about it, nothing at all. You can make him neither appear nor disappear. Just live, and be aware. That is all I can tell you."

I felt as if the oracle I had believed in had let me down.

"We are so led to believe in doing, all the time. But at my age, there is really very little I can do, so I see how unnecessary it is. I can pass that on to you. But I'm not sure if, at your age, you can manage it."

She leaned back in her chair, her eyes closed for a moment, and I felt that I had exhausted her. But then she opened them and said, "Come back when you like. But when we have finished our tea, I think it is time for you to go."

I wondered then if at ninety-four I might be in a room with an anxious young woman who was trying to puzzle out how to live her life, and if I, too, might say, *Do nothing*.

"Thank you, Amélie."

"Thank you too, Gaby. You, with the name of the angel Gabriel, the one with the fiery sword that cut things apart, the weapon of discernment. You will have it, I am sure of that."

I closed the door behind me, after kissing her on both soft white cheeks, and stepped out into the sunshine. Black clouds still massed at the end of the street, but there was this sudden rather eerie light, as if before a storm. Sky in the puddles, reflected; black tarmac wet with recent rain. I walked home, thinking of the masks. Of all the people we can seem to be, or who may exist inside us, waiting their turn to play and be played. I was not even halfway through my life; according to Amélie's terms, I was just a beginner. I had never had such a sense of the extraordinary possibilities of life before, of all that I was and could be, if I were to take up her challenge. Discernment? Was that really what was coming to me? But the knowledge was fragile too, could so easily be lost. I might fall asleep again and lose it all, this edgy awareness she had produced in me. I had been given the essence of one woman's long life, and it was vital not to let go of it, but it was also like walking along with a full bowl of something that could so easily spill and be lost. Where could I put it down? And if I carried it for the rest of my life, who, for God's sake, would I become?

10.

When you walk around a city, you inevitably see people who remind you of people you know. Once when I was a student, I saw a boyfriend of mine kissing someone else on a bridge in Cambridge, and the pain of that immediate physical jealousy went through me with the violence of heart failure. But when I came near, it wasn't him. It was a young man with hair like his and a jacket like his and a similar way of rolling along in blue jeans sagging at the waist and dirty sneakers. But the pain was real. I remember sitting down on a bench to recover. Someone I didn't know at all was kissing a girl I didn't know either, and I'd felt the sharp pain of it like an incision. It was the Doctor Zhivago thing again. He saw Lara from a moving tram, and it was not her. But it killed him, the shock of it, the feeling. Would he have died there had it really been her, the one woman, unique and irreplaceable? We don't know. So I went on thinking about my father in the streets of Paris, the dead ringer, whatever he was.

After midnight, after Yves had gone home to study for his oral, I stood at my kitchen window and saw a light on in the building opposite. Another insomniac, his or her light like a signal in the darkness. One other person, at least, was awake. I made some herb tea and sipped it, standing there. Remembering.

I had last spent real time with him in New York, on what turned out to be his last trip there, in the summer of 2003. He disdained the rest of the United States, as Françoise had said, but loved New York. After the destruction of the Twin Towers and the panic after September 11, 2001, there was that sense of fragility among New Yorkers; you felt it at once among people who lived there, the care for each other, a kind of deliberate tenderness that took everything seriously. New York was still scarred and mournful, even though the reconstruction of the city had begun. It lasted, this sense of its own vulnerability. Perhaps, as people said about London after the war, it would take a long time to lose it completely. It was like a person after surgery, no longer quite the same: stoical, solemn, grateful to be alive.

We went to my friend's play together, and the following day to the Guggenheim to see an exhibition of small still life paintings, grouped by subject. I remember how he moved from one to another, peering close, very intent on each one. I remember a particular painting of walnuts but not who painted it. He pointed, drew me to it. Here we could celebrate something that resonated between us, a passion for a kind of perfection, I thought. We were far from the chaotic warmth of the house in Norfolk and the gray reaches of the North Sea. Far from my mother, and her influence, I thought now. Did we talk about her? All I remembered were those small perfect still lifes, and the cold light outside the Guggenheim, the cabs lined up, the sky above the trees of Central Park. We were staying in the Village, near friends of his who had an apartment on West Tenth Street. The hotel we were in was comfortable, and he treated it like his club. There was a café with good coffee on the corner, and bagels. My father in one of his other lives, being a New Yorker, taking me with him to yet another place where he could be anonymous. As he had taken Françoise, apparently, to the Algonquin, because she wanted to go there. What did my mother do, when he was away? What lay in the gaps between people, the places where things did not work, or dreams could not be confessed, or the safety net of marriage was not enough to catch you as you fell? If I were to go to New York now, would I see my father there, on West Tenth Street, in the

Park, studying a perfect still life that he longed to buy? What happens to our multifaceted souls, if not multiple hauntings, a multiplicity of places in which to stroll after death, and be seen?

The light opposite snapped off, and I took this as a sign to go back to bed. The sheets smelled of Yves, and I rolled myself in them, and slept again.

In the morning, I sat in my old T-shirt, bare-legged, drinking coffee, dunking a heel of bread from yesterday. My cell phone warbled. It was Françoise.

"Gaby, I hope it's not too early. I was thinking about you. Are you all right?"

"Yes, fine. I had a rather rough night, so I'm waking up slowly."

"Me too. I mean, I was awake in the night. I was thinking about you. Can we meet? Are you free at all today? I have to see a doctor this morning, and I'll be in the *treizième*, not far from you. How about meeting for lunch?"

I thought of the rather old ham and wrinkled tomatoes in my fridge, and suggested my usual café. Like me, she was not a lunch maker, so I felt no obligation to cook for her.

"How are you? How's the leg?"

"Much better, actually. Thank God, I can get around better now. But I've had this appointment for ages. It's just a checkup, really. I've had the plaster off for days, it's great."

"See you at about one, then?"

I went to shower and found some clean clothes, black jeans and a flowered sleeveless top, and tied a scarf in what I hoped was a Parisian manner. In the mirror my face looked back at me, looking older with the circles under my eyes from the night. I rubbed in expensive French face cream, did my eyes, added lipstick, and thought, *This is how it goes from now on: repairing the ravages of time.* This is what everyone over forty has to do, before they go out. All this for my father's old lover, or rather, for me in her eyes. I was the only person left who could remind her of him, so I felt a certain obligation. Her admission of sleeplessness drew me to her rather as the light in the building opposite had: two lights signaling in darkness. I remembered that today was a strike day, and heard on the radio that the march was to begin at Bastille and make its way to Port-Royal in the afternoon, but presumably she knew about that and would get across town somehow before everything stopped, buses and taxis included. Forty years after the famous month in which I had been born, and still the marchers were in the street, stopping traffic and handing out leaflets, just as they always had and always would in France. After my years in America, I still appreciated it all, the extraordinary optimism of it, probably more than Parisians would whose days were being complicated by strikes and marches.

My eyes still aching, I slip-slopped down the polished stairs in sandals, clicked the door open, and went through the courtyard to open the big doors that once let in horses, carts, carriages, and these days opened for delivery vans and the garbagemen. Out into the street, bright light and water running down the gutters. Morning in Paris, startlingly beautiful, whatever the doubts of the night before. My heart lifting with it, the movement of people on the street, the fresh green of the early summer trees. I went down to browse in the market and the bookshop and sit in the little park until it was time to meet Françoise. Who would not choose to be a ghost here? Who would give the chance a second thought? No amount of pollution or dirt could undo the beauty of the light, the way it fell upon buildings, streets, trees, benches, human life. The way it made us respond. I thought, *So be it, Dad, if you chose to haunt this place, I understand, I get it, I do, and I'm not going to let it worry me anymore.* The cities of our hearts: Why would they not claim us after death, as they do in life?

⚜

She was a little late and arrived with a shopping bag, limping slightly. She put her big black handbag and the crisp paper carrier down on the chair next to me where I sat sipping water and feeling my stomach rumble. I half stood in the tiny space between chairs on this café terrace and we kissed on both cheeks, friends meeting for lunch, or a mother-and-daughter get-together, anyone might have thought. The waiter put down the menu and asked us what we wanted to drink, and we ordered with little fuss a *pichet* of red, and the bread came, and it was all very normal. I saw in the sharp light of today that her face was more lined than I had thought, and her hair more streaked with gray. But she had a fine profile, a thin nose, wide lips, and something very attractive or at least interesting about the little channel we all have that runs from nose to lips. I stared at her, and found her beautiful. She smiled back, a little surprised. "I'm having the goat cheese salad, what about you?"

I had been thinking about smoked salmon, but I said I'd have the same, to simplify things, perhaps to avoid a gap. I mostly like eating the same thing as the person I am with, as it feels as if one is sharing the experience more completely. The wine arrived, clear red in the midday light. Françoise poured our glasses, and we lifted them to each other.

"You know, you look so like your father. I hope you don't mind my saying so. His nose and mouth especially."

So, we had both been studying each other, finding likenesses, finding aspects to love, or at least admire.

"I was always told so. But then people told me I looked like my mother too. It's funny how likenesses work, don't you think, you see echoes of one person and then of another."

"Ah, but I never met your mother."

No, I imagine you did not.

The salads arrived, *chèvre chaud* with walnuts. Just what two women eating together on a summer day would order.

We talked about her doctor's visit, her leg and how it was healing, how dangerous the stairs were where she lived, very slippery, how it was good for everyone that European law was insisting on everyone in old buildings putting in elevators. We talked about my apartment, and how I liked the neighborhood. Then we looked at each other, and a moment's embarrassment passed between us.

This woman was my father's lover. Did my mother know about her? The questions still nagged at me. What were we all doing when he was away, and where did we think he was? I tried to remember if he had always seemed to be leaving. He left for work each day, and so did everyone else's father, so fathers not being there did not seem to be particularly significant. Women and children simply got on with life in their absence; my mother, with all her friends, one after the other at the kitchen table, drinking mugs of coffee, smoking cigarettes, talking, always talking, while the big pots of soup bubbled on the stove and homemade wines burped in their glass containers like different-colored potions in an alchemist's shop. The floor was quarry tiled and cold, but babies crawled and sprawled on it, and we older children had to haul them back from the fireplace or the open door, because the mothers were always talking so intensely over their coffee. That was what I remembered. That was what fathers did—they went away elsewhere, and when they came back in, all the talk stopped, the women scooped the babies up off the floor and disappeared, heavens, look at the time, and we still have nothing for dinner, Helen, see you tomorrow, Thursday, next week, at the meeting, leave the kids at my place if you want, let me know, okay, ciao.

How was it that my mother, a feminist, did not know what was going on? At this moment, I knew, of course she did. But she prevented herself from minding, she stopped all jealousy at its source. She was incapable of claiming him for herself because sharing, giving, being generous was what life was all about. *Sexual jealousy*, I could almost hear her say it, *was a thing of the past.* But she knew. She must have. She must even have covered for him, lied for him, told people he was at work when she knew he was in Paris.

I wondered how he traveled: Did he fly, or come on the slow boat train and ferry, in the cumbersome days before Eurostar and the tunnel? He must have flown; anything else would have been absurdly slow. I imagined Françoise waiting for him in Paris, opening her front door, and my father coming in out of the cold and fatigue of journeys, even short ones from London to Paris, taking her in his arms. Why had I not known any of this until now? How could I have been so unaware? When we are young, we accept the story we are given; we soak up its atmosphere. It is what has made us, and we don't think to question it. Children whose parents may have been quarreling for years are still stunned and shocked by the word *divorce*. We believe our parents' versions, as long as it is possible to do so. Forty years, in my case. I couldn't believe that none of us, none of my siblings nor I, had known.

"Gaby, where are you?" Françoise asked me gently enough, over the *chèvre chaud* on this warm summer day of 2008, with the trees in the little park thickening their foliage hourly and the sun on glass and metal making its sharp reflections.

"Thinking about him. My father. How ridiculous this is, us sitting here chitchatting as if he'd never existed."

"It's over now. I just wanted to know you, Gaby, it was important. You were the one he was always talking about, the one who made him laugh."

"I was?" Again, a new picture. Myself, suddenly become witty and amusing and more lovable than the others. *Thank you, Dad, for the belated compliment.* I was close to tears and rummaged in my bag for a tissue.

She said, "It's a hard thing, to lose someone that suddenly."

"Françoise, can I ask you, what did you think when you heard he was dead? I mean, did it strike you as strange, too sudden, even a bit unlikely?"

"He had a heart condition, you know. It wasn't really such a surprise. He wouldn't go and get fitted for a pacemaker, and it could have saved him if he had."

"I didn't know."

Had he told anyone else? My mother, at least, must have known. How strange, that my parents of all people, old hippies, people of the sixties and seventies, fanatics of truth and openness, should have been so invisible at the ends of their own lives. What had my mother been thinking about when the truck drove into the back of her car, slamming her into that wall? Had she been distraught, anxious, fighting down jealousy, or had it simply been a rainy morning, hard for the truck driver to slam on his brakes and have time to stop, and even a Volvo could not protect her against such an impact? How had my father lived since then with his unreliable heart, alone?

I looked at Françoise across our little round lunch table and knew I would simply have to let the questions go, because now there would never, could never, be any answers. I had not been paying attention. I had been getting on with my own life, in the way that people do. I had been in America, getting a green card, applying for citizenship, unable to leave the country while I waited for a slow bureaucracy to give me what I thought I wanted most. Nothing I could have done would have changed things. Now I imagined stopping my mother on her way out, too hurried and anxious to get to the supermarket, and saying to her, *Slow down, Mum, don't rush. And why not wait until this afternoon, when it's going to stop raining?* I could have been there, but I was not. Nobody was there. She did what she did, and it happened.

Françoise said to me, "Let's eat. We have all the time in the world."

I thought of saying to her, *It is here that he has come to find me. Maybe there is something I have to know, or understand.* But I started on my salad instead, and we ate for a few moments in silence while the traffic roared past us, the way it always does past cafés in Paris so that you eat in a haze of fumes, heat hung and gathered in the air.

Then we heard the shout, of hundreds of voices all at once, like a collective sonic boom. A loudspeaker, shouting into the afternoon. We both jumped.

"It's the *manif*," Françoise said. "The march. That's why the traffic's so thick, they must have closed the bus lanes. I just got across town in time."

"Where are they? That shout sounded quite near."

"Coming down Port-Royal, I think."

We ordered our espressos, and as they were put in front of us, with a tiny square of chocolate in the saucer of each small cup, we heard the growing roar of a large number of people all singing "The Internationale." I had never heard anything like this: people singing, as they marched, protesting against the government, against laws, against discrimination. The sound grew, and people sat silent in the cafés, put down their papers and coffee cups, and looked at each other, acknowledging something. This was what my parents had believed in; however little they had actually marched or protested in fact—my mother, I remembered, did go to Greenham Common on a couple of occasions and talked passionately about it, the women in the mud, the plastic benders they lived in, the police on horseback, the wire fence, the dogs. It was what bound them together. Old lefties, with an easy belief in change, in people's ability to make change happen, in governments crumbling and revolutions taking place. It was what they had dreamed of, it was what their marriage had been for, and the fact that my mother was giving birth to me in May 1968—not as she would have wished, or said she wished, being on the barricades—just made her more thoroughly of her time. "My daughter Gaby," she used to say, "a daughter of sixty-eight, a child of the revolution." Never mind that the aborted revolution was here in Paris, and she at the time in the hospital in Fulham.

"What are they protesting about?"

"Oh, everything. The French always protest. This time it's against Sarkozy's policies, people being paid the same for working longer hours, and about pensions. I totally agree, but I don't think singing

'The Internationale' is going to do any good. I voted for Ségolène last year, but that didn't do any good either."

"I know the feeling," I said. "But what else can we do? My parents would have said, *March, protest, shout, wave banners.* It was what their generation did."

"My generation too," Françoise said, smiling. "I am their age, nearly. We had ideals, and we were quite sure we were right. The only trouble was, it didn't work. We got Mitterrand and the thirty-hour week, and the country went broke. Now the left is all broken up, and we don't know how to react. The unions are struggling, I don't even think they will survive."

"This is on me. You gave me lunch last time." I drained my wine and a mellow early-afternoon feeling moved through me. It would have been nice to have met up with Yves and gone to bed.

"Have you met anyone since you've been in Paris? I mean, a man?" She might have been a mind reader. Or perhaps this is what everyone here thinks about after lunch.

"Yes, actually. A man called Yves. A friend of my friend René, who worked for my father long ago, in the London gallery. He and his girl-friend set us up, and it worked."

"I miss that," Françoise said. "Not just sex, though, of course, that is nice, but the closeness, the physical contact, you know, skin to skin? I have had it with others, since, but somehow nothing lasted. You get so used to the touch and smell of a particular man, don't you find?"

I thought then that two women who barely knew each other, going out to lunch in North America, would not have had this conversation. Also, that the particular man had been my father.

"Yes, it makes life so much easier, somehow. That nakedness, that sense of ease." I knew I was talking about Yves here, not Matt. Yves was happier naked than not, whereas Matt was usually wrapped in a towel or wearing his boxer shorts, his naked self not readily available. Even the fact that he showered so often seemed to veil him in cleanliness and the smell of soap.

"You are still married?" she asked me as the bill came.

"Yes. We've separated, at least for a while, to see how things work out. I was unhappy. It wasn't just him, I know, but I had to leave, so I came over here."

"What do you think you will do? Or is it too soon to say?" She leaned forward, clasped her rather wrinkled hands together. I noticed the ring, on the wrong hand.

The shouts and cheers sounded again, seeming nearer. There was a brief blare of music. A voice on a loudspeaker, shouting out something that neither of us could make out.

"I don't know. Something will make me decide one way or the other. I don't yet know what."

"Perhaps," she said, "you will be like your father, and have a divided life. Two lives in one. Two loves. Two homes. Is that possible?"

"Doesn't one have to win, in the end?"

"No, apparently not. What happens in the end is that we die. We leave the scene. I know, that seems a long way off to you, but it did to me once too. I thought we were going to be here forever. Everyone does, when we are young."

I was young to her, of course. I was my father's American daughter. I was the emissary from that other world where people did not have double lives, where infidelity was a sin, where life did not depend on how subtly you maintained your love affairs, where winning, not sharing, was everything.

She told me then that she had been there when he bought me the Chinese horse. That he had hesitated to go in and get it for me, but she had pushed him a little, go on, it would make her happy, your little girl who loves horses, and he had done it and brought it home for me. The invisible hearts of known stories: the stories turn inside out, and there, *voilà*, what you have felt but never really known. The invisible woman who is there with your father when he buys you a present and then pretends it all came from him. The half-truths and half-understood things. I felt sadder and more adult all at once, hearing this, remembering my joy when he brought the picture home and I unwrapped it from its crisp French brown wrapping paper. But there was nothing to be sad about, perhaps. He had bought it in the end because he was happy, because a beautiful young woman had been with him, her arm through his, telling him, go on, she'll love it, it's our present to her of today. Happiness had been passed on: surely that was what mattered.

"I have something I need your advice on," she said, just as the waiter came back with my change. Ah, here it was. The one thing she would ask me that I could not do.

"What's that?"

"I have a painting in my flat that your father left there with me, because he couldn't take it back to England. I think it's valuable. I didn't tell you when you came to lunch, because I wasn't sure then that you wanted to know any more. It's in the bedroom. But, really, it's yours more than mine. Will you come back and see it, and we can decide what to do?"

"What is it? What sort of a painting?"

"It's quite small. A still life. I think it's Dutch, seventeenth century."

"But he didn't give it to you, he just left it with you?"

"I think there must have been some problem in taking it back to the UK. He was going to come back for it, decide what to do. But he never did. It was only last year, the summer before he died."

We gathered up our bags and purses and said goodbye there on the café terrace with the traffic stalled in the narrow street beside us, the booming announcements from the distant demonstration still in our ears. In Paris you are always part of something else that's going on right next to you: someone's love affair, a big political event, a film being made, a demonstration. You never live just your own life, somehow, but are spliced in among all the rest of it, a small part of some invisible whole. Everything is always being interrupted: you have snatches of conversation as trucks roar past you, words cut off that might mean your life is changed forever; you kiss goodbye, and then hello again, and the roar of distant voices comes between you; you roll over in bed, as I did with Yves only hours earlier, and a saxophonist plays a volley of brassy sound down your street. Hours ago, days ago, yesterday, tomorrow: all are jumbled, relative. The past soars above you in its buildings and lies in deep layers beneath your feet. Your father looks at you across time and space, and the look means something, but you can't translate it, and a woman comes into your life who has been there all along, and a picture that hung on your bedroom wall in your childhood room for all those years has a provenance quite unlike the one you imagined, and a small Dutch still life is the next thing you have to deal with, hidden in the apartment of the woman who was your father's lover and is now waving to you a little distractedly as she limps toward the *métro*. Pigeons soar and swoop, swallows dart above you, the sky is Matisse blue in long strips of cutouts between the buildings, and you go home to a small apartment high up under eaves, that has become the hub of everything that matters.

I hadn't asked her about the apartment, the one I lived in. Did she meet him there, or was it only for him and my mother? Did my mother innocently suggest going to the Jeu de Paume or the new Centre Pompidou for an exhibition, or want to browse in the market in the rue Mouffetard, while he dashed across town to a rendezvous in Montmartre, saying he had to go and meet a dealer? Was there for him that breathless rush on the *métro* between women, for her that bland question, *How did it go, your meeting?* I imagined him dashing up steps, along concrete corridors, leaping on a train before the doors closed, squashed inside and breathing hard, hoping that the scent of Françoise had been adequately washed off in that brief shower. No wonder he had had heart failure. Hearts failed, perhaps, from too much use as well as too little. My father, that muscle, that pump: again, like Zhivago, staggering, falling, driven by love across distance.

11.

I stood in Françoise's bedroom and stared. It was small, the painting, smaller than I had imagined, and it was a copy or a twin of the one we had seen together in that exhibition in the Guggenheim. It was a tiny still life of walnuts, on a gray-blue cloth folded into ridges. The nuts were scattered as if a squirrel had left them, and what had fascinated the painter, I could see, was the way the whorls and ridges on them could be translated by paint. There was a silver nutcracker like a pair of bandy legs. The cloth was a real, rucked-up tablecloth, and the walnuts were knobbly and looked hard to crack. The light that fell on them came in from the left, as if they had been abandoned after a meal in an adjacent room. There was one nut that had been split open. I came in close, examined the slightly crazed surface of the paint. The kernel that had fallen from the open nut lay in two pieces only just joined together, like the human brain. I remembered how my father had peered at the little painting on the wall at the Guggenheim, one still life among others, pots, jugs, apples, kitchen implements, even leeks and carrots, all the ordinary things of life made to glow in the light the painters had seen. Still life, a celebration of the ordinary. *Las Bodigones*, the exhibition was called. It had been organized by topic, rather than in historical sequence, so the artists were all jumbled together as if what they had painted mattered more in the end than who they were. A Cézanne study of apples next to a Dutch seventeenth-century pot, a Cubist fruit bowl beside an Italian Renaissance heap of root vegetables. I had been brought up to respect the order of art history, to recognize painters by their connection with each other—Rembrandt, Ruysdael, Pieter de Hooch all knowing each other, the Impressionists lending each other money to buy paint as they lived together in Montmartre, Picasso and Braque bound together by their era and their friends and what was going on around them. Both my father and the Courtauld had taught me that historical period mattered, made art coherent. Shocked, I saw a new way of presenting things, and I remember commenting on it to my father. He'd said, "This is how they have organized the Tate Modern, you know. It's the new fad. I'm not sure I approve. But it does allow you to concentrate on the paintings themselves."

I saw him move from painting to painting with the absorbed attention of his profession. He was pretending not to care about provenance, influence, all the things I knew were at the heart of his work. You had to know these things, to know whether a painting was real or a fake. The brushstrokes, the signature were visible on the surface, but what lay underneath, the history beneath the paint and varnish, that was where the clues lay. Each painting was a palimpsest, more than itself alone, because painters used and reused canvases, and sometimes, with cleaning, details appeared that had been invisible before. The painting in the Guggenheim had looked newly cleaned; I remembered him pointing it out.

She came and stood behind me. I turned back from my examination of the painting and glimpsed a look on her face that was like a grimace of pain.

"What is it?"

"Nothing, don't worry. It's nice, isn't it?"

"Yes. Very nice." I wondered whether to tell her now, or leave it.

It was dark and highly varnished, its surface crazed like the bottom of a fine bowl. *Craquelure.* I knew the word. I tried hard to remember the one in the Guggenheim exhibition, and thought that the nuts were perhaps more scattered, the cloth smoother. It was not the same painting. But had the painter made several studies of the walnuts, even on the same day? This one could be the other's near twin. Or one of them could be a fake. I thought that this one was darker, probably simply because it had not been cleaned as the other had. Clues might be here that I couldn't see at present.

"How long have you had it?"

"He brought it here a few months before his death. Last June, maybe? He just asked me if I could look after it for a while, and that he would collect it and get it back to its owner. That made me think that he had not bought it. But since I don't know who the owner is, and your father isn't here to tell me, it's really yours more than it is mine."

In the museum, I had loved the smallness and intensity of these still lifes, and the way the painter had chosen subjects—walnuts, leeks, potatoes—that were at once so solid and so temporary. A seventeenth-century vegetable or nut wouldn't have a hope of still existing today; it was a particular product of its time. Everything rotted and went back to the earth, but this series of marvelous little paintings told us all we needed to know about eternity.

"But I can't take it. What would I do with it? You have no idea where it came from, none at all?"

"I know he found it here in Paris. That must have been why he couldn't take it abroad. We're very exacting here about art staying within the country, even if it isn't by a French artist."

I tell her, because here we are, two women who loved him. "I was with him when we saw it, or one exactly like it, in the Guggenheim museum in New York."

"Really? Do you know where the New York exhibit came from?"

"It was in someone's private collection. I can't remember what the name was. But I don't think it was American."

"The painting could have been borrowed for the exhibition."

"Yes, or there could have been two of them. Or even more. Or one of them could have been a fake. A forgery."

"I don't think the Guggenheim hangs fakes, somehow. They have a mass of experts. They would know."

"Could this one be a fake, then?"

Françoise frowned and stared closely at it as if for the first time, or as if she had never considered this. "I don't know. How do you tell? I should know, but I don't."

"You run a series of X-rays and see what's underneath. You examine the signature. You look to see if it's the original stretcher, and they can test the canvas for age, and look at even minute amounts of paint through a microscope. Even the rust marks from nails. But sometimes it's very, very hard to tell. I don't somehow think he'd have hidden it here if he'd thought it was a fake; he could have just taken it home and hung it on the wall and said, *It's a copy of one I saw in America, isn't it good?*"

I thought, *I wouldn't care if it was a fake if I managed not to care about the painter.* Once you had imagined a person in seventeenth-century Delft or Amsterdam scattering his walnuts on a gray-blue cloth, with the light coming in from the left just as in a Vermeer—conscious or unconscious influence?—then you wanted it to be real. If all you cared about was the surface, then a good forgery would do. I thought of billionaires who famously hid their real paintings in vaults, under lock and key, while the ones they hung on their walls were copies. When was a copy a fake? When it pretended to be the original. If you had the original locked up in your cellar like a prisoner whose cries you tried not to hear, you would still know your hung painting was a copy. Faking involves the imagination, a sleight of hand, while a copy is simply a

112

copy, isn't it, no malice or legerdemain involved? A forgery demands a signature, surely; yet even a signature can be faked.

Françoise said, "Well, it can stay here while you make up your mind. But I wouldn't feel all right about keeping it, long term."

"He didn't say he'd given it to you, did he? You're sure?"

"No, he said, keep it for me, I'm going to get it back to the owner. I'm sure that's what he said."

"As if he thought it had been stolen, maybe?"

"Who knows?"

She made coffee, and we went to sit at her kitchen table to drink it. Small cubes of sugar stirred into little cups, and she lighting a little cigar. Already we had become allies in a need to discover truth. We were on a trail set by my father, the pieces of his life scattered before us as if we were on a treasure hunt. Had all this been deliberate? No, nobody could know exactly when they were going to die. My father, the magician, the one who had done conjuring tricks at my birthday parties and laughed when a sharp child found him out and shouted, "I saw you! Mr. Greenwood! It was you!" and simply went on to the next trick. Handkerchiefs fluttering out of hats and sleeves, eggs appearing from behind ears. All that was easy enough to perform. But Dutch paintings? Sudden appearances of mistresses? Himself, even, as revenant, echo, copy, fake?

"We could take it to the Louvre, I suppose."

"But if it does belong to someone else, the person your father mentioned? We might be accused of stealing it. We have no papers for it."

"We could just tell the truth, that someone left it here."

"Somehow, I don't think the experts at the Louvre would swallow that," she said.

"Françoise?"

"Yes?"

"I just wondered—you saw him last summer, when he brought you the painting. How was he? Did he seem ill?"

"No, not really. He got tired easily, had to walk more slowly than he used to. But no, he seemed all right. Were you worried?"

"I've been thinking I should have been."

"Gaby, it was sudden. I had no idea it was going to happen like that. You have nothing to reproach yourself about, if that's what you are thinking."

"My sister told me he was living in a mess, seemed depressed."

"Oh, your sister. Hmm. His heart wasn't strong, I knew that, but he seemed fairly well. We had a good time. Don't worry about it. So, see you soon? You'll think about what you want to do about the painting?"

We kissed on both cheeks, and I left her flat and walked down the hill to the *métro* station, the bulk of Sacré-Coeur a looming presence at my back. We were in something together now, she and I. Was that what my father had wanted to achieve? I ran down the steps, my ticket in my hand, and went underground to come up like a mole on the other side of the city, on the Left Bank. Two sides of everything, even Paris. This is what he'd done, over and over, crossed the city, under the great river, to come up on the other side. I was following the way he had gone. Of course I was. I was his daughter, after all: not a copy, not even a reproduction, but with his genes in me mysteriously making me in his image.

What I knew of the business of testing paintings for their source and authenticity, I had mostly from him, picked up from idle conversations, questions, the sort of thing a parent hands on to a child without even knowing. It was not the sort of practical thing you learned at the high-minded Courtauld Institute where he had sent me. He had not been training me to follow him in his career but providing me with an education, a safe alternative to hanging out in a squat in the East End and stealing from department stores. Yet it had always been me, not any of my siblings, who was invited to art openings, private views, who was told about deals and offers made and the secret language of dealers, of how auctions worked, and when new techniques were found to baffle thieves, discover forgeries. How chrome yellow was not used in painting after the nineteenth century, for example, until the end of the twentieth, because it blackened quickly from pollution. How electron microscopes were used these days to scan paintings, as well as ultraviolet light, and infrared. How radiography can see through layers of paint, discovering hidden paintings underneath the surface ones: the true meaning of palimpsest.

Once he had said to me, "Every good dealer is at heart a thief." I was shocked, but I knew what he meant. The urgent desire to have and handle a painting, to contemplate that painter's vision in private; you would have to be a billionaire or a thief to indulge it. Or a dealer. He chose the middle way, meaning that he could hold on to things he loved for a certain time but was dependent on letting them go. He had the knowledge that gave him power. He could make a client want a painting and then not want it. He could, by simply raising his eyebrows, create sudden interest. His way of clearing his throat could send the price of a painting up by thousands; a downward glance of his could bring it down again. I had seen this, but more, I had guessed at it. He lived in the place between people's desires and the actual exchange of money, with a foot in both camps, understanding the longing to own, manipulating it, able to gratify it at will. A Gemini by birth, and by occupation: two of everything, a way of being he could hardly help, I began to understand it now.

At the root of it was the love of the thing itself, which he could never have afforded—unless he had become a thief. The passion for the way paint had been laid on, for the human touch that showed through the brushstrokes, the light of a particular morning in a man's studio hundreds of years ago, or yesterday. He had showed me, in galleries, the mark and the limits of a painter's skill; more, he had showed me something about himself. I had hardly paid attention, or so I thought, when I was young and easily bored, going around London galleries with him, being taken to Kettle's Yard in Cambridge, looking at Nicholsons and Alfred Wallaces and the sudden shock of a small Braque. I had complained when being dragged, as I'd felt it, around the endless galleries of the Louvre. But now I knew that the information had gone in; I had learned and absorbed what he had wanted me to learn. I could love what he had loved. That morning in the Guggenheim, he must have seen it as we both moved toward the same small canvases with the addict's light in our eyes. Had he hidden the painting of walnuts here in Paris for me to find? Had he used himself as a series of clues—his appearances a trail, leading to a treasure? Françoise and me as his acolytes? The painting, my inheritance that had been waiting for me all along—and the way to it, tortuous, complicated, like himself?

Yves said to me out of a long silence, that evening, "You will go back to America, won't you? To your husband?"

We were lying sprawled across my bed, swallows dipping and diving at the window and sometimes nearly coming in. The other day, one had flown in and circled the room twice and then flown out again through another window while I held my breath, hoping it would fly free. A failure of sonar, a sudden missed flight adjustment? Swallows can change direction on the wing, avoid obstacles, swoop back out and up into the air.

"Why do you ask? We already talked about that."

"I feel it. I feel you thinking about him."

"Not when I'm with you."

"Yes, when you are with me. You aren't entirely here. Part of you is elsewhere."

"No, Yves, I am entirely here." I came close to him again and began to show him the completeness of my presence: this, here, my hands and body, my mouth, my skin. He had been right. I had been thinking of Matt, but not sexually, not at all. Is anybody ever completely in

116

one place these days, with just one person, when our minds are full of e-mails to be read, voice mails, text messages, memories, plans, demands from far away made even without our consent upon our consciousness? We exist, each of us, at the heart of a complex web. The swallow through the open window: a thought, circling twice and then gone.

Matt had been sending me more e-mails: I miss you, when are you coming back to your senses, my life is better when you are here, for God's sake, Gaby, please. So I was in his mind; perhaps he dreamed of me too. I tried sometimes to remember him in his particularity and failed to do more than conjure his face in a photograph, and the parts of him: hands, buttocks, toes. The whole of him was unknown to me now. Change had taken place in both of us, and I no longer knew him in the intimate daily way I once had. I felt sad, recognizing this. This must be how people parted, not so much by announcement or decision but simply by allowing time and distance to do their work. The man with me on the bed was present in his entirety as well as his parts, erasing, or at least blurring, memory. A body in a smooth skin, marked with patches of dark hair that I knew as his particular geography, a movement toward me, an urge to scratch an itch suddenly, a penis that rose slightly and turned as we talked as if it wanted its own way into the conversation. The conversation itself, his accent, his slang, his questioning turns of phrase, his hands gesturing in the air. Soon the conversation would stop, because the penis had insisted, and we would be inside and outside each other again, feeling our way to the center of life where pulses and streams of feeling defined us, not words.

I said, "I'm here with you completely. This is real. You, me, today, here on this bed. If I think about Matt, he's on the outside of this. This is the present, you and me."

I remembered a time with Matt, when he had said to me, "Gaby, you aren't really here. What's up?" I had said, "No, no, nothing. I'm here, don't worry." At what point in our life together had I begun to leave? Had it been when my mother died, or long before?

Yves said, "Good. I only said that because I was worried that you would suddenly be gone."

"And you would mind if I did?"

"Of course. But you are married. That's not nothing, Gaby."

"People do get divorced."

"I don't believe you will get divorced."

"Why not?"

"I feel you thinking about him."

"But not in that way, really. We can't just eradicate whole sections of our lives. We can't just not remember. Of course I think about him from time to time." But, if my thoughts were elsewhere now, they were not with Matt but with the conundrum of my father's appearances and the painting he had left me.

"Yes, that's what I meant. So, I think you will go back."

I looked at him, lying so easily beside me, thinking of me gone. Was he pushing me into making a decision, so that it left him free? I wanted to say to him, *Don't ask me for answers I don't yet have.* Then I thought, *Oh, my God, we have not been using condoms.*

"Yves! No *preservatif*, what are you thinking? I didn't even notice, it was so nice, and now look at you, coming up again. You simply have to put one on. I can't believe we took such a risk."

"It isn't a risk. I have had a vasectomy."

"But why did you use one before, then?"

"Against the SIDA. The AIDS, as you call it. Just to be safe, to start with."

"You should have told me."

"I don't remember that we had any time for talk. Perhaps we should have."

I had had sex with him that first time without having any of the conversations you are supposed to have these days about diseases, others you had slept with, the chains of possible harm.

"No, that was crazy. So, we have to catch up now. Why did you have a vasectomy?"

"So I didn't have any children!"

"But why? You're young. You might want to someday."

"No, I know that I do not, because of being a child myself, and not wanted. It was one of the reasons that my wife left me. I didn't tell her I wanted it for myself."

"Oh." Then, "I can imagine she was pretty upset."

"Yes, well. It's over now. Do you want children?"

I looked down at the flat expanse of my stomach and the knobbed points of my hip bones at the place where I would never see the bump of pregnancy. "I think it's too late. It never seemed like a possibility. I was too busy doing other things. So we didn't really try."

"Your husband wanted children?"

"Yes, he did." Without thinking, I had used the past tense. I felt sad again, there on the wide bed in my Paris flat with Yves, at all the little Matts that would not exist, or at least not if he stayed with me. He had the young American's optimism still that everything would eventually turn out okay, kids would be fine, grandkids too. His vision of our future had included a backyard, football games, a barbecue, even a dog. He minded that the line of his name, even though it was an absent and unknown father's—perhaps for that very reason—would end with him. Yet he had accepted my lack of interest in children, for what else could he do? Again, the realization that being with one person taught you about another; Yves standing naked at the window now, looking out at the swallows, Matt somehow signaling to me, I'm here, I'm still here, from a distant shore. No, Yves was right, I could not be with him without also thinking about Matt.

I myself, at just past forty, could have been, could still just be, the conduit for children. The flat plain of my belly, the dark frizz at my crotch, the two lifting angles my legs made; I looked down at my horizontal self. What men see of us, that we don't see ourselves: the horizontal, the lax, the laid out, not the busy vertical self of most of life. A body for men to come into and babies to come out of. I had never before considered myself like this; I had been so busy trying to make my vertical life work.

"You should maybe go home and try," was what Yves said, naked, watching swallows.

"Hey, someone will see you, standing there like that," I said.

"It's not forbidden, here in Paris, to look out of a window with nothing on."

"There's Google Earth, don't forget. People at their computers in other countries can just zoom in to this street."

"Well, whoever sees me like that, they are welcome. I'm French."

"I'm not going back, not yet, anyway, and I really don't think I want to get into the business of trying to get pregnant. It sounds horrible, all bossy doctors and endless tests, at my age, and you have to spend a fortune if it doesn't work, and then it often doesn't work anyway." I knew that this was not it, not my real reason, because the fear was in me, a constant warning against being tied down, having to give up my own life for a child's. I sat up. It was as if I now had to convince Yves too that I did not want, had never wanted, children.

"No, I don't think you'll have to do all that. All that is crazy. Just think about it, though, what would it be like not to be born? Not to have a life? You know, I am beginning to understand my mother, why she kept me. It must have seemed crazy, to have a child with a foreign man who didn't want her, in another country. But she gave me a life. I'm grateful for that. Or I wouldn't be here with you now."

"But you still don't want to give somebody else a life? You sound rather keen on my doing it."

"When I was younger, and my wife wanted to have a child, it was like she was using me for it, you know? I was angry when I went and had my operation. I thought, I won't let myself be used like that." He came back to the bed, sat down, and took my hand. "You know, those swallows, they go to Africa and back, just like that, because it's in them to do it. They can't decide not to."

"So?"

"Nothing. I just wonder why you and I have met. Why it was so urgent when we got together. Was it just desire? Or, maybe, to allow each other to change? What do you think?"

"More than you just fancying my bony ass, you mean?"

"More, yes."

"Perhaps." I thought, perhaps we are conduits for each other, not destinations. Perhaps, yes, this is the way life is.

I told him then about my father, and the painting of walnuts. We sat in the growing dusk of that evening, with the windows wide open on the warm summer night, and the courtyard outside with its darkening trees and deepening shadows, its pigeons and swallows and house martins, its yellow lights coming on one by one as people came home, its open windows and shadows opposite opening wine bottles, holding babies, coming together and moving apart. We opened a bottle of cold red wine and sat naked in chairs, looking out. I told him everything that had been happening to me, because I wanted him to have my story just as I wanted to have his: his mother, his missing father, his grandmother in Lisbon, his day-to-day. Then we would truly have met; we would be in each other's lives, in depth, if not in length of time.

Yves said, his feet up on the edge of the window, his glass nursed against his thigh, "I envy you, you know."

"Envy me? Why?"

"Because you had a father who cared enough about you to come back and give you all this."

"You don't think it's crazy?"

"No, I think, like the old lady you went to see, that we see people sometimes because we need to and want to, but they also want to see us. I think your father wanted you to be here, in Paris, and to find his girlfriend and the painting, oh, and me, of course, and so you came. And he showed up and gave you a little wave, a greeting, a little hello, to show you what he had done."

"Really? You believe all this is possible?"

"Believe, I don't know, it's not really belief. It's just knowing that life is more complicated than we'll ever know, so when you get evidence like this, you might as well accept it, rather than fight it, say it's crazy, or you are crazy, or whatever. I know that here in Paris, all the history is jumbled up together, from the Romans onward, the whole city is built over, one thing on top of another, one thing removed to make room for another, people dying and killing each other and getting born, so close, so incredibly close, that of course it must make a difference to life. You understand? It's just a very intense environment. Maybe in the desert, in huge plains, in America, things are different. Cities are intense, people come to them for that reason. It's the kind of thing I want to—sorry, I'm talking a lot—the kind of thing I want to tell children; I want to teach them to let things in, not just categorize them or count them, but to be amazed, to be open to wonder, you know? Not to believe, necessarily—I think belief confines you, it's always about one system—but to open yourself to possibilities. I want to show them a world where there is hope, not stupid hope, but the hope from knowing everything is possible, there is depth, and width, there are alternatives always. I want them to have a big view. Everything gets so narrow, so limited. Buying things, making money, even politics, even love. *Ouf*, I'm talking too much, maybe. But, so, yes, why not a few ghosts, or strange happenings? 'There are more things in heaven and earth than in all your philosophy.' Right?"

"*Hamlet*. Funny, I've been thinking about him recently."

"It's not surprising, with your father appearing to you, only on rue Mouffetard, not on the ramparts of a castle. But really, your Shakespeare knew all this, four hundred years ago, and all we have done since is make him into a monument and forget what he says."

I leaned to pour more wine into his glass. The two of us, naked and warm enough on a summer evening in front of open windows in a darkening room, our bodies drying after lovemaking, our secrets open to each other, the world opening up to our words, it seemed, becoming both more complex and more knowable as we talked. I thought, *This is what I wanted, what I needed, and I didn't know it. This is what I have been traveling toward.* This openness, this sense of possibility, this ability to be still, in the present, and have the world fall open around me to be marveled at and understood.

Yves said, "I believe that intuition and imagination are simply another way of thinking. You know, here in France, thinking has been so rational and scientific. It's as if everything else has been marginalized. But when we create something, for instance, a work of art, a book, whatever it is, we are simply using a rapid and effective way of thinking. Imagination and thought are not separate. So your experience of your father is a thought process. Just as valid as any other. What you do with it is entirely your own business, and as for the painting, there's nothing you absolutely have to do about it. Take your time. It's been quite safe for a year, so it will probably be safe for a bit longer."

I looked at his vertebrae as he bent forward over his knees. His bones were near the surface, like mine. Our skins were thin; we were not padded against life. "You think I'm too keen to figure out what to do about all this?"

"Well, yes. It's very American, if you don't mind me saying so. Do nothing, for now."

"It's what Amélie said. And Françoise."

"Well, now, I'm suggesting it too." His hand on my bare thigh, feeling its way up, stroking, caressing. I inched toward him, put down my wineglass. "Yves."

"Yes. Shall we go and lie down again?"

Later that same night I said to him, incautiously, "I love you," and saying it in French made it quite different from the thoughtless American phrase that ends telephone calls, or even my farewell to Matt; and in response, he said, "I know, I know. It's good, isn't it?"

I know, I know. As if he had known I would, and I was expected, a welcome if temporary guest.

12.

The Fête de la musique, when music is played on streets and in concert halls and parks all over the country, takes place on the shortest
night of the year. The light that evening was extraordinary, even for
Paris. We had walked all the way up the rue Mouffetard to the Place de
la Contrescarpe, the streets packed, rock bands on every corner, belly
dancers on the rue de l'Arbalète, the little square itself with its leaning trees a mass of people, with little kids letting off firecrackers and
squirting plastic streamers all over everybody. We escaped down the
empty streets to the Arènes, where there was nobody, only the ghosts
of Romans and animals in the sand, and on down to the square outside
the Jussieu *métro* where four middle-aged men were playing jazz outside
one of the cafés. On to the Institut du monde arabe for the famous
Egyptian singer in scarlet satin who had drawn crowds, families, whole
clans to sit on the steps and dream of North Africa, and then down to
the Seine. Notre-Dame behind us in a blur of golden light. Turner, I
thought, should have been here now. The sky over the river, the sky
reflected in the water. Sunset in a mist of gold. Little puffy lit clouds
floating over the Seine where we walked and then sat to watch the tango
dancers on the quai Saint-Bernard. The couples: he proud and rigid,
profile set, she tucked in against him, her legs following his, their bodies
welded together in the dance, her feet in high-heeled strappy shoes. A
black man and a woman with a helmet of dark hair, eyes almost closed,

their bodies moving like one entity. Her silk dress on her thighs, her stepping feet, the muscles in her legs, the way his head turned, and hers snapped around to follow.

"Do you want to dance?" Yves whispered in my ear.

"Not with those people, we'd look like idiots. Later, maybe." I had never seen such a sexual dance as that tango, with that particular couple, he in his black shirt with his hair in cornrows and his motionless profile, she in her crimson dress, her hair slicked, her face a white mask against his shoulder. The big pleasure boats went past, and the diners waved at us, and the water lapped its wake against the stone walls, and the tango dancers danced on, as if this were all there was in life. When we got up to go, our buttocks were cold and our legs stiff with sitting on stone. Around us on the sloping grassy banks, the picnics, the wine bottles, the sausages and cheeses, the children munching chips, and the couples passing a bottle from lip to lip. All down the river, the boats disappearing into golden light. The *Atalante*, the *Jeanne Moreau*. Ripples on the water like bronze. It was a night that would surely never end. We walked on, right down the quay to cross the main road and come back past the closed Jardin des Plantes; we leaned in through the railings to sniff up the cool green scent of locked gardens, plants left to rest and grow on their own with all the visitors shut out. The smells of grass and dew. My feet in sandals were sore, and I held Yves's arm as we walked on back to René's place for a late supper.

Out in the streets the next morning, the green-and-yellow vans were forking up garbage containers, and men with huge hoses were squirting water down the pavements. The noise of the big cleanup, the morning after, but the cafés were quiet and empty, and the wet cobbles in the square gleamed, where nobody walked on them. I went down to the Place Saint-Médard to buy bread. Yves had left early in the morning, to study. Last night we'd danced, at one in the morning, in this very square, under the yellow lights and the brief darkness beyond them, among the crowds that surged homeward and the musicians putting away their instruments. Under the trees beside the little park next to the church, we had moved for a few moments in each other's arms, to the last flirtatious sounds of the trumpet before it was put away. A last note, a last twirl, then good night.

I stood in line for my baguette and walked back home again with the warm loaf in its sleeve of paper under my arm, and it was only as I turned my key in the lock that I felt the onslaught of grief again like a sudden urge to vomit, a physical reaction that would not wait. I ran up the shallow stairs to the third floor, let myself into my flat, dropped my bag and the bread on the table, and fell down sobbing onto the sofa. I howled aloud, as I had in my first days in Paris, and I hiccupped and slobbered, and ran into the bathroom to snatch up a whole roll of paper to try and stanch the flow, and my whole body shook with the violence of grief. In the bread shop, standing in line with my euro in my hand and the smells of warm pastries and bread wafting around me, I had been fine. I had paid and taken my bread and walked up the street quite calmly, and then it had overtaken me. The unbearable nature of existence, the terrible paradox of life and death, the razor-blade-thin divide between them. My mother smashed against a wall. My father facedown in a puddle. And all my memories of them both, alive, loving, moving through the world, so vividly with me still that I could hardly convince myself that they were dead. As I would be one day; as we would all be. After I'd thrown my soaked and wadded pieces of paper on the floor and gone to the kitchen for a glass of water, I was sufficiently calm again to realize that I had felt this before and would feel it again. I had been happy, self-forgetful, last night: death had let me go free of its weight. I had walked up the street with my lover in the daze of the present, the fullness of life. The wave that came and knocked me over one more time was just that—another wave. I could take its buffeting, its salt splash, and stand upright again, quite easily now.

⚜

In spite of this new sense of my own resilience, I found the whole business of my father's random appearances too strange and disturbing to
let go. In Shakespeare's plays, ghosts were there to announce impend-
ing events, or to warn you of something. As were storms and tempests,
cataclysms of nature. We seem to know more now: the hurricanes and
tsunamis and bushfires and earthquakes that are consuming our world
ever more frequently are not because of gods being angry, we know that
much. But still, they warn us of something inside ourselves, a desire
to consume too much, a thoughtlessness about the world. So they are
still warnings, just about the future rather than the past. If the ghost
appearances were messages of warning to me, what were they telling me?
I couldn't imagine. But that they had drawn me to people who were
giving me the benefit of their views on life—Amélie, Yves, Françoise,
René—was undeniable. Even Matt, when I had told him, had come up
with his theory of the dead ringer, the double, the man who looked like
my father but was not him.

I called Françoise, as I had not talked to her since the day we had looked
at the little painting together. I thought, *That painting is the clue. It is
what connects us.*

"It's still here, waiting for you," she said. "Are you coming to get it?"

"All right. When's a good time?"

"Any time. I'll tell you what I've found out. The painter was
Spanish. But it was probably in Holland because in the sixteenth
century, the Spanish ruled the Netherlands under Philip II, so some
Spaniards probably still lived there. Including, maybe, the man who
painted the walnuts. These little paintings of still life objects were called
bodegones. Originally that meant paintings done in bars or wine shops.
They showed the existence of the transcendental in ordinary objects,
ordinary life."

I said, "I remember, that was the name of the exhibition. Yes, the painting we saw was an exhibition with El Grecos and Picassos. Why did we think it was Dutch?"

"Because the Dutch took up the still life theme in the seventeenth century and particularly liked still lifes of very ordinary things. But it was probably the Spanish who took their *bodegones* with them when they conquered the Netherlands, and after William of Orange liberated the country, the style of painting lived on. Yet I think the symbolism changed. If you look at the objects lying around in say, a Vermeer, you see that they nearly all represent something. They are everyday life, and they are more. They are not religious, though. You can't say they are purely symbolic, the way you can with medieval paintings, nor can you say they are simply the things that happened to be lying around. These walnuts—do walnut trees grow in Holland, by the way? I was looking at them closely, and what they look most like to me is the two halves of the human brain. Do you think that is too far-fetched?"

"No. In fact, it was something that had occurred to me too." I was in the street, walking home down the Gobelins, and it seemed strange to be having this conversation while traffic passed, kids came out of school and were shepherded home, and a large van stopped right on a crossing and started disgorging furniture wrapped in plastic. A hoist was being set up, going vertically up to the top floor of a building, to take the furniture in through a window. I stopped to watch, fascinated at the accuracy of the whole operation.

"So. What shall we do about it?"

"Everybody has been telling me to do nothing, it seems. But I'm not sure that I have to obey them."

"Well, I've put out some feelers with somebody I know who is very good on forgeries, fakes and copies. He's coming to look at the painting the day after tomorrow, so if you want to come and meet him, do. His name is Fabrice Corte, and I have known him for years. He will tell us at least something, probably whether or not it's a good fake, or the real thing."

"Okay, what time?"

"I've asked him for a drink, at seven. See you then?"

"See you then. Ciao, Françoise. And thank you."

"There's just one thing. I thought I should warn you. He does have a certain resemblance to your father."

I walked up the steep street toward Sacré-Coeur, pressed in Françoise's code, came through the art nouveau doors, and started up the winding polished staircase, one worn tread at a time, thinking of all the thousands of feet that had come this way, up and down for centuries, before me. As Yves had said, the present is piled upon the past in Paris: stairs, steps, streets. New furniture being shot up into the air, to inhabit ancient buildings. Hidden rivers beneath pavements. Marble and ancient brick beneath concrete. We walked on our modern streets high above the medieval walkways, and even higher above the Roman roads; we turned corners and passed the sliced sides of buildings that gave way into Roman amphitheatres; we confronted history itself. Bears and lions in the arenas, people being torn to pieces. You could always ignore these things, of course, and go down streets simply looking at shops. Now I went up Françoise's oak stairs thinking of the recent past, my father on these very steps, about to reach her door, myself walking in his footprint. I wasn't thinking about the man I was about to meet.

"Gaby! Come in. Fabrice is here already." She stood aside to let me pass, and I went in to the sitting room with its windows above the street, and a man stood up to shake hands with me. I couldn't believe what I saw. Fabrice Corte had white hair, a tanned face, a slightly Roman nose, and he was wearing a black jacket above a white collarless shirt. I took his outstretched hand and stared. "*Bonjour*, monsieur."

"*Bonjour*, mademoiselle. I am so happy to meet you."

"Yes," Françoise said. "There is quite a resemblance, isn't there? People used to think that Fabrice and Peter were brothers."

I let go of his hand. "You knew my father?"

"Of course. We were in the same business. I respected and liked him, even when we argued over the interpretation of a painting. He used to bring things to me to verify and then insist on his own version. I used to say, Peter, I don't know why you bother coming to see me, because you already know what you want to think. You look very like him, by the way."

I said, "So do you." I heard my voice shake.

"Yes, I know, sometimes people used to mistake us for each other. Not Françoise, unfortunately." He smiled at her.

She was carrying a tray with a bottle of Ricard on it and glasses. "Fabrice likes pastis, I hope you don't mind? I have some wine in the fridge, if you prefer. But he comes from Corsica, you see, so I have to indulge him."

So could that have been Fabrice Corte on rue Mouffetard and coming out of the Closerie des Lilas? Could I possibly have looked at this man and seen my father? Looking at him now, I couldn't even remember what my father had looked like. Features I had known seemed to be here in front of me, but played in another key. My father's nose had not had quite that Roman bump. Nor were his eyes that deep, dark brown, more hazel, like my own. But the white hair, the build, the searching look, the set of the shoulders under the jacket, and the craggy neck in the collarless shirt all seemed familiar. Or, nearly familiar. A shade off, a touch different. My father was English; this man's gestures were not his, nor did his sharp glance upward at a listener have my father's amused and speculative air.

Fabrice took the offered glass and topped it up with water, and I took mine. Françoise handed out olives in a little bowl and asked him, "Now, so you want to see the painting?"

"Of course. That's what we are all here for. Except, of course, I am trying hard to get used to being in the same room with Peter Greenwood's daughter, who looks so like him, a feminine version, of course."

I didn't say that I, too, was trying hard to get used to being in the same room with him. The most disquieting aspect of him was that he was annihilating my memory of my father; because he was here, alive and real before me, my father was fading. As I'd noticed with Yves, memory fades in the presence of new information, even as it is evoked.

Françoise went into her bedroom and came back with the little painting, which looked smaller than ever in her hands. Fabrice took it and turned it, looked at it closely. He turned it around again. Then he looked up. "I think it's just as well you didn't show it to anybody at the Louvre, because it's very good. It may well be the real thing, not a copy, and in that case, it belongs to somebody, and we don't know who. That person might be very upset to have lost it. That person might almost think that it was stolen."

I said, "You mean, my father might have stolen it?"

"Well, I don't want to insult him, and dealers very rarely steal things; it isn't in their interest. But could he have bought it? Could someone have left it with him for safekeeping, or to be valued? We don't know. We do know one thing, though, or I do. It does have a twin; there is another one by the same painter, and it was the one exhibited at the Guggenheim in that exhibition a few years ago. So at least that is clear. As in Shakespeare, twins are tricky, you never know which one you are dealing with."

Shakespeare again. Does everyone in France grow up reading him, while everyone in England has taken him for granted? Is he the hidden genius who lies beneath French civilization, after all, and are Corneille, Racine, Molière, Victor Hugo, all of them, only second-rate influences? Twins, ghosts, storms, gravediggers, mortality; in the end, everyone had to go back to Shakespeare.

Fabrice handed me the painting, and I felt impossibly moved once again by the way those nuts had been painted. I was back in the Guggenheim beside my father, listening to his slightly lecturing voice. "Walnuts are symbolic, of course, but who cares about symbols when you have the thing itself in all its essentials? The smallest thing on this earth, a nut, a seed, and here it is for us, just the way it was four hundred years ago. Most of the nuts still closed, just one cracked open."

The one cracked nut lay open like a little boat, its edges turned smoothly. Somebody had just cracked it and was perhaps about to start on the others. I looked up at Fabrice Corte and said, "He took me to the exhibition; it was the last time we really spent time together. He told me about the painting. We both just stood there in front of it and were amazed by it together."

"In that case," Fabrice said, "he must have meant this one for you. He found it—somehow, somewhere—and he left it here for you. Don't you think so, Françoise?"

She nodded, looking at me intently. It was like having parents again. It was like being the child between two adults, all at once being allowed to understand. The world was falling into a coherence it had not had since I was young, when something had fractured that I had not had the time or opportunity or maturity to appreciate. I was being shown another way of seeing things, and yet it was not unfamiliar, only distant. I saw my parents together in that messy kitchen in England where I had grown up between them, the child of all his children who looked most like my father. I saw the massive farmhouse table, always covered with pots and bowls and half-sliced vegetables, those still lifes my mother needed, those sacred things. I saw the two of them stand together in a doorway, his arm around her, a farewell kiss, and then goodbye. I had watched, and known, without knowing it, that my father had somewhere else to go, and that it was not just the world of work. I had received all these messages at that time, as I was growing up, but I had not been able to interpret them. They had been in me, because I had observed, watched, meditated; it is what children do. I had had to wait until I was forty, and had lived for years in another country, and was married and even separated myself, to see what his message was. You can love people and leave them, as he did. You can have more than one life. We are multiple beings, each of us, and we can come and go in the world, appear and vanish, be there among crowds on a street and then gone again, love more than one person, do more than one thing with our lives.

"The only problem is," Corte was saying, "that somebody else may want it too."

Françoise said, "It's been here for a year, and I never heard of it going missing anywhere."

"So, I'll take it with me, have a look at it under X-ray? I'll get it back to you by the end of the week. We might do a test on the actual paint too. You know, a forgery is often easy to detect because paint that has not had centuries to dry will flake off. Recent forgers have used plastic, and before that they even used Bakelite. But it's easy to discover. Don't worry, we'll be very careful."

We watched while Fabrice wrapped it in bubble wrap, scotch-taped the ends, and placed it in his briefcase. I could see that the act of stealing a painting this small would not be hard. What would not be easy would be deciding what to do with it afterward. Like a person in a witness protection program, it would have to stay permanently out of sight. If I accepted it, would I be trafficking in stolen goods, or simply inheriting something my father wanted me to have? I would have to rely on Fabrice to tell me what to do. For some reason, this made me uneasy. I thought of my own brief career as a thief in London when I was a teenager. It was called shoplifting, not stealing, and we had all done it, making it a kind of competition. It was to make myself feel better: to feel that power, that intense secrecy, the fear of being discovered, and the glow of success in getting away with it. What the objects had been, I could hardly remember; they had not been the point.

"So. I must go. I have a dinner appointment. Thank you so much, Françoise. This has been most enlightening. A real pleasure." He took my hand, with a very small inclination of his head, his eyes on mine.

"Well, thank you for coming, Fabrice, I appreciate it," Françoise said. Again, I thought, how can she not be amazed and moved, even silenced by the likeness? Perhaps she had become used to it, and that might mean she saw him often.

I felt my question grow in me; I had to ask him: "Before you go, monsieur, can I ask you something? Were you by any chance on rue Mouffetard on a Monday in late May, when they were making a film about Paris in the fifties?"

"I don't think so. Why?"

"I thought I saw you. I'm sure I have seen you before."

"Ah, but isn't it because I look rather like Peter? A lot of people have remarked on it. We used to joke that we could stand in for each other and no one would notice. Anyway, I rarely go to the Left Bank."

"Did you, ever? Stand in for each other, I mean?"

"I don't think so." He laughed, a little uneasily. I had overstepped some line with my question. I had been too inquisitive, too soon. Goodbyes had been said already. This man had a formality about him, I saw too late. Françoise sucked in her breath.

"Well, I'll contact you at the end of the week, Gaby, if I may call you Gaby. Do you have a mobile number? I'll give you a call."

We saw him out. I knew I should leave too, but I had to ask Françoise: "He is astonishingly like my father. Don't you agree?"

"Yes, but being French not English makes him very different. They are not at all alike in character. And his eyes are much darker, and he isn't so tall." She would know. She saw me looking at her and said, "Since you asked, he hasn't stood in for your father, nobody could do that, but yes, we have become friends, over the years. And I think you can trust him with your painting."

My painting? I thought, *How can it be mine?* I can't take it anywhere. Unless I live with it here in Paris. Or carry it around with me in a shopping bag, the way Fabrice Corte had just tucked it in his briefcase. The way I used to walk nonchalantly around with a bag of stolen goods from John Lewis or Selfridges, my head in the air.

I wanted to ask Françoise, *Was it because he reminded you of my father, was that the attraction?* Or, *How could you, after my father died?* But I said neither of these things. People did what they did. I knew the surge of physical attraction, the way it came up and grabbed you, with a smell, a memory, a certain movement, a certain light, even a mistaken identity, like the boy I had seen kissing a girl all those years ago on a bridge over the Cam. But I did want to know: Was that Fabrice in the street that time, and on the Right Bank when the bus nearly stopped, and outside the Closerie des Lilas? ("I hardly ever go to the Left Bank." Why?) The only way I could know was through recovering my own visual memory of my father, and since I had seen Fabrice, that had faltered and been changed. I doubted that I would ever get it back.

At the end of the week, Fabrice called me. "Bonjour, Mademoiselle Greenwood. How are you?"

"Fine. You can call me Gaby."

"We did some tests, the X-rays and the paint test. There's nothing underneath it. It's the real thing, just as I thought. Seventeenth-century Spanish but probably painted in Holland. The canvas is seventeenth-century Dutch. You can tell from the density of it, the rust marks too. The white paint is lead, on the meat of the open nut. You know the painter Francisco de Zurbarán? Well, he painted some marvelous still lifes, with symbolic meanings to the objects in them, religious ideas, some people think, lemons meaning purity and so forth. I must admit that allegory bores me, but the painting is wonderful. He was a friend of Velázquez, and he had several younger followers. This is one of them, a painter called Guido Ferrer. The best known de Zurbarán are from the 1630s, '40s. This one's a little later. The fact that he signed it with initials rather than with his full name could mean that it was not entirely his. It sometimes means, school of, or pupil of, as you probably know. It's not incredibly valuable, because he never became that well known, but there you are. It's real, not a fake, although it may well be a copy or another version. Quite often, an artist would paint several versions of the same subject. If you were to sell it, you could probably raise about eighty thousand euros."

I listened hard, my phone to my ear. I hadn't expected a lecture, and I was reminded of being back at the Courtauld, taking notes for a final exam. "But whose is it? Where did he get it?"

"I'm afraid that is something I haven't been able to find out."

"Then I couldn't sell it even if I wanted to. Which I don't."

"No, I suppose you couldn't, or not easily, anyway."

"So are you giving it back to me, or Françoise?"

"Françoise says your father left it with her for safekeeping, but as far as she is concerned, it's yours, you should have it. So, where do we meet? Can I come to your place? Where are you?"

I gave him my address and the code. Then I sat down to wait. I thought of Matt and his dead ringer theory. Was Fabrice the original, the real man I had mistaken for my dead father, so that the talk of ghosts and revenants had been sheer superstition? The fact of such likeness was so disconcerting because it undermined the whole idea of uniqueness. Two paintings, so alike as to be hardly distinguishable from each other, that was one thing. Two men who resembled each other this way, quite another.

He came up the stairs once I had pressed the buzzer to let him in; I heard his footsteps slower on the last flight, and then he arrived at my open door. "Come in."

He was checking something on his cell phone. Then he clicked it shut, held out a hand. "Nice place."

"You haven't been here before?"

"No. Why should I?"

"I just thought my father might have invited you."

"Oh, of course, it was his. No, we never socialized much. It was mainly professional, our contact. And I live far from here, in the sixteenth arrondissement."

I took the wrapped packet from him and set it down on the coffee table. Apart from the tape coming unstuck at the corners, it looked exactly as it had when I had last seen it. I had no idea what I would do with it, but for the moment my attention was on him. I wanted to say, *I can't believe you haven't played around with your likeness to my father, that it wasn't something you both may have used in some way.* But, of course, I couldn't say it.

"Did you meet my mother?" I could, at least, ask him that.

"Oh, yes. A couple of times, at private views, that kind of thing."

I wondered what my mother would have thought, if she had felt the same shock. Or do you, when you love somebody and live with him for years, become immune to thinking anyone else resembles him? Does intimacy insist on the particular? In Françoise's case, the likeness between the two of them seemed to be erotic, a draw. In my mother's, I knew it would not have been. If my father were present today, there would be no question for me; I would know, of course, which one he was. But in his absence, there was that uncertainty—was he like this, or like that, how was he different? The idea of cloning human beings is ultimately repugnant because singularity is the essential human quality. We are, because we are unique. I found it hard to look at Fabrice Corte, and hard not to; he smiled at me quite frankly and opened his empty hands as if to say, *I can't help it, it's just the way things are.*

"Well, thank you." I didn't know if I could call him Fabrice.

"Do you know what you will do with it?"

My turn to open my empty hands. "Keep it here, I suppose."

"As long as you do not try to take it back to America. Then, there could be complications."

"Oh, well, I'm here for now," I told him, wanting to sound as vague as possible. I also wanted him to leave, so that I could examine it at my leisure. "Thank you for your opinion."

"I will be in touch, soon. I will find out what I can. Au revoir, Mademoiselle Greenwood."

"Gaby, please. Au revoir."

Just as the appearance of Fabrice Corte, alive now, did not wipe out the reality of my father's life, Dad's long affair with Françoise could not alter the reality of his life with my mother. Or so I hoped. The next question was, what was the reality of my own life? Was I no more than the child of my parents, the inheritor of the situation here in Paris, the passive recipient of a possibly stolen painting? Was I a fake, or could I be authentic? Who would vouch for my originality, when all I had done in my life was escape, react, refuse?

I poured my glass of wine and sat down with the omelette I had made—only eggs and limp parsley left in the fridge again—and watched the swallows as I ate my solitary meal. Yves was spending tonight at his mother's, as she wasn't well and so had summoned him. What was it that our generation found so hard to learn? Our parents had loved passionately and often wrongly and had had babies by mistake and affairs and messy houses and bills that could not be paid, and had somehow been forgiven; they had survived all this and were not blamed. Yet the world they had hoped for had not come about, and we were the inheritors of that failure. For us, it seemed that there was little leeway. We dared not stray, or refuse to conform. We had to be careful, or we would come to grief. This was the message of these days, and it was the one I'd instinctively fought against when I was younger with my rebellions, my fugues. Sex was dangerous, we heard, money was always short, you had to earn, work late, pay your taxes. We had been told: *Be serious, life is difficult, time is short. The world is in entropy.* But now, thinking of my parents—the extraordinary generosity she must have had to keep him and go on loving him, his own fidelity both to the other woman and to her—I was struck by a graceful ability to live life that these days seemed almost out of reach. What would we become, without this possibility? How would we grow beyond our limits, become the people we were supposed to be?

It was nearly dark outside when I went into the bedroom and looked at the wrapped parcel that lay on my bed where I had left it. My gift from my father. It lay there as you might place a sleeping baby, right in the middle of a bed where it could not roll off. I fetched scissors and began to undo it. I would simply hang it on the wall and live with it, and see what happened. Fabrice could investigate its real owner or find out where it had come from. I would simply accept that here it was. I found a nail and a hammer that someone had left in a cupboard in the kitchen—my father in unusually practical mode?—and I drove the nail into the wall and hung my piece of the seventeenth century, its loving certainties, its perpetual dangers, its appreciation of the everyday, right where I could see it. It struck me as the first change I had made in this apartment, the first action I had taken to install something of my own. My painting. My walnuts, whatever they symbolized. There.

Fabrice telephoned the following day. His voice made me feel nervous; why was he getting back to me so soon?

"There is a list which exists, you know, of all the paintings worth a certain amount, and who the owners are, throughout the world."

"And?"

"The painting that was in the Guggenheim is in the private collection of a certain Anton Freiborn, a foundation now, which lent it for the show in New York. It was probably sold to him in about 1906, or at least to the person in the US who sold it to him. Your painting, as far as I can discover, is the property of a woman in Holland, a Marth ten Bruggencate. So where do we go from here?"

"You think my father got it from her?"

"I think he may have been asked to sell it for her, and was not able to find a good enough buyer, and thought that if he left it in Paris and came back later, he would have the time and the contacts to sell it."

"So it can't really be mine."

"Well, I think we already knew that, Gaby." It was the opposite of what he'd said to me at Françoise's the other day.

I thought then, my father wanted that painting, he had no intention of finding a buyer, he wanted it for me, just as he had wanted the Chinese horse for me, all those years ago. Thinking this, I felt that I knew him better than ever, in the way we know the hopes and desires, even irrational, of those we truly love.

A quick memory: My father showing a drawing of mine to a colleague who came to lunch. In those days, far-off now, I drew. I was ten or eleven, and I drew horses. I knew their bodies and their flying manes, their hooves and their eyes, by heart. I was in love with horses; I wrote stories about them but also drew them obsessively and from the clarity of my passion. A painter came to lunch, someone my father was representing, and he looked at my horse drawings because my father had shown them to him. "Gaby is the artist of the family, see. She's the one who draws and writes all these stories. I'm sure we are going to have to be proud of her one day."

The artist, who was famous, looked at my drawings and appreciated them. Maybe he was being kind to a little girl, one of the millions who draw horses and love what they draw. But that my father showed him my work, in all seriousness—that was what mattered.

My painting, my walnuts, the one he had chosen for me. No, I was not about to give it up, for all the rich women in the Netherlands who might think it belonged to them.

I held my phone and heard Fabrice waiting at the other end. "Well, if she wants it back, you'll just have to let me know. I'll hang on to it here for the moment. It will be quite safe."

Quite safe, I thought, as long as I don't return to the United States. Quite safe as long as I stay here, both myself and the painting in hiding.

"*Bon.* So, we will wait to see what happens?"

"I think that would be logical."

"So, goodbye for the moment, Gaby. You will get in touch with me if you should change your mind?"

I stood opposite it and looked and looked. The surface like the leather of a finely creased glove; the high varnish of the time, more yellowed than the one in New York, for this one had certainly not been cleaned. The gleam on the silver of the nutcrackers, duller, the edges of the nuts themselves less clearly tinged with light. But as I looked at my painting, the memory of the other one faded. You can't keep two images of the same thing, slightly different, in your mind at the same time. One, the one you can see and touch, has to cancel out the other. That thought again. I stood with my glass of wine and, at my shoulder, in the Guggenheim museum, my father murmuring about symbols and the transcendence beneath ordinary life and the way the early alchemists had sought the philosopher's stone, the true metal, and the way artists had always, over the centuries, sought the eternal in the temporary, and that that was why we were drawn, over and again, into the contemplation of what they had done. The search, restless and eternal, for the eternal in life, the transcendent. The failure, repeated, to lay hands on it for long. Glimpses made across centuries. The fascination of the clues, hunted up with an almost erotic intensity. Why he did what he did, why he spent his life with other men's paintings, why he loved them so.

What did we do afterward, that time in New York? Did we walk down Fifth Avenue? Did we stroll through the Park, talking about art; was he finally able to unburden himself to me, explain himself, show me what drove him? And was I listening? Did I pay attention? Or was

I worrying about my flight and whether Matt was waiting for me at home, and whether I would make my check-in time at LaGuardia? So many things crowd in, always, to fill the crucial moments of our lives with ephemera. We never know which moments will turn out to be the vital ones. I do remember going into Bloomingdale's and pretending to want to buy something, because I wanted to use the restroom. I remember coming down the escalator and seeing him in the men's department turning over a pair of leather gloves but not buying them because as soon as he saw me coming he was ready to go. There was a sarcastic remark or two about my returning to Florida, a conspicuous lack of interest in my husband, a sudden firm but nearly lingering pressure on my cheeks as he kissed me goodbye. I think I walked down to the subway station without looking back.

13.

When Yves came to my apartment the following evening—it was July already, a Tuesday, and he had been to an evening class in computing— he was in a strange mood. I poured him a glass of cold wine from the refrigerator while he showered, and he sat slumped on my sofa under the picture in its new place, in his T-shirt and underpants. "You don't mind? It's so hot."

"Of course I don't mind. You can sit there nude if you want to."

"This is the famous picture, then?" He jerked his thumb backward; he had not really even looked at it properly.

"Yes. Yves, what is the matter?"

"Nothing. I'm a bit tired, that's all."

Un peu crevé. Like a tire with all the air blown out of it.

"Yves. You can tell me."

"*Ouf*, I don't know. You're going to leave, so why should I bother?"

"What do you mean? I'm not at all sure that I'm going to leave."

"You have a return ticket, don't you? You will go back, to your husband. We won't see each other again."

"I don't know if I'll go back. Either to my husband or the States. If, or when. Does it matter?"

"Of course it matters! You should know! You should know which man you want to be with. It isn't like—I don't know—choosing between two desserts, after all."

"No, it isn't. And if it were just a matter of desserts, I could have both." I felt annoyed that he should accuse me of such frivolity.

"But you can't, can you? One is in the United States, one is here."

"It hasn't mattered up until now, Yves. You said so yourself. It was for cheering us up, you said."

"Well, that was then. I don't feel at all cheered up now. I feel you will go back to the United States, and that will be that."

"Maybe I will, just to see what's what, clear things up. But it needn't be final."

"Gaby, there is one thing I don't think you realize, it is about me, whether I sit here waiting for you to show up one day, putting my life on hold, being treated like a, I don't know, a gigolo or something. I'm a man, Gaby, I have some pride, I don't want to be just someone else's leftovers, a dessert at the end of the meal, you know what I mean?"

"What brought this on? Did I get something wrong, is there something I haven't understood? You said you might be getting a job anywhere, after the exams. You said we were together in order to discover things, not to be a couple forever."

"Well." He swirled the wine in his glass, took a big swallow, and leaned back, his arms behind his head, the black hair of his armpits just showing beneath the white of his T-shirt. He smelled of my soap and shampoo and something else, a metallic tang I had never picked up before. The scent of fear?

I said gently, like walking up to a frightened horse, "Yves, tell me. Really, I want to know. I have made no decisions. I want to hear from you. If something has changed, tell me."

"You really think you can have this double life you dream of? Like your father?"

"I don't know. I hadn't thought about it. My husband would certainly be horrified by the idea, and now it seems you would too." I thought of my parents and Françoise, the delicate distinctions and the hard decisions, the pain that must have been there for each of them, if not all at the same time.

"Would you stay with me, Gaby? Would you leave him, leave your life in America, stay with me? No." It was less a proposal than an assertion of the difference between us. He was not looking at me as he spoke, but down at his knees, bony and boyish under their sheen of black hair. "I don't think so. You with your apartment, your valuable painting."

"What do you mean?"

"Just, you don't know exactly who I am, I think. I wanted to teach philosophy, I told you, but of course I can't do that, and anyway, what's the use of it when the whole world, France, at least, is going downhill fast. I want to teach kids, now, because someone has to. Someone has to show them something that isn't computer games and drugs and supermarkets. There's going to be a whole generation of people who simply have nothing, the way things are going, and if I can reach just a few of them, even, before they give up and go and work stacking shelves in the nearest supermarket, I want to do that. Even if their lives are shit, afterward, I want that chance."

"Well, I want it for you too."

"Ah, but you wouldn't want to be sent to some crappy suburb with me, would you?"

"No, probably not. But, Yves, this wasn't meant to be a long-term thing. Was it?"

"No, no. But I have come to like being with you. And you said, the other night, that you loved me."

I had said it with the gratitude that comes with being well loved, physically; it had come from me like an exclamation, not a commitment. "In a way, I do. Yes, it's true. But not for marriage, not for staying together. I said it because I felt happy, because you had made me happy." I looked at him where he sat with his head bent and felt appalled. Was he saying that he was in love with me?

Then Yves said it: "I like you a lot, Gaby." *Je t'aime beaucoup*, not the same as *je t'aime*.

He said it seriously, not as a plea. I felt intense relief. "Oh, Yves. I like you a lot too. You know I do." I remembered him saying, almost impatiently, that time I said I loved him: "I know, I know."

"But."

"Yes, but. I'm just not sure what I want, you see. I can't be that certain. I married Matt in a hurry, years ago, I told you, and I don't want to make any more decisions in a hurry. Do you understand, I can't, not just like that?"

"I think so. So, you need more time?"

"Yes, I need more time." I said it, but what I felt inside was a panic like being in a room without an open door. Why do men always want to close the doors, whatever they may say about freedom and choice? I need more space. I need all the space there is. I need you to hold me lightly, so lightly, and to trust life for the outcome. I need you to do what probably nobody can do: love me and make no demands.

We went to bed together quite soberly that night and held each other under the white tent of the single sheet, an embrace that seemed to me valedictory. High in the sky beyond the unshuttered window, the swallows swooped and circled. On the wall in the salon, my little painting hung on the pale-gray wall, strangely small all on its own. The change had moved in with us, the shift had happened. I kissed him with all the tenderness I could find, on his neck, on his shoulders, while he curled against me like a boy finding refuge. We lay like that into the small hours, a gray light filling the room, nothing shut out, nothing held in. I could not tell how the morning would find us. I was weak inside with my feelings for him, for his vulnerability, for his confession of it, yes; but on the outside, where it mattered, I knew now that I was strong.

Fabrice called when Yves was in the shower, to invite me to lunch. I stood at the window watching light spread down the façade of the building opposite and heard his slightly southern voice with its rolled *r*'s. He asked me if I had ever been to Le Train Bleu restaurant at the Gare de Lyon, and I said no.

"Then we should go there. Your father would have wanted you to go there, I am sure."

"But we're not going anywhere. Isn't it just a restaurant for travelers?"

I knew of its existence, had imagined it was something to do with the grand days of travel, when the blue train actually took people to the Riviera. I'd thought it might even have been closed down by now.

"No, not at all. It is a national monument, and the food there is still very good. Will you meet me there, say, at one?"

I agreed. Why not? People were inviting me to lunches and meetings these days; it was as if a crowd of well-wishers had emerged from this city to help me on my way. We could talk about art; we could talk about my father. With Fabrice sitting opposite me, I thought, I might well get nearer to discovering exactly who it had been, on the rue Mouffetard, outside the Closerie, on that quai beside the Seine. The known face of my dead father—the dead ringer; the doppelganger; the ghost; or simply Fabrice Corte in his old jacket from the seventies, doing his shopping, going about his life, even venturing onto the Left Bank.

"Who was that?" Yves, naked except for a small white towel, his wet hair on end, coming out of the bathroom.

"Fabrice Corte. Inviting me to lunch." I did not say where.

"Watch out for him, Gaby." It was what Françoise had said, Françoise who was his friend. I knew what Yves meant, also that my going out to lunch with this man annoyed him, as it would have annoyed Matt. But perhaps there was some possible danger that was not sexual, not to do with a middle-aged man taking a younger woman out to lunch?

I said, "Don't worry, I will."

⚜

I met Fabrice on the station platform as we both headed for the grand winding staircase that leads up to the restaurant. No point in assuming he came here for his lunch normally; nobody would do that. He had wanted to impress me, to give me a treat. I had taken the bus across the Seine and got off in front of the Gare de Lyon with its grand façade, its huge and beautiful clock. Inside, on the platforms, voices boomed about trains to the south, Aix and Marseille, the TGVs in their stalls like gigantic horses about to be kicked into movement.

He stood aside to let me go in first. Up a level and through the doors, the painted ceilings, the scenes from all the French colonies of the past, Tunis and Algiers, Tangier, Marrakesh, and the paintings of the Thames in London, with Westminster and St. Paul's, and the boats going out of the port of Marseille. Caryatids clutching their heads held up the ceiling. The weight of conquest upon them, the permanent headache of occupation. The waiter let us in by undoing a small golden rope from a hook. "You are here for lunch, monsieur? This way, please."

White tablecloths and napkins, polished glass, silver. The trappings of the colonial past.

Fabrice ordered smoked salmon and a turbot soufflé, without asking me; I simply nodded when he told the waiter of our choice. He also ordered the wine, a bottle of Saumur. I wondered if he was used to women sitting opposite him simply agreeing with his choices, and presumably being paid for. It felt strangely restful.

"Now, Gaby, I have asked you here not only to admire the ceiling, or for the décor, as you must have imagined."

"Something to do with going somewhere on a train, maybe?"

"No, no, we aren't going to *le midi*, much as I would like to. One day you must go to Corsica, which is where my family comes from. You can take a boat from Marseille. It's a beautiful country. No, I have something more about the painting. I have something to ask you. I thought we could combine it with a nice lunch, rather than over the telephone."

"Sure. I always like a nice lunch. This place is spectacular."

The waiter, who was probably Fabrice's age, came back with the bottle, poured an inch of pale gold for Fabrice to taste, and when he nodded, poured some for me. The naked caryatids with their headaches looked down on me. The boats went out in all directions, assured that the world was still French.

"Very good. I thought, since you said you had never been here, it would be nice."

"Yes, yes, it's great." I wondered if he would wait until we were eating for him to tell me.

The smoked salmon came, with lemons and capers. The butter was in little curls.

"Gaby, I am going to have to ask you to give up your painting, or there may be trouble."

"Why? What sort of trouble?" I'd guessed that this would be coming—some variety of threat.

"It is being looked for. It is known that it is somewhere in Paris."

"The Dutch woman?"

"She is dead, actually."

"Dead? But you said—"

"I know. I didn't know she had died. It was fairly recently. It is her heirs who are looking for it. It would be easiest to be able to put it somewhere—somewhere where it may be found. So neither you nor I will be implicated."

I took a mouthful of my wine. I said, "Fabrice, if somebody wants it, they have to come and get it from me. I am not just going to give it up. As you said yourself, my father wanted me to have it, and now I do."

"But he wouldn't want you to be accused of stealing it."

"Well, I won't be. Any more than Françoise would have been."

"Gaby, let's have our lunch and then talk. It's no good talking on an empty stomach. Look, have some salmon. Do you like the wine?"

"Yes, it's perfectly lovely, and so is everything, and the waiter makes me think of somebody in a 1940s film, but I am not even going to think about giving you back the painting, sorry, because it was meant for me. So, don't even ask me again. If Mrs. Ten Whatsit's heirs want it, they can come and see me. I didn't steal anything. I have a completely clear conscience. Right?"

Silence. We cleaned up the smoked salmon, and the little soufflés that arrived next were like chef's hats puffing out over their rims, and nothing I have eaten was ever so delicious. Fabrice frowned and ate, and avoided my eye. I washed soufflé flavors with delicate wine into my throat and felt at once liberated and elated. Here, in the restaurant of Le Train Bleu, with this man thinking he could buy me and change my mind, I would assert myself at last.

"You are your father's daughter," he said. "Stubborn. But I don't think you quite realize what is at stake."

"Yes, you are right there, about my being his daughter. Including being able to handle it. Thank you for bringing it to me, Fabrice, and thank you for everything, but you do understand, I can't possibly give it up now."

The ships went out in all directions, down the Mediterranean, to Africa. The ceiling was held up by naked slave women, and I was down here, a twenty-first-century woman, staking my claim to property, refusing to give in.

"Do you want a dessert?"

"No, I don't think so. Just coffee, please."

"You're sure? They are very good here."

"No, really." I had seen the desserts being served to some Japanese tourists on the other side of the room, but wanted to give Fabrice the impression that I was not a woman to be bought with sugar and cream. I was sure that Françoise would have refused a dessert.

"*Deux expressos.*"

The waiter went to bring back our tiny gold-rimmed cups, with brown sugar in cubes.

"I have to ask you something, Fabrice, if you don't mind."

"Go ahead, Gaby. I'll answer if I can."

"You looked to me when I met you very like my father. Now I can see there isn't so much of a resemblance. But have you ever, at any time, pretended to be him?"

He looked at me and stirred his coffee with a tiny spoon. I thought of how small, perfect things were always appearing between us: the painting, coffee cups, sugar cubes, the things of everyday life. *Las bodegones.* "You have asked me that once already, and the answer is the same, no, I haven't. Why do you ask?"

But there was no point in continuing. I had refused him the painting; he would refuse me the information. I would never know now if he was there at those times. Check, checkmate. My father again, showing me chess moves. He unfolded the bill for our lunch at Le Train Bleu, just as the early afternoon TGV to Avignon and Marseille was announced down below, and the steam trains of the past blended with the clean efficiency of the trains of the present. The caryatids and the seagoing ships would remain the same, decade after decade, always being renovated now that they were a national monument; and men would invite women to lunch here and give them delicious mouthfuls of soufflés and smoked fish and the best wine; and one would ask, and the other would refuse, and that was simply how it went: the past disappearing into the present, the present the only place where you could say yes, or no. Yes, I will do what you want, I will gracefully fit in with your plan. Or no, and make yourself somehow less a woman, less deserving of that fine lunch.

"One thing, Fabrice."

"Yes?"

"Why does all this matter so much suddenly, when it has hung on Françoise's wall for over a year?"

"Because nobody knew it was there. Because nothing moved, nothing changed. It was—how can I say it—sleeping. Invisible. Now people know."

"Because of you."

"Because you asked me, you wanted me to find out. So, I did. And now, it is in the open, it is, well, awake."

"But you could lie and say you don't know where it is."

"I could, yes."

"So, will you?"

"You are asking for my silence."

"Yes."

"Normally, my silence costs something."

"Ah. But I don't have anything. No money. Nothing."

"No, Gaby, you do have something. Do I have to tell you what it is?"

If I hadn't been trying to be sophisticated here, I would have said to him, *I've no idea what you are talking about,* or, *Are you trying to get me into bed?* But the whole aura of this place, with its outdated images, its glorious colonial past, and our sitting at this table opposite each other, after such a remarkable lunch—well, it all made me want to appear more worldly than I was. I wondered then if the Dutch woman and her heirs were an invention of Fabrice's. Nothing was what it seemed to be; I would appear other than I was.

So I stared at the coffee spoon I was playing with in my left hand, twirled it a little, and said to him, "Well, Fabrice, I will have to think about that."

It was a ridiculous thing to say, as I had no idea what I meant. It was a line out of a bad movie, in which two people played manipulative games with each other in a grand restaurant. It wasn't my style at all; and I suspect he guessed.

Fabrice paid the bill with the discreet ease of a man used to paying for expensive lunches for women who are not to be allowed to know how much they cost, and smiled at me as soon as that was done. His smile was that of the one with the power. But I could see, it was a habit. I was not intimidated. Then he said something that interested me. "You know, Gaby, that a forger is nearly always a failed artist, and he does it out of a kind of revenge. It's like saying, look what I can do and get away with it. It's a calculated insult to the rest of the world. A forger is nearly always ambitious, frustrated, a person whose talents have not been recognized."

"But you said my painting is not a fake, that it wasn't forged."

"No, but I wanted you to know this. We tested your painting's actual paint, comparing the way paint changes color over time, and it's seventeenth century, no doubt about it. Also, the canvas and the boards. The only thing in doubt is the signature. No, I wanted you to know about forgers just for general information, about life. They are people who didn't get what they thought they deserved, in some way. You see?"

Was he referring to my father, who was a dealer, not a forger? Dealers, Fabrice himself had said, are very rarely forgers. My father, who may have forged not a signature on a painting, but his own life? Who had at least attempted to duplicate himself, and was still doing so, in his appearances to me in Paris? And if so, how did Fabrice know?

The effect of all this food, wine, and convoluted French was enough to make me nearly fall down the elegant staircase that curved down to the station below. I held on to the banister and took my time. I couldn't wait to get away from Fabrice Corte, go back home, take off my clothes, have a shower, and fall on the bed, alone.

"You aren't worried, that you might be accused of stealing it?" Yves wanted to know. I had given him a very brief account of my lunch with Fabrice Corte, leaving out how delicious it all was, and how confusing, and he had grumbled again, "Don't trust that man."

"No, because I haven't. I feel completely innocent, and I am."

"Well, don't be too innocent. People play games, you know, and especially with valuable paintings, you have to watch out."

"How do you know?"

"Well, it's about the money, isn't it?"

"For me, it's about the art. As it was for my father. It's got nothing to do with the money at all. Anyway, it wasn't so much, if it's really seventeenth century. Eighty thousand euros, Fabrice said."

"It would amaze me if that was all. I think he's seriously underestimating it, probably on purpose."

"Yves, the only point of the painting for me is that my father left it to me because of our last afternoon together and what we both felt for its twin. That is it. I am not in the slightest bit interested in how much it is worth."

"Ah," he said. "You, no. But other people will be, you can be sure. And Fabrice Corte, well, I think he is a man who gets what he wants."

"Yves, do you think I'm crazy to think it was him on the film set, and at the Closerie, and on the Right Bank walking down toward the Pont Neuf?"

"Him?"

"Fabrice. Not my father, after all."

"Hmm, no. What would be more crazy would be to go on thinking it was your father. Did you ask him?"

"No, partly because I'd refused him something he wanted, partly because he has the right to walk about Paris as much as he wants, without being questioned about it."

"If it was Fabrice, you don't have your ghost. Maybe you want your ghost."

"Maybe I do." Like *Hamlet*, I thought: Having a ghost makes the whole thing viable. No ghost, and the play would be a story of hasty adultery and a sulky boy's objections. It needed the ghost, and, perhaps, so did I.

We did not discuss my going back to America or staying here. It seemed that the night we had slept together curled around each other in the gray light had brought that conversation to a natural end, at least for now. He looked at the painting with more interest, and I thought, he wants to be on a par with Fabrice Corte, he wants to be knowledgeable, powerful, all the things he is not, that I love him for not being. I felt I had reached a state of truce, in which men had laid down their arms and I, who had been battling for my very existence, was the one with the strength and balance to live at the heart of it all. I had not given in—to Yves's anxiety, to Fabrice's greed and manipulation. I wanted to tell someone this, someone who would understand.

Matt called me that evening—midafternoon in Florida, ten o'clock in the evening in Paris. We had not spoken since my four a.m. call. It was July 4, and I had not even remembered the significance of that day in the United States.

"How are you?" He sounded careful, a little unsteady. I listened with attention to the change in his voice.

"I'm okay."

"Really?"

"It's turning out to be a very interesting time, yes."

"Well, I can't say the same for me. Gaby, I miss you."

"I miss you too, Matt." It was not true, but I wanted to be kind to him. I wondered if he missed me more, surrounded as he probably was by barbecues and family parties, if this was what had brought on his call.

"How would it be if I came over?"

"To Paris?"

"Yes. I'm owed some vacation time. I could. Then we could—see."

In my mind two worlds collided; space and time eclipsed. I shuddered, hoped he could not hear my intake of breath.

"I don't know. Could you leave it a while?"

"Well, yeah, I can't come immediately. I can't just disappear, the way you can."

Touché. I said, "Let's think about it?"

"I worry about you. What are you doing over there? Aren't you lonely? How do you live? You know, I just don't get it. Shit, I decided not to say any of this. You're free to decide, Gaby. I'm trying to leave you free to decide, and it's hell, if you want to know, but I'm leaving it up to you. So look, you think about it, and let me know, okay? Because I think we need to talk, and not on the phone."

If the two worlds were to collide, then what? I could hardly imagine Matt here in Paris, but people flew from the United States every day to land here, and it was entirely possible, even easy, to do so. And no, I did not want it: not now, not soon, perhaps not ever.

14.

July, and summer rain had darkened the leaves of the trees in the little park outside Saint-Médard. The children were out of school but had not yet left for vacations elsewhere in France, the smallest ones playing on the slides and climbing frames while their parents, who all looked surprisingly young, sat on the benches. A young man with a shaved head and unlaced sneakers and a little knapsack with his daughter's things in it, a snack, a change of pants. The little girl with hair in tight black bunches sticking out sideways, who shouted to him from the top of the climbing frame. The black woman with the tight black T-shirt and green baggy pants, the mother? An American child stamped through puddles, counting out loud in English, spattering mud. The young woman next to me on the bench frowned and got out her sandwich and said to me how annoying he was. The mother, in Birkenstocks, not saying anything until everyone had frowned and withdrawn their clean shoes away from the splash. The American mother said, "Honey, people are trying to read and eat lunch. Maybe you shouldn't do that." The child took no notice.

Yves came through the gate with bags of groceries, a baguette under one arm, and rolled copies of newspapers, and sat down beside me. We watched children fall over and cry and be picked up, children call out for parents to admire them, children hugged and held and let go again: the whole pantomime of a certain way of life that we had excluded ourselves from. Our generation, reproducing itself without us. Yves unrolled *Libération* and *Le Monde*.

"They have liberated Íngrid Betancourt, did you know? No, of course, you don't watch TV. We watched for hours last night. I can't believe it. And she was so amazing, so warm and grateful, so happy to be back in France. Do you know, I cried when she spoke. I don't know why, it just touched me so much. She is such a beautiful woman. And how can she be like that after being tied up and locked up for years?"

I reached to look at the photographs: Íngrid Betancourt, the French-Colombian journalist, who had been imprisoned for years by FARC in Colombia, first shackled to a wall, then embracing her daughter in the open air. The caption said that she had never given up. But how did you do that, when every day was simply hours of discomfort or pain, days, weeks, years of imprisonment, being insulted and even tortured, being systematically deprived of hope? I read over Yves's shoulder. Yes, she had been tempted to despair. Some days, it seemed impossible that life would ever be any different. And yet, in a small corner of her spirit, she had kept hope alive. Her thin face, her long dark hair tied back, her dark eyes. Reaching to embrace her daughter in the sunlight, freed at last, who knew how, would she ever know exactly how it had been done, I wondered? Would she even know what deals had been done, threats made, promises offered?

Yves said, "It gives you hope, doesn't it?"

"Yes, but for what? For a world in which that never happens again to anyone? I don't think so." I thought of how I had lived for years only a couple of hundred miles from Guantánamo Bay, where men were held in such conditions you could not even bear to imagine them. Where they died, because life was unbearable when hope was gone. I looked at Íngrid Betancourt's dark eyes on the page and thought, nothing matters but the freedom to come and go, to make choices. Nothing counts but freedom. And I have it and have always had it, and what would I have done in Íngrid Betancourt's position? How would I have known how to survive? Not just physically, but as a person who could come back home and love people and smile and laugh in the sun?

In the little park today, the children ran around, and the adults ate sandwiches and read newspapers; sun spread across the benches so that there was little shade, and the big bell of Saint-Médard struck twelve. I took Yves's hand and held it on his knee.

"You know, you were right, I do have to go home," I said.

"You mean, back to the apartment? I'll come with you, but today I can't stay long."

"No. Home, to America. I mean, at the end of the summer."

"Why? What happened? You suddenly decided?"

"I have things to do." Matt's phone call had stirred some guilt in me that I hadn't known was there. I had, after all, left him to deal with every aspect of our shared life. "I can't just be here endlessly recovering. I have to go back, at least to sort it out."

"But you have a life here too." He turned my hand over and then clasped my fingers with his, interlaced to keep me close. "You have this, with me. You said, you just needed some time, to think."

"Yes, and it's wonderful. It's been exactly what I needed. It always will be, these weeks, this summer. But I can't just be a visitor in your life."

"A visitor who stays stops being a visitor. You can commit yourself to something. You can choose exactly what you want. People do. My mother, for instance, has never felt at home in France, but she chose to stay here, for me, because I would have a better chance. She even worked as a cleaning lady so that I could be here."

A little Vietnamese boy ran up then and threw himself onto Yves's knee and then looked up, scared to see he had collapsed on the wrong knee, the wrong man. His father was sitting on the next bench, and he smiled to us at the boy's mistake, and held out his arms to his son, who stared back at us, appalled, when he had reached safety. Yves smiled back and waved, making faces at the boy. What were we doing in this place full of other people's children? Saturday in the park, the market full of people, crowds at the bread shop, couples beginning to settle into the cafés for lunch, two by two, lovers, friends, wives and husbands, mothers and daughters, all meeting each other at the cramped little tables, reading menus, choosing wine. I kept hold of Yves's hand, and at last I said, "I didn't mean it to be so sudden. I'm sorry. I'm not going anywhere in a hurry. Yves, let's go and have lunch at the café, let's be one of those couples sitting opposite each other, can we?"

But he looked at his watch and said, "You know, today, I have things I have to do."

I knew then that, as I had turned a corner, away from him, he was doing the same. I couldn't blame him, and neither could I ask him to change his mind. Here, again, was the hard edge of reality, and I had to welcome it.

"You didn't ask me about my exam results." He stood before me in his black jeans and white T-shirt, pulled me to my feet.

"When did you get them? Yves!"

"Yesterday."

"Well?"

"Well, I passed. Both written and oral."

"That's wonderful. Congratulations. That's brilliant." I knew by now that the exams for a teaching qualification in the public sector were hard, and that many people failed them.

"So now I'll be able to get a job in the autumn, I hope. It may be anywhere in France. They just send you where they need you."

"So it may not be in Paris?"

"I hope it's in the new towns, in the outskirts. That's where it would be toughest, probably, but also where I could do some good, maybe. At least I could try, like I said. I've had a lot of good opportunities that others don't get, and I want to use them. But no, it could be anywhere. I may well not be around here for long."

"So, it isn't just me who has other things to do."

"No. Just, you said it first."

An afternoon in a park in the *cinquième arrondissement*, with other people's children around us, other people's lives. The clock of Saint-Médard chiming, pigeons skidding down into the dust. One day, one afternoon, in a life that was not to be ours to share.

"This"—he gestured in the space between our bodies—"this is forever. Even if we don't see each other again. I am sorry about the other night. It was unfair, I know."

"How do you feel now?" I asked him cautiously.

"Now—well, I can be a bit more adult about it."

I, too, since my lunch with Fabrice Corte, had been feeling more adult, as if I had won an important point. But Yves, in the park, in the July warmth, close to me, his smell, his touch, the sound of his voice. Matt, at the airport in Miami, telling me he loved me, telling me again on the phone, as if these words themselves were a magic spell. The belief we all had in love surviving absence, memory transcending time. The way we longed for it to be true, the old romantic pledge: that this—this, here, now—is forever.

The bells, the shadow of leaves on the gravel as the sun came out, a child in a pink smock falling over, being scooped up, held and kissed, the man in the white singlet, African, holding his child, a pigeon landing, the Vietnamese father opening a pot of soup for his little boy, the bells, the newspaper images, Íngrid Betancourt, Yves's invisible mother: What was it but the entire world around us that made us move on into the next moment, inexorably becoming who we needed to become?

July 14 came and went, with the Firemen's Ball in the Place Saint-Médard and fireworks arching over Paris, but Yves spent it with his mother, as she was still not well. I stayed in, reading and trying to write. I have never liked national holidays, and having avoided July 4 in the United States, I was not keen to take part in Bastille Day.

Fabrice called me a couple of days after the holiday and left a message that he needed to talk to me. I ignored it. He sent me an e-mail. A text message. Then, feeling I was perhaps being too rude to someone who had, after all, paid for a memorable lunch, I wrote an e-mail back. *Desolée*, I had been ultra-busy, missed his messages, what could I do for him? I knew he wanted the painting back, and guessed that someone was putting pressure on him to deliver it and that there was probably money involved. The Dutch woman's heirs, perhaps. Or someone else. The next e-mail said that I should deliver the painting to him at his office, near Opéra. What, walk about the streets, get on the bus with it in a bag under my arm? There was no way I was going to take it down off my wall now—or, at least, not yet. Getting on a bus with the painting in a shopping bag might yet be the safest way of transporting it across Paris, but I wasn't going to do it. Let Fabrice Corte pursue me a little longer, let him sweat. I felt angry with him, and didn't know why—maybe because he assumed so easily that I would do what I was told?

His next communication announced that he had to go to Corsica the following week, and that he must see me before he left. I wrote back that I would meet him if necessary, but that I could not give up the painting, which had been left to me by my father and which was none of his business, since Françoise and I had called him in as an expert and he had already given us his opinion. I asked him to send me his bill. Then I called Françoise and told her what I had done.

"Ah, Gaby, I'm sorry now that I even thought of asking him. But he's a fairly old friend and colleague, and I thought we could trust him."

"It seems that someone got in touch with him when he began investigating the painting. Apparently the Dutch woman died and her heirs want it back. At least, that was the story. What can I do?"

"I know, you can stall for time. Send it to be cleaned. Get in touch with someone from Sotheby's or Christie's in England. You are English, after all. Get them to take it."

"That's an idea. Do you have any addresses, by any chance?"

"No, but I'll try and find out." She paused. "Actually, I do know one person at Sotheby's, a friend of your father's. Gaby, just one thing. Are you doing this because you miss your father, because you associate him with the painting? I feel I ought to warn you that you have no real right to it by law. Peter was only the dealer who had it at the time of his death."

"I'm doing it for the same reason that you had it. Because it was what he wanted. And I'm pretty sure that it's the right thing to do."

"Even if it's illegal?"

"Well, they have to prove ownership. It was left in my father's care. Fabrice tried to threaten me, but it didn't work, I told him so." Yes, I thought, trying to sound like Ingrid Bergman in *Casablanca*; but it did seem to have worked—for now.

"Gaby, you sound like a different person, if you don't mind my saying so."

"Well, maybe I am." I'd stood up for myself against a bullying man, in French, and so far, got away with it.

She called back with the home number of the man who worked at Sotheby's but who lived in the English countryside and whose job was to identify paintings hanging in obscure English houses and list them and their degrees of authenticity. "He was someone your father knew well. His name is Simon Jakes. I thought he might be a better bet than someone at their head office. He'll probably have more time for us."

I called the number in England and heard a tentative English reply. Then, "You're Peter's daughter? How simply marvelous. Just let me get my diary, and we'll make a date. Where are you in Paris, the same flat?"

"You've been here? You know it?"

"Yes, ages ago, used to go out on the town with your dad from time to time. Always glad to skip over to Paris. You free any time next week?"

"Yes," I said, amazed. He was going to get on the Eurostar, he said, and pop across. I was going to meet someone who had been to this flat, been out drinking with my father, for whom none of this seemed problematic.

"Terribly sorry about your dad. I'm still shocked, and you must be too. What a shame. I'd have come to the funeral, if only I'd known about it. What was it, heart?"

"Yes, his heart." That extravagant organ that had made my father beloved by so many, most of whom I had never even met in his lifetime.

"Great man, your dad. Well, can't wait to meet you. Tuesday all right? At the flat, are you? No problem. Gare du Nord, RER, Port-Royal, then down the road. Know it like the back of my hand. Remind me, though, there must be a code by now, no more nice old beady-eyed concierges dressed in black. Bye for now. Au revoir." He pronounced it *ove-wire*.

I put clothes in to wash and tidied up, and then stood for a long moment in front of my painting. "You're going to England," I said. "Officially, to be cleaned." The painting needed it, if the one in the Guggenheim had been anything to go by. Its surface was blackened and stained in places, and the bright silver of the nutcrackers looked tarnished. If some angry heirs were to show up and accuse me of theft, I would simply say that I'd had their interests at heart and had sent it to the best place I knew to be cleaned.

I had had no more sightings of my father since I'd had the painting. I wondered if this were a coincidence. I had reached the stage of believing, almost, that it had been Fabrice I had seen three times on the streets of Paris. I was in a state of mind to discount ghosts and revenants as explanations of current phenomena; I felt I had my feet back on the ground. I hoped that Fabrice Corte, in Ajaccio, was about to have a good long summer vacation until at least the end of August, as French people were supposed to.

✣

As I waited that Tuesday afternoon for Simon Jakes to ring my doorbell, I felt composed, contained, almost Parisian. He was so English, it made me smile. Untidy clothes, blond hair falling sideways, a rosy face and blue eyes, a grin that showed slightly discolored teeth, and a big warm hand that clasped mine and held on to it. "Gaby Greenwood. How wonderful to meet you at last." He was so unlike Fabrice Corte that I felt like hugging him.

"Come in. Can I make you some coffee?"

"You wouldn't by any chance have a cup of tea? I'd kill for a cuppa, metaphorically speaking, of course."

"Of course. Earl Grey or Lapsang?"

"You wouldn't have any builders' tea, would you?"

"Twinings do?"

"Lovely. Milk and two sugars, please." He sank down on the sofa, and immediately his eyes came to rest on the painting on the wall opposite, and he stood up again, dragging his long limbs that seemed wrapped in folds of denim and corduroy out of the depths of my sofa. "Ah, so that's our baby."

"Yes." I stood over the kettle, found tea bags, a mug, milk, and sugar.

"Very nice. Very nice indeed." He stood close, stroking his upper lip, looking. "Ah. Thanks. Lovely. Nothing like a cuppa. Now, you said this came from your father?"

"Well, he'd left it in a friend's flat. In Montmartre. She was keeping it for me. I didn't exactly inherit it. I more sort of inherited the responsibility for it. Dad was keeping it for someone, to sell. Now some Dutch people are after it, because the woman who owned it died. I guess she was the one who wanted to sell it in the first place, but they want it back, I suppose for probate or something, or to sell it, I don't know. If they exist, that is."

"Hmm. Complicated. So you are temporarily taking care of it?"

"I think my father meant me to have it. There was a twin, in the Guggenheim, in an exhibition we saw together. He loved it, I know."

Simon Jakes stirred sugar into his thick brown tea and said, "But there's a difference between loving a painting and owning it. You know that, I suppose?"

"Well, yes. But Françoise, my father's friend, was keeping it for me. She said he intended me to have it too."

"Françoise Lussac?"

"You know her? Oh, yes, of course, she suggested I get in touch with you."

"I've known her on and off for years."

"Simon, how well did you know my dad? You said you used to come here and go out drinking with him."

"I came here a couple of times. Yes, we went out together, Françoise too."

"So you knew about her and him."

"Well, yes, didn't everybody?"

"Not his family. Not me. Not my mother, probably."

"Ah. Yes, I suppose he was a man who kept things in compartments. Safer that way, I suppose. So, you came here and met Françoise, and the beans were spilled, eh? I thought you lived in America, by the way."

"I did. I mean, I do. I came to Paris to think some things out." Then, I decided that, of all people, I would trust him. "Since I've been here, I've seen my father three times in the street, and no, I'm not mad and I'm not on anything. What do you think of that?"

He stared at me, his sandy eyebrows lifted, that lock of gray-blond hair falling nearly over one eye; from his height, above his shabby clothes, he gave me the serious look I needed. From the depths of some aristocratic conviction about treating everything and everybody with politeness, he gave me his calm attention. "Did you really? How extraordinary. Everyone said he was dead, but you know, I somehow doubted it at the time."

"You did?"

"Well, it was all so hushed up and hurried, wasn't it, and the funeral rushed through and nobody he knew invited. I was a bit upset, to tell you the truth, and I'm sure I wasn't the only one."

"You mean, you think he could still be alive?"

"Well, if you saw him in the street, he must be, mustn't he? Unless you believe in ghosts."

"Or Fabrice Corte."

"Oh, him. Yes, of course. But surely you wouldn't mistake him for your father?"

"I don't know. I just don't know anymore. When I met him, I felt as if I couldn't remember what my father really looked like."

"Oh, but Fabrice, he's just school of."

"What?"

"School of Peter Greenwood. Your father was the real thing. Gaby, he knew more about painting and painters than anyone I've ever met, and he was completely self-taught. You could trust his opinion utterly. He knew what he had, and he knew its worth, and he could smell a dud a mile away. Corte just goes off to other experts. He knows the techniques, but he hasn't the feel for it."

"He suddenly wanted to take it away again, to give it back to the heirs of this Dutch woman, he said, Marth someone. Then he disappeared off to Corsica."

"So, he's out of town. That's a help. And who suggested you get in touch with me? Françoise?"

"She thought you could take it to England, to get it cleaned."

"And so I could." He waved a canvas bag at me, like a deep shopping bag with buckled fasteners. "If it wouldn't annoy the French, who are also very good at cleaning paintings."

"But nobody knows it's here, except Françoise and Fabrice Corte and me."

He sat down on the nearest chair, straddling it with his arms along the top, his long legs spread, his feet in the kind of suede shoes that you don't see often these days, with trailing laces. "Ah. And Corte is in Corsica. You're sure?"

"Yes, he left yesterday."

"Well, in that case, the coast is clear. Have you got any bubble wrap by any chance, and perhaps brown paper? Luckily nobody examines anything much on the wonderful train. But I want to know one thing, Gaby, if you don't mind. What is your part in all this? What are you doing this for?"

"I want to take over from where my dad left off, that's all. I don't mean, to be a dealer. I mean, to look after this painting. It needs cleaning. And look at the state of the frame. And it should be properly valued. That's what you do, isn't it?"

"Yes, that's exactly what we do. Good. Well, let's wrap up our little beauty, shall we, without more ado?"

I fetched the bubble wrap and brown paper that had covered the painting when Corte brought it to me, and watched him wrap it. I handed him Scotch tape and string. Simon put it in his canvas hold-all and did up the buckles. *"Et voilà."* His French accent was terrible. "Now, I'm fearfully sorry, but I shall have to take the next train right back. I've a client waiting for me in a house in Sussex simply stuffed with potential goodies, and I swore to be there by six, before the light goes. But I'll be in touch soon. Thanks for the tea."

"Just a minute. I have to ask you. You seemed to think that my father might not really have died. Please don't rush off. I really have to know why."

Simon Jakes sat down again, the bag on his knee, like someone waiting at a bus stop. He placed his hands on top of the bag and folded his fingers together. "Well. Sometimes people do that. They fake their own death. Some people have just done it in England, this summer, in fact. The man was supposed to have died in a boating accident, body never found and so forth. The wife was to collect on his life insurance, then they were both to scarper off to Panama or somewhere and live happily ever after on the dosh. Only it backfired, and she ended up in court. Now, obviously that's not what happened with your father, and he'd never have done it for the money, but I just had a hunch, especially when you told me you had seen him. He was someone who wanted more out of life. He may have felt he deserved more than what he had. He was once a very fine painter, you know. It's possible—just faintly possible—that he'd have wanted to disappear and sort of . . . pop up somewhere else. And be someone else."

"You make him sound like a rabbit going down a rabbit hole."

"Gaby, I can't know, obviously, so please don't take what I said for gospel. But why not phone me, if it happens again?"

I was remembering something. A phrase hung in the back of my mind, recent, in French, a man's voice, who was it? Fabrice Corte, at lunch, saying that a forger was nearly always a disappointed man. But nobody thought my father could have been a forger of paintings, or even signatures. I had never even known he was, as Simon said, a fine painter. He must have stopped before I was old enough to know. Or had he? All I had seen of his were the sketchy little drawings, almost cartoons, that he had left for me from time to time: a drawing of me tidying my chaotic room, once, and another of me looking absurdly Gothic in black clothes, later on. A scribble that was me taking the current dog for a walk, with sun and clouds, one time when I had sulkily refused to do so. But paintings?

"I will take it straight up to London with me in the morning," Simon Jakes said, maybe sensing my apprehension. "And it will be cleaned and valued, and we will get in touch as soon as that has happened, and send you a bill." As if the sending of the bill would validate the whole transaction. I thought of Corte, carefully pocketing the bill from Le Train Bleu. "Now, don't worry. It will be safe as houses. Then, we'll get in touch with those Dutch people; it would be easy to find out if they exist, and tell them the exact worth for probate purposes and ask them for their instructions. And if there aren't any, we'll know we have Corte to deal with. All right, Gaby?"

"But what about me?"

"You will have done your bit. Very responsible, actually, the best thing you could have done, handing it over to us. And you know, it strikes me that if it were found to be a fake, after all, it would be very much easier for you to keep it."

"I don't follow. Why?"

"Well, it would simply have, let's say, less of a footprint. People wouldn't want it back so much. Have you ever heard of a famous forger called van Meegeren?"

"No. Why?"

"He painted some very bad paintings, also some halfway good ones, that he managed to pass off as Vermeers. He bought seventeenth-century canvases, removed the original paint from them, ground his paints exactly the way Vermeer did, and believe it or not, used Bakelite to fix them. He really worked at it. He was obsessed. Amazingly enough, nobody ever challenged him or even did an X-ray, he was so convincing. There was a particularly bad one called *Supper at Emmaus* that nobody in their right mind now could accept as a Vermeer. He sold one called *Christ and the Woman Taken in Adultery*—terrible painting—to Goering during the war, and the fact that he admitted the paintings were forged actually saved his life. Selling the Dutch patrimony to the Nazis would have been treason, a capital offense, whereas selling forgeries was merely clever. See what I mean?"

"I don't see how it connects with me."

"No, just that sometimes it is more convenient for something not to be real."

"But Fabrice Corte said it was real!"

"And so I believe it is. But if only you, me, and Corte knew that, it would be more convenient."

I let out the long sigh I had been holding in. It was all beyond me, but suddenly I thought, it would not have been beyond my father.

"Simon, I want it back. On my father's life, I want it back. Real or fake, I don't care. If you value your friendship with him at all, you will bring it back to me, or I will come and steal it from you in England."

"But, of course, Gaby, you will have it back whenever you want. I'll get in touch as soon as it's done. Scout's honor."

"And I'm not doing anything wrong. I'm not selling things to the Nazis."

"No, no, of course, I just wanted you to be aware of what the possibilities are. True art lovers, Gaby, are people who are prepared to love a painting because of what it is and what they feel about it—sometimes against all the odds. There aren't many of them. But you know, a very large proportion of paintings in art galleries are forgeries, and then, it's more convenient to pretend that they are real. I'm just saying that this woman's heirs probably will love your painting a lot less if they think it's a copy. That's all."

"So what's the difference between a copy and a forgery?"

"A forgery is masquerading as something it is not. But in a way, you see, it's art's shadow, its other self. The false has to exist in order for the true to be itself. A copy is anodyne, carries no shadow. We do live, increasingly, in a world of copies. Or am I getting into deep water here? Anyway—look, I'm afraid I must depart. Tempus fugit, you know. The mighty Eurostar waits for no one. Thanks for the tea."

He was already sliding away from me with his slightly blundering politeness, glancing at his watch, thinking about his train. An ungainly middle-aged Englishman with floppy hair and a look of Alan Bennett about him, his jacket flapping, a canvas bag hooked over his shoulder with my painting in it, striding off to identify yet more found paintings in somebody's attic, to pronounce on the false and the real. I closed the door behind him, breathed out, and felt the disappearance of my painting, sharp as loss.

⚜

There was a blank space on my wall beneath the nail where it had hung: absence, visible now, where once there had just been a wall. Yves noticed it immediately. "Gaby, your painting's gone."

"I handed it over to a friend of my father's, who works at Sotheby's. It's going to be cleaned. And I think he knows that if I don't get it back, there'll be trouble. Now, how was your day?"

"Not so interesting. I went all over Paris looking for a computer for my mother. She wants to learn how to use one, and every secondhand one I looked at was fucked. I'm going to have to buy it new. There's a deal now for getting TV, phone, and Internet access all in one, and she wants to go online. My mother, imagine! Still, it's a good idea. It will link her up to the outside world at last. When even my mother is online, we're really in a science-fiction world." He came over and stood behind me, rubbing my shoulders, his hands easing lower, coming around my waist. I leaned back against him, enjoying it, but more as if he were a masseur than a lover. I felt as if we had already said goodbye. Maybe in buying his mother a computer, he had also said goodbye to her, freed himself into becoming a son who could go and live at the other end of France. If I myself were to leave Paris, I would be leaving not only him but my father, who walked these streets but presumably not those of any other city, especially in the United States. Or was it possible that he would wait for me outside the gates of Central Park in New York, or in line outside the Met? That he could pop up, as Simon Jakes had put it, anywhere at all?

"Come, let's go into the bedroom." He pulled me by the hand, and I went with him, and yes, we found each other again among the tangled sheets, our bodies remembering and saluting each other, but our minds, I was almost sure of it, elsewhere.

"Gaby," he said at last, "where are you? I can't find you today."

No fooling this man, I thought. "I'm sorry. I'm distracted."

"I'm sorry I can't undistract you. What is it?" He sat up, naked at my side, his fingers moving across the top of my spine.

"I feel as if I've been going around in interlocking circles and as if there's something at the center that I'm never going to find."

"Your father?"

"Well, myself too. What it all signifies. What I do next with my life."

"Gaby, you know, I think you have to stop worrying about it, and something will become clear. Your mind keeps working away at it, you keep on asking other people's opinions, but, really, you know, I think it might be better to relax and simply be here. Here, in this room, today, with me. This is your life, even if it never happens again. In fact, it won't ever happen again. It's a one-off, even if we meet again, even if it's tomorrow. You told me this yourself. Be here, Gaby, be present. Be happy. Don't fight me off. You are so well loved, you know; that's the heart of it."

"You love me?"

"Yes, of course. But not in the way of wanting to keep you, don't worry. And so does your husband, I imagine, and so did your parents, and so do René and Marie-Christine, and so, I'm sure, do many other people I don't know. You have to accept it, Gaby. You are such an intellectual, you ask so many questions, and God knows, so do I. I've spent my life asking them, the hard ones, and not letting myself off the hook. But we're here to please each other and also to teach each other, I think. Let yourself feel loved, Gaby, and it won't matter so much about your father being dead or alive."

We sat with the sweat cooling on our joined flesh, and for a long moment I tried to let in what he said. It had the freshness and simplicity of reality. It wasn't a construct. It wasn't out of the past, or even connected to a future. It wasn't about pretending anything, or covering anything up. It was about us, in this room, this evening, now. We lay down again and held hands, while the light beyond the shutters changed and darkened. Outside, the nights were growing just perceptibly longer. I felt an extraordinary peace settle around us, and tears leaked from the corners of my eyelids that he licked up, leaning over me, his tongue washing the saltcellars of my closed eyes.

15.

August: Paris was emptying itself of its residents and filling with tourists. Everybody who lived here was about to go on holiday or had already gone, the days were hot and still and the evenings blue with fumes and dust, even with less traffic in the streets. Most of the shops in my neighborhood were closed, with grim metal grilles pulled down over the windows. Some of them had their windows covered with brown paper on the inside, so that the look was blind, where not fortified. Down below in our street, beneath our opened windows, tourists trundled suitcases on wheels as they searched for their hotels. It was another season, one of migration, one of change.

Françoise went to Brittany to stay with her family and was then going to treat herself to some thalassotherapy on the coast. René and Marie-Christine were staying on in René's father's country house in Touraine, and begged me on the phone to join them. Yves was going to Portugal to see his grandmother there and was then going to a windsurfing school near Arcachon. He, too, begged me to go, saying how I would love it. August in Paris seemed to nail a roof of heat above the city, in spite of impromptu beaches along the Seine, and bicycle lanes everywhere with people bicycling on the free bikes that had appeared in ranks everywhere, and picnics on the worn grass in the parks. I refused all invitations and then felt bitter and alone. But there was something to see through, here, and I would not know for sure if I went away. There was still a question, and there was still a chance.

I heard nothing more from Fabrice Corte, who was presumably in Corsica for the month of August. Nobody sent me a bill from Sotheby's. No Dutch people arrived on my doorstep to demand their painting. In August in France, everything gets forgotten, let go, postponed. Only at the *rentrée*, when the schools reopened, would anyone begin to send e-mails, ask questions, send bills, knock on doors, demand answers. I drifted in the heat, breathing in traffic fumes, dawdling like a tourist along the Seine. I went to the Jardin du Luxembourg and visited the lovely statue of the Mask Seller, and stood amazed before the huge golden sculpted head of the Prophet that gazed back across the formal gardens into a yet unknown future, out of an inscrutable past. I left my windows and shutters open all night and let the dawn wake me and birds swoop through my dreams. I wrote brief, cryptic poems on old yellow legal pads brought from America for that purpose and then in French notebooks with squared paper. I sat at cafés on narrow pavements in streets where I had never been before and drank pastis as if I were in the south, drowning it with water, or Campari, with orange juice as if I were in Italy. I took cold showers, walked about the flat naked, bought a fan at the local *quincaillerie* and spent an entire afternoon trying to put it together. I thought of sleeping in the air conditioning of Florida. I thought of going back there—but to what? I felt as if I were in a giant oasis, a mirage, a city that only existed in people's imaginations, a city abandoned by its inhabitants, created by the fantasies of foreigners. I heard the voices all around me: American, English, German, Japanese. I felt deprived of language, with no one to talk to. Even the cinemas had given up changing their films and were showing the same tired old ones. The market on rue Mouffetard turned into a display for tourists and the one on Port-Royal on Saturday mornings had shrunk, leaving only a few tired sellers of tomatoes and lettuces. I began to forget why I was here, whether I had made a life here, after all, if any of it was real.

I longed, in the absence of reality, for the *rentrée*: for sensible clothes, chill winds, new books, films, newspapers, people going to work. My return date was not until late September. August stretched around me, a desert, a purgatory. Yet it was what I had chosen. There was a reason, even if I had forgotten it, why I was here. I missed Yves. I rolled across my bed in an ache of longing. I flung my hands out to the very edge of the mattress and turned into the pillow to search for a new cool place. I understood why they had all gone, only too well. It was a necessary migration, leading to a necessary return. It was the way life was, had to be. It was like the order of French meals, one thing after another, and coffee at the end. It was the narrative of the French year, as inevitable as spring or winter, a season abandoned, emptied, left to rot. No wonder people died in Paris in August without anyone noticing.

In the middle of the month, a call on my cell phone: Simon Jakes's English voice breaking open the silence. The English don't vanish entirely for the whole month of August. They have holidays but are quickly back on the job.

"Gaby, how are you?"

"Almost nonexistent. Everyone here is away. I should have gone too. But somehow, I couldn't. I couldn't leave."

"Well, I've got the painting for you. It's been cleaned, it looks wonderful, and it's been valued. Two hundred thousand pounds, approximate probate price. That means it's worth far more on the market. But the odd thing is, we've not had a squeak out of those Dutch people who were supposed to be so keen to have it back. D'you think they exist? Ten Bruggencate, the name was, not an unusual one, and they were supposed to be at an address in The Hague. What did Fabrice tell you about them?"

"Nothing much. That they were the heirs of the woman who wanted to sell it, who'd left it with Dad. Marth, her name was."

"Perhaps she didn't want them to have it."

"Who knows. I can't get anything out of anyone here. The whole place has ground to a halt until September."

"Well, I don't think that's true of the whole of Europe, is it? Gaby, are you all right? You sound strange."

"It's just that I haven't spoken to anyone for so long, I suppose." I leaned against the wall in my underwear, feeling the fan cool my knees as it turned.

"Well, I've got the picture for you, since nobody else seems interested. What do you want me to do?"

"Can you keep it for me, Simon? I'm coming to England, to see my sister, I've decided. In a few weeks. I'll let you know."

"Of course. Just let me know. Keep in touch, tell me if you need anything? Oh, and by the way, forget what I said about suggesting it's only a copy. We aren't going to need that now."

"Thanks, Simon, I will."

A last time. There would be one, of course, and then I would know. It was what I was waiting for, without ever admitting it to myself. I couldn't leave Paris without knowing, however crazy that might seem. All my other reasons for being here had dropped away, and I felt very much alone. I walked through the familiar streets of my neighborhood feeling like a ghost myself. My brief clothes fluttered about me, I walked in sandals, just another foreigner with no right to be here and no particular role to play. I felt insubstantial, light, skinny with not eating meals, since nobody invited me out and there was nobody to cook and eat with. I was pared to a sharpened sensitivity; I walked like a cat in the night. At sunset and in the long twilights, I walked up to the Observatory and all around Saint-Jacques; I walked up to the Contrescarpe and down rue Descartes and rue du Cardinal Lemoine toward the Seine. I walked for miles all along it, lit boats and barges passing me by, lovers against the stone walls leaning and kissing endlessly, eating each other up, their breath in their joined mouths and throats, their legs intertwined; I walked where I had walked with Yves on the night of the Fête de la musique, all along the quai Saint-Bernard and back past the Jardin des Plantes and its locked gates, its high fences, up rue Buffon; I crossed the river and walked on the Île de la Cité, the Île Saint-Louis, along the Canal Saint-Martin. I stood among all the hundreds of visitors in front of the cleaned façade of Notre-Dame. I walked to the Marais and watched young foreign men in twos walk entwined; I sat on a bench in the Place des Vosges and stared at the statue of Louis XIII on his horse under the tired trees and the picnickers and couples stretched out on the grass with their bottles of wine and water beside the fountains, always couples, always kissing; I joined the crowds, the flashes of cameras, the kisses, the exclamations. I was in it yet alone, engulfed yet wary. I was walking to wear myself out and feel the city wear me into its warm stones, its polished cobbles, its leaf surfaces, its glimmer of water under bridges, its stained morning skies. I walked, and walked home again, and let myself in late to fall across my stripped bed in the glare from the streetlights and the beam of the moon. I walked until I was unsure that I existed, I was thin as a shadow, silent as a shadow. I was becoming a shadow of my former self. I slipped into churches, Saint-Julien-le-Pauvre, Saint-Ephrem, Saint-Eustache, Saint-Sulpice, Saint-Étienne-du-Mont, Saint-Paul des Marais, Saint-Jacques, Saint-Louis-en-l'Île, Saint-Médard, all the saints of Paris. I lit candles for my dead parents; I stood against cool stone walls and breathed in the scent of incense and asked for an answer, why some people died and some were left living, and why life was the fragile thing it was. I wanted answers, meanings, truth. I had let go of the solid things, my painting, the still life in it, my objects, my *bodegones*. I had used them as I could, gained the strength from them that I could. I wanted, now, the essence of things, and I wanted to be shown it once and for all, in this febrile search through the days and nights of August in Paris, my loved and deserted city. I talked too much in the bread shop, the only one left open in the quartier. I loitered to talk to the man who sold me a newspaper. I longed for someone, anyone, to address me by my name. I did not call Matt, as to do so in this state felt too much like failure of nerve. I walked, thought, gabbled requests for cheese and fruit in the market, sat in the cool dusk of the churches of Paris while my superstitious candles burned and guttered and the saints said nothing. I sat and stared at Claude Monet's enormous water lilies in the Orangerie. I even stood in line to slip in to the glass portal of the Louvre among the international tourists, the Germans, the Americans, the Japanese. I felt invisible, almost surprised to be asked to buy a ticket, as if I were a ghost myself. I began to write lines of poems, but they, like the candles, guttered and died out. Words, which attached me to the things of life, seemed such frail connections, in any language. In the city the heat built up to what is called *la canicule*, which at least gives discomfort an explanation and makes of excess temperature a solid reality. *Ah, c'est la canicule*, meaning, it isn't just hot, and it isn't just me.

Then one afternoon in late August, as I came home up the dusty empty street, I knew from an unexpected surge of energy I felt that this stage of my mourning was over. I was ready to move. I telephoned Simon Jakes to say when I was coming to England to collect my painting. I called my sister, Marg, in Cambridge. Speaking English, even into a telephone, made me feel at last more real, an actual person. I thought of calling Matt, just to break the silence, but where he was, across the globe from me, it was still the middle of the night. And what could I say?

16.

I bought my ticket for the Eurostar at the Gare du Nord and, with just my small overnight bag, boarded the train with hundreds of other English people going home. It was strange to be surrounded by the English, with their pale holiday clothes, their clunky footwear and patchy tans, couples who had been for a weekend in Paris, families coming back from farther south, with their accents and expressions and ways of dumping down their belongings in all directions and pulling out messy picnics as soon as the train began to move. I was one of them, and I'd forgotten. I wasn't American or French, but I'd been away long enough to be surprised, shocked even, amused and critical. A woman with long blonde hair waving over her shoulders, wearing a tiny pink top with straps that cut into a painful case of sunburn and boobs that bulged like freckled apples, sat down beside me and let out a huge breath, as if she had been punctured.

"Phew, never thought I'd make it. Bloody taxis. They don't let you on, you know, if you're more than half an hour late. Never thought I'd get here." She closed her eyes and leaned back, and I sat still and stared at my own knees in their dark jeans and wondered how to respond. No Frenchwoman would ever sit down beside a stranger and let out all the air in her like that and flaunt her breasts as if they were on a plate. An American might sit down and ask me after a few moments where I was from and where I was going. But my big pink gasping neighbor with her eyes closed as if she had only just saved her own life made me want to laugh or run. At last I opened my copy of *Le Monde des Livres* and pretended for a few minutes to be French. Then that seemed both absurd and unfriendly, so I said after rather too long, "Got held up, then, did you?" and heard all about the disastrous taxi ride, the driver who had taken her all around the houses, couldn't find his arse from his elbow, and dumped her at the wrong side of the station, could I believe it. I said that Parisian taxi drivers often took foreigners the long way around, and she said, you can say that again, bloody nerve, and then closed her mascaraed eyes again so that I felt I could go back to reading my paper.

"Understand all that, do you?" she asked after a few minutes. The train began to pick up speed and move smoothly through the northern suburbs.

"Well, yes."

"I never could pick up languages. I can ask for stuff to eat, that sort of thing. But read, no way, José."

I began to like her, and folded the page with the review of a new book of philosophy that I thought would be hard going anyway.

"D'you live there, then?" she asked me.

"Yes."

"But you're English, right?"

"Yes."

"I couldn't live anywhere but England. Not really. I mean, the price of everything's going through the roof. I know everyone's buggering off to Spain and France and everywhere, but I couldn't, not where I can't talk to people. Talking's what counts, really, isn't it? But I suppose if you can speak French . . . Why d'you go there, if you don't mind my asking?"

I thought I'd leave America out of the equation. "I was left a flat there. By my parents. So I have somewhere to live."

"Wow, lucky you. I've been down south, that's where I got this tan, then just had the weekend in Paris. Can't wait to get home, though, now."

⚜

Home. I sat and wondered where home was as the train hurtled closer to the coast of northern France, and in a few minutes would disappear under the Channel and pop up—as Simon would say—in England. England, that I had fled from, that I had missed, that was now full of a ragged emptiness where home had been. The keys to the Paris flat in my bag, a French mobile phone in my pocket, two passports to choose from, two very different-looking photographs, one in each. My American and my English faces, both of them far too young for the face I had today at forty, thin with not eating, with a good French haircut, plucked eyebrows, skin that needed suddenly a lot of expensive face cream. The train plunged forward into darkness, and my neighbor let out a small squeak, as if she had not expected anything of the sort, and we were under the English Channel, which is also French and called *La Manche*.

My sister, Margot, was there to meet me at the station, off the slow, grimy train to Cambridge from King's Cross. She looked like me, although in another version: taller, heavier, with eyebrows so dark they made dramatic punctuation marks across her face. I'd forgotten those eyebrows; they were my father's legacy to her, and his had remained dark even while his hair turned white. Her hair, in a chunky bob, was beginning to be streaked with gray. We would all go gray early, while our faces still looked young. She opened the door of a dirty Peugeot and let me in on what felt for a minute like the wrong side. We'd kissed, two cheeks in the way people now did in places other than France. She'd looked at me, hard, and then away.

"Gaby. My God, how long has it been? Since the funeral?"

"I know. Only, what, eight months?"

"But we hardly even saw each other then."

I thought, we saw each other as much as we ever had. The wake, or whatever you call it, had been organized by her at our parents' house, and we had grimaced at each other over the sandwiches, had a brief, tearful hug on parting. Now it sounded as if Marg minded, as if she had even wanted more.

She started her car, hands rather worn looking as though she gardened, or did pottery. I had no idea what my sister's life was like. But, as if a door in the past opened, suddenly I was back in the room we had shared, with a line drawn down the middle, her dolls and neat art projects on one side, my chaos on the other. Three years between us, she the older, and here it was again, that consciousness of her superior age, knowledge, experience. She would always be out ahead of me, winning races, mocking—even if the race was to have children, and the prize a family everyone could envy. I'd dropped out, but I still felt it: Marg the success, the gold standard by which I had to measure myself always.

"Great haircut," she said now, turning and backing the car to drive it out effortlessly into the stream of traffic that moved into central Cambridge. "You look wonderful. So thin!"

"Yes, well, I've hardly been eating."

"In France?"

"Everyone's away," I said. "It's August."

"So you don't eat? Well, I hope you're going to eat my roast lamb, because I got it specially for you, and it costs an arm and a leg these days. We have pudding too, apple crumble. You up for it?"

"Of course! Actually, I'm starving, I just had a mini sandwich on the train."

"Good." She drove down Mill Road toward Parker's Piece, and it all looked familiar and strange at once, the way places do when you have been away for years. Especially places in which you were young. Before the house in East Anglia, our parents had lived here in a tall, thin house on Maids Causeway, and we had been to a kindergarten somewhere on Parker's Piece and played out on its then-huge expanse under the sky.

"So, you've been in Paris all this time?"

"Only since May."

"And have you left Matthew, or what?" My sister, I remembered, always went straight to whatever she thought was the point. I watched her hands on the wheel and saw she was wearing a ring of our mother's. Oh, there was so much that had never been said; would it be said now, or would we drift over it, vague and noncommittal as we all could be, the way our mother had drifted around kitchens all her life, helping people to food, smiling, not saying? Margot would ask me this directly, had I left Matt, but would she ever say what she felt herself, or what challenged, worried, scared her? She was so like our mother. Everything was always all right, then suddenly you were dead, crushed between the weight of an unknown person's truck and a brick wall.

"It's complicated," I said. "I'll tell you." I'd thought I was solid enough, calm enough, after the months in Paris, and now I was not sure.

When she showed me into the house in Newnham that they had bought, she and Jude, her husband of nearly twenty years, I saw my mother's kitchen again, my mother's living room. It was nearly impossible to go in, and for a moment I hung back. But the smells of roast lamb with rosemary and garlic were wonderful, and there was Jude hugging me, and the boys, Adam and Fred, coming in from the garden, and it was impossible not to be drawn in. As it was always impossible not to be drawn in to my mother Helen's rooms, with her hugs, her cooking smells, her wide, aproned waist, her beaming face. "Gaby, darling, how wonderful!" How had Marg not noticed? Or did she not mind? Was it what she wanted, was it the way she saw her life? Evidently, it was. Jude was a handsome man, with a broad face and big brown eyes. His sons resembled him, had changed into teenagers, and even seemed to have grown taller since the funeral.

"Have you seen Hugh and Phil at all?" Our brothers, one like our mother, the other mysteriously like nobody at all. Phil could have been anybody's son.

"Not lately. We talk on the phone, e-mail, you know, everyone's so busy. But aren't you going to see them?"

"I haven't time. I have an appointment in London, and I have to be back in Paris on Thursday."

"But that's no time at all!"

"I'll make it longer next time. Promise. Tell them. I won't leave it so long."

Fred, leaning forward for bread—a basket, a sliced homemade loaf, as my mother would have provided—asked me, "Do you still live in America?"

"Well, yes. When I'm not in France."

"America's not fair," he said. "They kill people. They have wars. So why do you live there?"

"Chip off the old block, eh?" Jude said, smiling.

I said, "I know. A lot of people there think the same as you. That's why we're having an important election."

"So are you going to elect the cool black guy? Is he going to stop the war?"

I hadn't been prepared for this from someone who had been a small child in such recent memory. "I hope so. We'll see, in November. I'll write to you. Do you have e-mail?"

"Of course. Okay, yes, please. I want to know if he stops the war."

"Me too," I said.

"More lamb?" Marg said, just as our mother would have done, calming conversations that might get out of hand. "This is a lovely wine you brought, thanks so much."

It was a 2005 Bordeaux, from the wine shop down my street. The boys both wanted a taste, and sipped thoughtfully, as if they were going to be asked to comment. Jude filled my glass again. "It's wonderful to have you here, Gaby, even if for so short a time."

I thought, so this is what it's like, my family. This is what I was too scared to come and find, in case it no longer existed, or in case it would swallow me whole. *Drink your wine, Gaby, eat your dinner, talk to your nephews, accept it for what it is, because it has hurt to live without it, because it is part of who you are.*

After dinner, Jude said to me in the sitting room, "Really, Gaby, it's lovely to see you. We've missed you, you know. Marg in particular."

I looked out at the rainy garden beyond the French windows, the heavy heads of hydrangeas drooping, the sodden grass. August in England.

"We haven't seen you since your father's death."

"I know. I'm sorry. After the funeral—Dad's—I thought I could never come back to England. But, actually, I couldn't stay in the United States. Really, I left home a long time ago, after a series of awful fights with our mother."

"I've often wondered what happened, Gaby. Did you and Margot have a fight too?"

I looked into his kind face, his brown eyes, and sighed. "I was an awful person when I was young. Marg was always the good one, the one Mum approved of. Dad sort of got who I was, even when I was at my worst. But he so often wasn't here." It was true. The memory of absence. Our mother, bitter, often angry—with the self-centeredness of youth, I had never wondered why—waiting in the house on her own. How had I not remembered this before?

"It seemed easiest just to stay away. But I won't do it again. The boys change too fast, for one thing."

Marg came in with mugs of decaf coffee, which I declined. She looked baffled for a moment, and I said, "I'm just so full, and I wanted to keep the taste of the crumble, that's all. It was so delicious."

Fred and Adam had sped off on their bicycles, wearing yellow slickers and flashing red lights. I sat down with my sister and her husband on a sofa that had surely belonged to my parents, a warm rusty orange with brown cushions. There was silence. Then Jude got up to put on a CD of Bach cello suites, and we sat and let the music cover and fill us. The sound of the cello seemed to be drawn on my skin, and a huge feeling grew inside me. He was a good man, this husband of my sister's. He understood things without asking, he trusted his intuition.

When I lay in bed in their spare room later, I heard them move about the house the way parents and house owners do, closing doors, opening windows, drawing curtains, turning keys, going at last into their own room to rumble to each other in the endless private conversation of married people who are in it for the long haul. I let out my breath in a big sigh like that of my blonde neighbor on the train. I could let go. I was in my sister's house, and something was being carried on here, continued, honored, that I hadn't realized I had missed.

It was only over the clearing away of breakfast that she mentioned Matt again, and I told her. "I couldn't bear it, and I thought I couldn't bear him. But it wasn't him, Marg, it was me. It's taken me months on my own to understand, just a little. I was in a state after Dad's death, and I blamed it all on him. It really wasn't fair. I had to leave, and I honestly think he may have been relieved to see me go."

"Why Paris?"

"Well, there was the apartment. It seemed to be waiting for me. But you know, Marg, there's nothing of Mum's there, nothing at all. It felt as if she had never even been there."

"Well, she didn't go there after she found out about that lady friend of his. And I think he had the whole thing redone, redecorated."

"You knew about her?"

"Mum told me. She told me not to tell anyone. It was once when he was away, and she thought he must be with her, the other woman, and I found her crying in the kitchen. I must have been fifteen. She said it was very important that none of the rest of you knew, because the family was the most important thing. So, of course, I said I wouldn't tell, and I didn't."

"God. Marg, do you think they were mostly happy together? She and Dad?"

"You know, I think they were, on the whole. It's something I know I couldn't have done—accepted that whole situation. But they weren't like people today. They were kind of heroic, their generation. They tried to change society, and they tried to change themselves. Heroic and a bit mad. If they thought they ought to accept something, they got on and did it. Or tried to, anyway, with a few tears now and then. I think it was because they were brought up after the war, and there was a sense of having to put up with things. Then there was this kind of revolutionary stuff in the sixties. They really thought then that people were capable of change."

She leaned against the counter, her back to the sink, the plates all stacked in the dishwasher, the window behind her fogged with steam.

"And we don't?"

"Well, Gab, I don't know about you, but no amount of revolutionary fervor would enable me to put up with Jude having another woman for years and years."

"I see what you mean." I had avoided talking to my sister for years because I thought she hadn't changed, would never accept me as an adult. Now we were talking as women, as equals.

"She could have gone back to work. She could have done anything. She chose to stay in East Anglia and do this kind of earth-mother thing, and of course it was great for us—we had everything we ever needed. But what about her? And just when she was getting a bit of life for herself, she got killed by a stupid bloody lorry. It wasn't fair." Marg closed the dishwasher and turned it on. I thought, how fairness counts with her, still; I remembered the boy at dinner: "America isn't fair." Nothing was fair, and surely you had to realize it once you were no longer a child.

"Gaby, I hated him, from that day on, the day she told me. And I'd been so jealous of you, because you were his favorite, and I couldn't tell you the truth about him because you were only young, and she had made me swear not to. But Dad was a shit."

I stared at her. "Really?"

"Really. He took advantage of her. He used her money, her energy, her good nature, her love for him, and he just took what he needed."

"I thought he loved her. I remember. When we were children, anyway. Marg, he did love her."

"Yes, but what if love isn't enough? I mean, what is that sort of love, really? You have to be able to think about someone, respect them, give up things for them, think about their well-being. And all he did was flit about Europe with this French floozy, and dabble in dealing pictures. I'm not even sure he wasn't a bit of a crook. You know, when he died, in that puddle, facedown in a puddle, what a way to go, I thought, *Good riddance.* I didn't want to have him on my hands. I didn't want to look after him in his old age, and I didn't want to put up with any more of his shit."

"Marg, I had no idea." Was this what I had come all this way to hear?

"Well, I know you didn't, but here we are in our forties. How long are we going to go on pretending? Hugh thinks the way I do; he told me. He got what Dad was up to, with all those endless trips away, mysterious phone calls, and so on. Phil, I don't know. Phil keeps things to himself."

"Well, hey, thanks for telling me. I'm amazed."

She had her arms folded across her chest now, her stance so like our mother's, and a frown drew down her startling eyebrows over her equally startling blue eyes. She was beginning to look lined, and there were those white hairs, but she was a looker, my sister, and her fierceness showed it to me again.

"No point in beating about the bush. We were all enveloped in his kind of ghastly myth. The great Peter Greenwood. Well, I was over it by the time I was a teenager, I can tell you. But you never saw it, did you, Gaby?"

"I loved him," I said. Immediately tears began sliding down my nose and into the corners of my mouth, and I drew my sleeve across my face to wipe them away.

"Yeah, I know." She said it gently, and there was a silence between us, in which raindrops slid down the kitchen windowpane, and tears slid down my cheeks, and she stood with her arms folded and then unfolded them, came across to me in two steps, and gave me the first long hug we had exchanged for very many years.

After we had drawn apart again and I had found a tissue in my jeans pocket and scrubbed my face, I said, "I met her, in Paris. Françoise, Dad's lover. She isn't a floozy, Marg. She's nice."

Marg said, "Well, of course she is. Women are. I expect she had crap to put up with too. It's Dad I was furious with." She looked at me. Conversations in kitchens, between women, between meals and dish-washing, on the way to the next thing. Was this what our mother had left to us? Outside, the trees still dripped, but there was a brief patch of blue sky, and watery sun. "What's she like?"

"Good-looking, sixtyish, works for *Le Monde*. An art critic. She doesn't cook. She lives in a high-up flat in Montmartre, and she had a broken leg. She told me she was quite happy with the situation. She hadn't wanted more of him."

"Well, I can understand that. A little of our dad went a long way. Why do you say, she doesn't cook?"

"Well, she doesn't."

"Unlike Mum, you mean."

"Well, Mum wasn't an art critic either. Just to say, I suppose, they are, were, not a bit alike. But then, why should they be?"

"But they both let him carry on his double life."

"Yes," I said. "And if they all knew, really, was there anything wrong with that?"

"Oh, the lies, the pretense, the disappearances, the way we never knew where he was, that was all. I know I was just young when she told me, and I was always her girl, where you were Dad's. But there was something just so—so shitty—about the way it all went on under our noses, hypocritical, I suppose, hidden, secret, nothing ever being said."

"Well, sure, we all went in for the *non-dit*, as the French say. Not saying. That was part of the pact."

"That's exactly what I mean," Margot said. "And it's what I can't stand."

"You have changed."

"No, I haven't. I'm just not part of their regime anymore, that's all. They're dead, and so I can say what I like. So can you."

Their regime. Yet did she know how exactly she reminded me of our mother, how her whole house, even her kitchen implements, did? Mum never had a dishwasher, that was all. Also, my sister worked full time now as a psychologist for the local authority, visiting disturbed children in schools. Maybe that accounted for her talk of the regime.

"What about you and Matt? Since we hardly see each other. Do you mind me asking? I always liked him but found him pretty immature."

"Me too." I smiled at her. "But then, so was I. I married him in a hurry. The way I ran off to the States. So, I honestly don't know. But I'll go back, yes, and then we'll see. He's a good guy, but I'm not sure that we should be married."

"You never wanted kids? I often wondered."

"No. No, I didn't. I had a sort of allergy to families, to the whole idea. But lately, getting to know people in Paris, talking to all sorts of people, I don't know. It's probably too late, anyway."

"Gab, are you having an affair? You look so—sort of sleek."

"It's just the haircut," I said. "And not eating much. I squeezed myself into these French jeans; I bought a few new clothes." There were some things that were going to continue being unsaid.

"Well, I should go to work. Help yourself to anything, feel free. The boys will be back around three thirty and probably go straight out again. See you later." On her way through the front door, she said, "Gaby, I'm so glad you came."

❖

I was glad too. Fifteen minutes with my sister, and something had happened—we had really talked to each other. It was all so much easier than I'd feared. Maybe there was nothing to be afraid of, after all. I went into the sitting room and lay on the orange seventies couch, thinking about her and Dad. A person came into this world and was loved and hated, admired and criticized. On one hand, there was the love that came from people as different as Françoise, Simon Jakes, André Schaffer, and me; on the other, my sister and my brother's disdain. He had been one person but had deliberately created what people called a double life. Was that simply because he wanted to live more than was allowed to him? Was he trying to increase his life exponentially, to make the most of it, or was it partly unconscious, just the way he was, from the beginning on? Had he been born wanting more than other people, in the way of experience? Had he known instinctively that he was going to die at sixty-five, not eighty-five, not ninety?

Marg said he was a shit. Shit, shitty—a word she used a lot. Marg was a child psychologist. Why that, of all things? Marg had duplicated much of our mother's life, and was her champion. Was that because Dad had bought me, not her, the Chinese horse? Was it because of the chance of going into the kitchen one afternoon, home early from school, and finding Mum in tears? Chance, or choice. Genes, or environment. The throw of a dice, or destiny. You couldn't know. But this morning I had glimpsed the other side of it, a picture that I had thought was one-sided. Nothing was one-sided. Jude could yet fall in love with another woman and not tell the fierce and exacting Marg. Anything could evolve from this fleeting time, the present. As it had out of all the fleeting presents which were past. The question now was not what our parents had been to each other or even to us, but what we would do with it.

✦

I asked Marg my question that evening as she searched in the cupboard for bottles of various aperitifs and set glasses out on a tray. Jude had not yet come home from a run, and the boys, as she had said they would, went out again as soon as they came in from school, leaving clothes like shed skins thrown down in the corridors.

"Marg, did you actually see Dad dead?"

She looked at me, a bottle of vermouth in one hand. "What?"

"Did you actually see him? After he'd died."

"Well, yes, I did, actually. I wish I hadn't. It was one of those moments when somebody asks you something and you respond automatically. The undertaker asked me, and I said yes, and followed him into a disgusting sort of parlor place with a coffin open and Dad in it. But it wasn't him, not really."

"What do you mean, it wasn't him? Hey, give that to me, you'll drop it."

"Just that he didn't look anything like himself. I still felt that I hated him, but there was nobody there to hate. You know, a body really is an empty container at that point. Nothing like a live person. He was waxy white, the same color as his hair, and his face had sort of sagged, so he looked all nose, no mouth and chin. He was dressed in a dark suit. Frankly, it could have been anyone. I took one look and ran."

"You mean, it really could have been someone else?"

She looked at me across the tray, which she put down on the coffee table in the sitting room. "Well, no, obviously it was him, only it wasn't him anymore. It was not a person. It was vile, actually, and I will never, ever do that again if I'm asked to."

"Did he leave you anything?"

"Only what we all got for the house and the few investments he had left. You mean, something personal?"

"Yes. Something just for you."

"He left me a letter. I've still got it. It was a sort of apology. He knew that I knew, you see. He said he hoped I would understand sometime, and that he was sorry he had hurt me, as he knew he had. I don't know what I was supposed to do with it. It would have been more to the point if he could just have said it, and I could have answered. But no, not our dad. He had to have the last word. Vermouth or sherry? Or, we do have some pretty good single malt."

"Oh, a drop of the hard stuff would go down a treat."

She fetched the Macallan from some far corner where it had been hidden from the boys.

"Why did you want to know all that?"

"Well, I'd sort of missed out, I wasn't here, and I only got to Norfolk in time for the funeral, and by that time so much had already happened. To be honest, Marg, I wasn't sure that he had really died."

"You mean, he might have pretended, like that fellow who was supposed to have been in a canoe accident and then showed up in Panama, living off the life insurance? I wouldn't have put it past him. But no, he did die, Gaby, and it was a strange death, all alone out there on the marshes. It was his corpse in the coffin, even if it wasn't exactly him."

"A dead ringer," I said, and she laughed. We drank tots of the good whisky, chasing thoughts of death away: a surreptitious toast to our dead father, and to ourselves. I didn't ask any more about the letter, and I didn't tell her about the painting. This was enough for now.

17.

Simon was waiting for me at St. Pancras, at the new coffee bar just inside the entrance for Eurostar passengers. He was so obvious, so large: six foot two, I should think, with his long legs sticking out from under the little table, his clothes falling off him as they had in Paris, an open jacket, a misbuttoned shirt, a tie that was at half-mast, his laces dangling, and his messy gray-blond hair falling sideways over one eye. I greeted him with a couple of cheek kisses, and sat down. "Where is it?"

"Gaby, you don't trust me? Here." He pulled the same canvas bag with straps and buckles out from under the table. It looked like something to take on a safari, perhaps to hold ammunition. "You'll need to put a label on it, to take it on the train. Everything has to be labeled. And don't let it out of your sight, don't even go to the loo and leave it in the luggage rack, right?"

"Simon Jakes, you must think I was born yesterday. Of course I won't. Hey, thanks for coming, I hope it didn't cut into your day."

"My day was ripe for being cut into. I always like coming here, anyway. Dear old John Betjeman, don't you think he'd have been proud? He virtually saved it on his own, you know. In the seventies, they wanted to pull it down. And now look at the old girl, all poshed up and European."

The red Victorian stone that had once looked like old meat was indeed beautiful, pink and clean behind the sheets of heavy glass.

Columns rose up out of the floor to support new ceilings, elevators went up and down like mercury used to in thermometers, and everyone was hushed and small in the giant spaces that had been imagined first in an era of steam trains, reimagined for a century of fast new trains to take over from air travel, the ideal of a Europe that would have no borders.

"Hmm, good job." I was hardly paying attention, so pleased was I to lay hands again on that canvas bag. It was oddly exciting, meeting Simon like this and taking possession of my stolen goods. He was looking nervous, his gaze going to the announcement boards, the queues of the returning French tourists with their carrier bags from Harrods and Crabtree & Evelyn and their souvenirs from Camden Lock, as well as all the people who lived in France and worked in London, and vice versa.

"What's the matter, are you afraid of being caught?"

"No, no, of course not, we aren't doing anything wrong, just a little unusual, that's all. I don't want you to miss your train. You're flying back to the States from Charles de Gaulle, right?"

"Probably, yes. I do have a return ticket."

"Well, if anyone asks you about this little darling, just say that it was a present to you from your father. Play the innocent. Don't go into details."

"Oh, I rather thought I might say, *Hey, I stole this from the Guggenheim.*"

"Gaby, don't even joke about it. I'd better go, I've got an appointment. Sorry to dash. Hope to see you again soon. And good luck!"

As I boarded the train and sat down, the bag on my knees, I thought that all I had done was remove the painting from Paris during the month of August, when nobody would have looked for it anyway. If anyone was going to get excited about it, it would be now, at the *rentrée*. The Dutch heirs might just have come steaming back from their holidays to hunt up the thief who had their painting. They might be in Paris, waiting for me. So too might Fabrice Corte. I was probably going right back into the center of an ants' nest of intrigue. But I had seen Margot, and been with my family, and as I watched England disappear and waited for the twenty minutes to pass before I emerged again in France, I knew that it was what I'd needed to do. I was connected to those people, herself and Jude and my two gangly nephews, more than I really was to anybody else in the world. I'd sat in their house and felt at home. I remembered Marg's sudden hug, and the way I had dropped tears onto her T-shirted shoulder. I wasn't a lone person foraging in the world, the way I had often felt since I had left Matt. It made a difference.

At the Gare du Nord, I went down underground to the RER station and got on the train, my overnight bag rolling on its tiny rollers and my canvas bag slung from my shoulder. Nobody stopped me, or asked me what I was carrying across Paris, and even as I walked back down Port-Royal, I felt at ease, at home here too, a person who had somehow gained weight and heft in the world.

Back in the apartment, I kicked off my shoes, placed the canvas bag on the couch, opened it up, and got out the bubble-wrapped, parcel-taped package inside. It was surprisingly light. For a second I wondered if Simon had cheated me, and filled the parcel with plain cardboard, or a print, or even a note saying, *Ha! Ha!* But no. The painting was here, in its cleaned frame that shone dully but beautifully in the summer evening light from the windows. The canvas was as bright and vivid as it must have been when first painted. It was like a different thing. It was so beautiful, so absolutely present, so real. The walnuts were real walnuts that someone picked up yesterday. Their shells were still damp and thick, not easily cracked. The opened one showed a little of its snug white meat, juicy and new. The nutcrackers were silver, bright where the light caught them from a window on the left of the painting that had surely not even showed before. Whoever had cleaned it had done it with such care, love, and skill, he or she must have adored it. I was on my knees before it. I was its first and only owner, its worshipper. I understood why people paid fortunes for paintings, and if they couldn't do that, stole them. I was on the side of thieves and capitalists, both. All that mattered was to be able to feast your eyes on such exactitude, such finesse, such love for the created world. It was nearly dark before I got off the floor, and placed the painting back on the nail that still waited for it, in the middle of the otherwise blank wall. I didn't even want to leave the room in which it hung, but I made myself my usual omelette and a salad, poured a glass of wine, and sat down at the table opposite it. It was mine, it was my gift, my inheritance, from the man whose other daughter said he was such a shit; while Simon Jakes had said he was the real thing, Peter Greenwood, Fabrice Corte is only school of. Was I school of? I didn't care. If my coming to Paris had been to lead me to this, it was enough.

I called Françoise. "Guess what I've got? You have to come over and see it. I'm just back from England. Are you free tomorrow? Did you have a good time? Did they massage you with seaweed until you begged for mercy?"

"Something very strange happened, I have to tell you."

"Tell me tomorrow, okay? Same time and place?"

18.

I dreamed that night of a funeral, only I didn't know whose it was. People had been dying around me for years, in all sorts of different ways. They lay down one night and simply did not wake up; they were crashed into, like my mother, in the prime of life; they were found facedown in puddles with heart failure, like my father. I woke and wondered if the manner of our death is set aside for us, to suit our character. If we actually court it, unconsciously. If what we flee from is what gets us in the end. Or if it is all random, a mess of objects bumping into other objects, cells multiplying for no reason, muscles giving out, a simple entropy. The only sure thing is that it will come to all of us; only, not the time, not the place, not the conditions. All that survives us is what we make: art, the painting on the wall, the sculpture, the line of a poem, a book that never goes out of print, a line of music. And the things of this world that have slow growth and are in no hurry to get through life: the Cedar of Lebanon in the Jardin des Plantes, for example, which stands there massive and solid, its bark hard as metal, its branches roof to the sky. Planted by Jussieu, a man before he was a *métro* station, in 1734, from a seed brought to him from England by an English biologist called Collinson. The seed of a tree from the Middle East, brought from England to Paris, planted in the garden that was planned by scientists, growing solidly there for the last 270 years. Trees are cut down so fast these days, by huge screaming electric saws; you can kill a tree as fast as you can kill a person. It's rare and beautiful to see one which is living out its natural span. I would go to visit the Cedar of Lebanon when I wanted to feel life going on; I would place my hands on its rough bark and touch the strength of its old growth.

But here I was in the middle of the night, suddenly awake and thinking about death, and the life of trees. I rolled over and reached for my phone. There was a message from Yves. Where are you? When are you coming back? And one from Matt, who had called yesterday from the United States. Where are you? When are you coming back? I lay on my back in bed and watched the yellow patterns of car lights roll across the ceiling from behind the shutters. I got up and stood in front of my painting in the moonlight that came in through the living-room window. Full moon. Ah, that was why I was awake.

Those walnuts would have dried and rotted and been thrown away centuries ago in some Dutch garbage bin; those nutcrackers which would have tarnished and been broken and eventually been lost in some household sale. I saw that it didn't matter. What mattered was the vision, and the ability to carry it out. Because all of us had lives that were more or less the same, people wanted the same things, feared the same things, they loved and hated, had families, fell out with them, they were greedy and selfish and generous and pure, they were just people. I and my father and Fabrice Corte and René's grandmother and Matt and Marg and my mother and Yves and all the people I had not even met yet were essentially all in the same mold. You saw one part, and then another. You chose whom to love, whom to hate. You took sides, because life demanded it. You loved your father, you despised your father. You were Gaby or you were Marg. It was all part of a complex pattern, I thought, and when people judged each other, it was ridiculous because, really, they were judging themselves. No wonder everyone wanted paintings like this. It was the only way to understand the briefness of life and its inevitability. Birth, then death. Two sides of the same thing. The split brain. The snug nut that held it.

⚜

I went urgently to see Amélie the following morning. She opened her door at my knock, and led me into her aquarium-like space, with light filtering through the green plants on the windowsill, the low light of September, golden and still. Just a flicker on one wall of something that moved outside—a branch that blocked the sun and then let it go. As if her indoors were an echo of the outdoors, always, with the movement from the street outside, the flashes of light from the windshields of passing cars. She peered, took my hand, kissed me on both cheeks.

"So, how was England? Did you enjoy seeing your family?"

"Fine. Yes, yes, I did. We all got on well. My sister and I haven't always done so. And I discovered something about my father."

"Ah. Sit down, Gaby. Will you have some coffee? Tea?"

"Coffee, if you're having it. Let me do it."

"No, no, I can still make coffee." She set a pan of water to boil in the kitchen and put out two small porcelain cups that were nearly transparent, like children's teeth. Sugar in brown lumps. Two tiny silver spoons.

"What did you discover?"

"Well, that my sister had always detested my father for making her lie to us all about his love affair. She saw him as a terrible person, while I just loved him. She made me think for a minute that I'd only loved him because I didn't know what he was doing. But I realized that you can love someone without it really mattering, how they behave, I mean. He was the same person. It was up to us if we loved or hated him. It still is."

"Like the masks I showed you," she said. "Do you remember? The masks of tragedy and comedy. Beauty and ugliness. Two sides of the same thing. So, your father was an ordinary man, then, and some people loved him, others hated him. Congratulations."

"What do you mean?"

"Well," she said, "as far as I can see, then, you will be rid of his ghost."

"Because he was like everybody else?"

"Well, yes. Don't you think so? This is such a familiar story. And possibly—forgive me if I'm speaking out of turn here—you may see your husband in the same way. What do you think?"

"It's possible. You mean, one thing shifts and so everything shifts?"

"Isn't that how things work?"

When I left her place, I wanted to walk, just to feel my way back into Paris and stretch my legs as well as my mind: up Port-Royal past the military hospital at Val de Grâce; past the street market where mushrooms of all sorts—*cèpes* and *girolles* and others I couldn't even name, the colors and smells of September—were laid out on the stalls; to the corner where the *métro* station is and the Closerie across the street winked its mauve lights from behind the dark leaves of late-summer trees. Where I had, months ago, believed I had glimpsed my father from a moving bus. The trees were beginning to turn in the Jardin du Luxembourg, and since all the schools had begun again, there were no children scooting up and down on the gravel paths between the flower beds. I walked past the great fountain where sea turtles spit water to splash over the greenish flanks of the mer-horses and up to the naked women who hold up the globe of the world, and on down the avenues of chestnuts. I crossed wet grass and came to the alley where I glimpsed the huge golden head of the Prophet at the far end. That wonderful sculpted head gazed out over the gardens, toward the boulevard Saint-Michel, bigger and calmer than everything around it. There were a few people reading on benches, there were dog walkers, runners, tai chi practicers uncurling their slow limbs to balance beneath the unmoving branches of the trees, there were the readers and the kissing couples, but fewer now, as it was September, people were back at work, and there was a slight chill in the air.

I thought about what Amélie had said. One thing shifts, and then everything shifts. The season had changed, yes, but also all the pieces of my life seemed to be sliding about and realigning. I thought of Matt. I thought what it would be like to see him again, clear of all my feelings about my parents' deaths. He, and his whole country, had borne the weight of my misery. But there was no way, I knew it now as surely as I knew seasonal change, the onward roll of the earth, that I could go back to him.

Then I saw a man move ahead of me between the trees on the left side of the lake. For a moment, I thought I was hallucinating. But no. A man in a black jacket and jeans, with white hair. He was walking quite briskly as if enjoying the exercise, perhaps on his way to a rendezvous. I followed, of course. As I walked faster, turning up behind the trees, keeping him in my sights, the distance between us began to shrink, and I thought, Corte: it has to be him. He must have come back from Corsica. I slowed down, to let the distance between us increase, but not so much that I would lose sight of him. I walked in my sneakers on grass, ready to duck behind a tree if he were to turn around. I did not want to talk anymore about paintings, particularly mine. Now that it hung on my wall, cleaned and gleaming, as beautiful as it had been when it was first painted, I didn't want him even to see it. But I followed him like a spy, walking slow and then faster, my breath just appearing on the slightly cooled air. I tracked him down the path between the trees, past the giant sequoias and the statue of Baudelaire, then turning to the right to walk behind the tennis courts, past the marionette theatre, keeping always a few yards of distance between us, careful on gravel. He was about the same height as my father, his white hair curled down close to his collar, he wore a knotted red scarf today over the black jacket, and he walked easily, like a younger man. I remembered my father's fast, sinuous walk, the way he moved, and realized that I had only met Fabrice Corte in rooms, in the restaurant; I had not had the chance to observe him at large, moving in landscape. He swung loosely from the hips as he walked. A first few leaves drifted down, yellow and crisp in a gust of wind, and the figure of the man in the black jacket turned abruptly in front of the Palais itself, with its bored gendarmes lounging in twos, to walk down past the Orangerie and toward the gates that lead out on to rue Bonaparte and then to rue de Vaugirard. Had he remembered something suddenly, a shop he had to go to, a meeting? He had something under his arm, white, that was possibly a rolled newspaper; that was surely enough to make him a real person, not a ghost? I had walked after him for long enough to be sure now that he was real, solid, a man just taking a walk before going to some business meeting, perhaps, or to a gallery down one of the side streets by Saint-Sulpice, perhaps, or even a café because he had suddenly thought that he wanted a coffee. I watched him go. I thought about what I would say to him—it could be entirely polite, banal, and off-putting, the way you could be in French, giving nothing away. He was somebody I did not have to have in my life, because I had got what I needed, the painting, my father's final gift, and with it my own sense of myself, at home in whatever life I chose. For a moment I had imagined walking up fast and silent behind him, as in the game of Grandmother's Footsteps that we used to play when we were children, tapping him on the shoulder, and saying some sharp, profound, incontrovertible thing in French; but I couldn't think what that might be. I could let it be entirely social, of course—*Did you have a good time in Corsica?* I could say, *I'm sorry, I thought you were someone else.*

Really, I only wanted to be sure that it was Corte, so that I could finally let the whole thing go, ghosts and likenesses and faked deaths. I saw him move toward the tall gates and the traffic beyond them, and my resolve failed me, simply because I could not carry it any further. Once he was out of the gardens and on the street, it was already too late. I saw him turn right, toward rue de Vaugirard. He crossed the street without looking left or right. I stood on the pavement just outside the gates and saw him go. I thought, it doesn't matter that much; I have everything I need, now: the painting, my restored life. He's obviously a real person. Ghosts don't carry newspapers. There are no ghosts, anyway. There are only the sliding planes of our existence that intersect at certain times and places; there are only states of desire and grief that let us imagine for a moment, perhaps, that reality is not as it is.

I turned back into the gardens then, crossed behind the lake, walked between the crisp, slightly browning trees past the statue of the seller of masks and the one of George Sand reclining and then Rodin's one of Stendhal, and went out through the other gates onto the big intersection at the top of boulevard Saint-Michel where the 27 bus route goes back down to Claude Bernard and home. It was after eleven by now, and I had a lunch date with Françoise, and I didn't want to keep her waiting.

19.

Françoise and I sat at a table outside our usual café, the wine lists in front of us and today's specials chalked up on a board. It was midday, and the church bells rang it out. We had come from our different directions, waving at each other across the square, coming around the arcing water of the fountains to meet. She was wearing a very beautiful silk scarf, tied in a certain way that I wanted to learn. It was September, the *rentrée* at last, time for everyone to start wearing scarves tied in a certain way. She was also in new jeans and a white shirt with a loose green linen jacket. She still walked with a slight limp.

"You look great!" Two kisses as we leaned into each other, and then the settling into chairs, folding of hands on the table, glancing at wine lists.

"So do you, Gaby. How are you? I must say, the thalassotherapy was incredible, you should try it sometime. But, perhaps, only after you are about fifty. At your age, one never gets as tired as I was earlier this summer."

"Don't bet on it. I could have done with a dose of seawater and mud this summer. Everyone was away, and it was so hot. I'll never do Paris in August again if I can help it. But tell me, what's the strange thing you were going to tell me?"

"Something happened, a bad thing. Fabrice Corte is dead. He was killed in Corsica, just before he was going to fly back, apparently. I only just heard."

"I don't believe you. How could he be? Killed? He can't have been!"

"I don't know. No idea. Whatever one thought of him, it was an awful shock to hear it. He was shot."

"How did you hear?" My heart was hammering inside me, I felt slightly sick and sweaty, as if I had drunk too much of Amélie's coffee.

"It was on the news. Art dealer killed in Corsica, in his hometown, Ajaccio, just before getting on an Air France plane back to Paris. He apparently met someone in a bar in Ajaccio for a drink, before getting his plane, and was not seen again until he showed up on the steps of a police station, dead. People were talking about it at work. I don't know anymore. Awful, isn't it?"

"Françoise, I just saw him, in the Luxembourg, this morning. He walked out into the rue de Vaugirard, carrying a newspaper. I'm sure it was him."

"You can't have. It can't have been him. He died yesterday, Gaby."

"Well, it was either him, or—someone who looked very like him."

"Peter, were you going to say?" She pronounced his name *Petair*.

"Look, am I going crazy? I don't know what to think. I thought I had it all worked out. My seeing my father all over the place, then concluding it must have been Fabrice, and now it can't be either of them. Françoise, I saw my sister when I was in England, and she told me about seeing him in his coffin before the funeral. He really is dead."

"What do you mean, he really is dead? Of course he is. Have you only just accepted that?"

"I wasn't sure. It sounds crazy, I know. I kept on having sightings of him here in Paris, earlier this summer. He kept making appearances. I didn't tell you, because it sounded so insane. I thought you might be upset too."

Then she sighed and looked away and said, "I did too, soon after he died. I thought I saw him everywhere. But it's a phenomenon, Gaby, it happens. I discovered that, especially when you never saw the person dead, or even ill. People look like each other. We see what we need to see, perhaps. The mind plays tricks, kind tricks, even. It slides a film of emotion across our eyes, so we see what we want to see, not what is there. It must have been the same for you."

"I thought I was going mad, or he had faked his death, or he was a ghost, or even that it was Fabrice I saw each time. And now he's dead too. Everybody I told about seeing my father had a different explanation. René's grandmother said, a ghost. Yves thought that he was just the kind of person who would fake his death and pop up somewhere else. So did Simon Jakes. Even my husband thought he might be—what's the word in French for a double?"

"Un sosie?" she suggested.

"Really? What a strange word. I didn't tell you, because I knew you loved him, and it would have hurt."

"No," she said. "Nothing like that hurts me anymore. I know I have to live without him, but then I did that part of the time anyway. There were six months at least of every year when I never saw him at all. It's qualitatively different, of course. But you can train yourself to accept, you know. Even to accept a death. Then the sightings, or appearances, tend to stop."

"But what about Fabrice? Is it possible that he faked his death?"

"Look," she said, "we're never going to know. He is a peculiar person, Fabrice Corte. Or was. I'm sorry I ever got you involved with him. It seems to have made everything more complicated. I just think there was a whole other side to him and his activities, and I was naïve not to see it before. In Corsica, it could have been something entirely to do with his family, you never know. Probably nothing to do with his activities in Paris."

"Did you like him because he looked like my father?"

She looked at me, perhaps wondering if it was a criticism. "Initially, I didn't see it, because I loved your father, and when you are in love, the person you love looks like nobody else. Then, of course, I realized. And, lately, the resemblance seems even to have increased."

"He took me for lunch at Le Train Bleu, did I tell you? It could have been incredibly romantic."

"Knowing him, I'm surprised it wasn't. But perhaps it wasn't, because you are your father's daughter, and he had to respect that."

"It was business," I said. "He wanted the painting. I expect he put lunch on an expense account, anyway."

There was a silence between us for a moment, perhaps as each of us decided that there were certain things which had to be let go. "But, Françoise, I've got the painting. You must come and look at it after lunch. It looks incredible now, it's been cleaned, they did a lovely job."

The young waiter came, we ordered a *pichet* of Brouilly and the *coquelet* with fried potatoes, as we were both hungry.

"What are you going to do with it?"

"Keep it. Tell nobody. Never let anyone in the art world into where I live. Oh, and carry it around in a shopping bag if necessary. Have it with me always, to remind me of what matters."

"And what does?"

"Art," I said, raising my glass to her in the mellow sunlight of a new season. "Life. Seeing things a certain way. Valuing the small, transient, precious things and knowing how to make them eternal."

"*Dis donc,*" said Francoise, and raised her glass in return. "You sound just like Peter. He produced a clone." Our glasses clinked. "Gaby, this has to be a toast to the living!"

"The living!"

"And the future. Enough of the past!"

I knew, as we grinned at each other in the sunlight and raised our glasses, that something else had begun. It was as clear as a letter in a mailbox. I could hear the words that would begin a new poem, that were beginning to shift and move themselves inside my head. In my brain, where perhaps the two sides connected, in that membrane, thin as the skin that divides the kernel in a walnut, something had at last begun to form that was not misery, that was not loss.

The plates were set before us, crisp potatoes and little roasted birds. We drank our wine and ate our lunch, the traffic circling around us, the water in the fountain juggling light, the September blue of the sky, a different blue, coming down between the crooked houses of medieval Paris. We were very small and temporary sitting there, but we were together, my father's lover and I, and we were friends. After lunch, we would go and look at my painting, and she might ask me what I was going to do next, and I might even tell her, because I knew that the rest of my life was waiting for me, uncertain and yet full of possibility, only just out of sight. But for now, the pigeons were flying down into the square and people were crossing the street, wearing their scarves tied in a certain way, and the church bell struck the half hour and the fountain water played. The light was changed, yet everything was very bright and still at the center, as if it had all been cleaned while we were asleep.

ACKNOWLEDGMENTS

I would like to thank the following:

Dendy Easton, for sharing his knowledge about paintings and forgeries.

The Van Gogh Museum in Amsterdam, for a timely exhibit on dating and authenticating paintings.

Kimberley Cameron, for the insights, persistence, optimism, and constant availability that make her such a wonderful agent.

The writers of Key West, especially Kathryn Kilgore for my room at the Artists' and Writers' House and Alison Lurie for her thoughts on ghosts.

Allen Meece, my husband, for his support of me, even when it means I spend months away in France.

Miranda Brackenbury, my daughter, for her careful reading of the manuscript.

The team at Lake Union, especially Miriam Juskowicz, who first loved this book, and Danielle Marshall, its editor.

Christina Henry de Tessan, who worked tirelessly to help me pull it into its final shape.

ABOUT THE AUTHOR

Photo © 2014 Nancy Spiewak

Poet and novelist Rosalind Brackenbury is the author of *Becoming George Sand*. A former writer-in-residence at the College of William and Mary in Williamsburg, Virginia, she has also served as poet laureate of Key West, teaching poetry workshops. She has attended the yearly Key West Literary Seminar as both panelist and moderator. Born in London, Rosalind lived in Scotland and France before moving to the United States. Her hobbies include swimming, reading, walking, and talking with friends. For more on the author and her work, visit www.rosalindbrackenbury.com.